VOYAGE
OF THE
SNAKE LADY

VOYAGE
OF THE
SNAKE LADY

THERESA TOMLINSON

An Imprint of HarperCollins*Publishers*

Eos is an imprint of HarperCollins Publishers.

Voyage of the Snake Lady
Copyright © 2004 by Theresa Tomlinson
Map copyright © 2004 by Alan Tomlinson

Library of Congress Cataloging-in-Publication Data
Tomlinson, Theresa.
   Voyage of the snake lady / Theresa Tomlinson. — 1st American
ed.
      p. cm.
   Summary: After living peacefully for some time following the
Trojan War, the Moon Riders, a fierce tribe of women warriors, are
driven from their home by Neoptolemus, the avenging son of
Achilles, and must fight for their lives to survive storms, shipwreck,
and strife.
   ISBN 978-0-06-084739-5 (trade bdg.)
   ISBN 978-0-06-084740-1 (lib. bdg.)
   [1. Amazons—Juvenile fiction. 2. Amazons—Fiction. 3. Wild
horses—Fiction. 4. Horses—Fiction. 5. Mythology, Greek—
Fiction.] I. Title.
PZ7.T5977Voy 2008   2006100471
[Fic]—dc22   CIP
                                                              AC

Typography by Hilary Zarycky
1 2 3 4 5 6 7 8 9 10
❖
First American Edition
First published in 2004 in the United Kingdom
by Corgi Books, an imprint of Random House Children's Books

For my mother, Joan Johnston

TABLE OF CONTENTS

Author's Note

I FIRST BECAME fascinated by the fabulous legends of the warlike Amazon women when, as a schoolgirl, I studied *The Histories* of Herodotus in Greek Literature classes. At the time they seemed to be nothing more than exciting and rather shocking stories.

Many years later, a BBC 2 *Horizon* television program called "The Ice Maiden" renewed my interest in the warrior women. The program recorded the discovery, by archaeologist Natalia Polosmak, of the frozen mummified body of a young woman in the Altai Mountains, believed to have been a high-status priestess or storyteller. I was impressed to hear the female archaeologists relating this find, and other burials of women with weapons, to Herodotus's stories. It seemed that the Amazons might, after all, have been real nomadic tribeswomen who lived, rode, and fought long ago in the area to the north of and surrounding the Black Sea.

My interest in the subject was fueled by Lyn Webster Wilde's fascinating book *On the Trail of the Women Warriors*. I felt inspired to try to write a novel for young adults, based on the ancient legends of the Amazons but also taking on board some of the new ideas that modern archaeologists were bringing to light. The result of this project was *The Moon Riders*, published in 2003.

I became too involved with my heroine Myrina to let her go, and soon found myself looking again at the legends for inspiration for a second "adventure."

Herodotus relates the story of the battle between the Greeks and the Amazons at the River Thermodon and tells how the defeated women were captured and herded into ships. According to Herodotus, the women overpowered and killed their captors, but as they knew nothing of seamanship, they were blown across the Black Sea to the land of the Scythians. Here they met, fought with, and eventually intermarried with a group of Scythian men, thus creating the origins of the Sauromatian tribe, whose women were always known to ride and fight. Though this story is usually set in a slightly later time period, I felt that it fitted well with the aftermath of the Trojan War.

The continuation of Iphigenia's story is based loosely on Euripides' play *Iphigenia at Tauris*. Another book— *Warrior Women: An Archaeologist's Search for History's Hidden Heroines* by Jeannine Davis-Kimball, Ph.D., with Mona Behan—supplied more inspiration and helped me to believe that the fierce nomadic tribeswomen of the Black Sea areas really *were* Herodotus's Amazons.

The KBR Horse Net website provided helpful information on wild horse behavior, and another website, www.pefkias.gr/, helped me to envisage the Mycenaean ships. http://users.cwnet.com/millenia/scythwrd.html gave me some ideas for ancient Scythian words.

Though most versions of the story have Cassandra killed by Clytemnestra after the fall of Troy, Dares the Phrygian's version sees Cassandra released by Agamemnon to live on, close to her lost city. Dares's telling claims to be an eyewitness account of events but seems to be rather discredited by modern historians. However, it was from this version that Chaucer took his inspiration for *Troilus and Cressida*. I decided that if it was good enough for Chaucer, then it was certainly good enough for me!

The ruins of the temple of Sminthean Apollo (Lord of the Mice) are situated in the southwest corner of the Biga peninsula in Turkey, not far from Hissarlik (believed to be Troy). Homer's *Iliad* refers to this temple as being the home of the priest Chryse and his daughter Chryseis. I thought this temple would make a good refuge for Cassandra, allowing her to live on as the priestess of Sminthean Apollo. After all the misery and hardship that my heroines had suffered, I felt the need for a happy ending!

THERESA TOMLINSON, NOVEMBER 2003
www.theresatomlinson.com

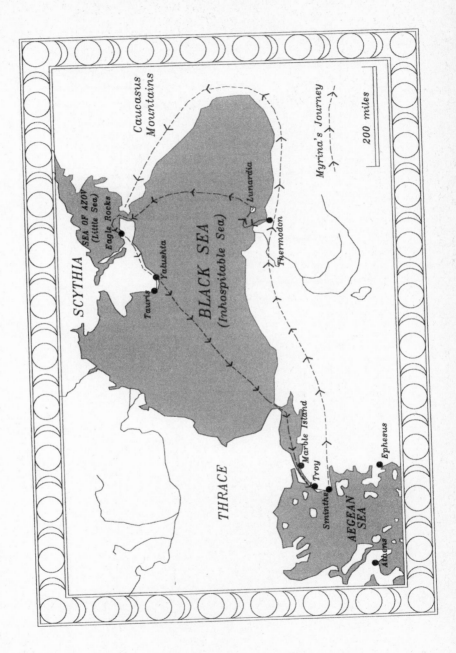

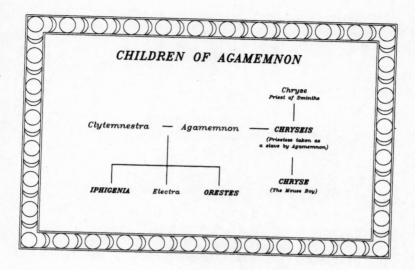

CHILDREN OF AGAMEMNON

Chryse
Priest of Sminthe

Clytemnestra — Agamemnon — **CHRYSEIS**

*(Priestess taken as
a slave by Agamemnon)*

IPHIGENIA   *Electra*   **ORESTES**

CHRYSE
(The Mouse Boy)

Prologue

CASSANDRA SAT BESIDE a dark pool, still as a stone, staring into the water. Chryse, the Mouse Boy, sat with her, watching, concerned at the intensity he saw in her face. Many feared the quiet priestess with the strange mismatched eyes who'd once been princess of the ruined city of Troy, but not twelve-year-old Chryse.

Some years had passed since a warship that had once belonged to the great conqueror Agamemnon had sailed in sight of the tiny island of Sminthe. The Mouse Boy could remember only too well how his mother Chryseis, priestess of the sun god, had snatched him up into her arms and run with him to hide in the cave of Apollo, close to the beach. She'd clamped her hand over his mouth so hard that it hurt; but it hadn't been for very long. They'd watched from the shelter of the cave as a small boat was rowed toward the shore. Two men jumped out and splashed through the shallows as they dragged the vessel up onto the sand. They had quickly ditched their cargo and rowed back toward the warship.

When she saw the cargo they'd left, Chryseis had cried out with doubt and then joy. She'd released her child and left him to toddle after her, while she ran down the beach, her arms open wide. The cargo had been the Trojan princess, left on the beach, her few belongings stashed in a sack.

Since then the three of them had lived peacefully together in the island temple of Sminthean Apollo, two priestesses and a child whose only playmates were mice.

But now, as Chryse watched the color fade from Cassandra's cheeks, he felt a growing unease. The pool darkened to inky blackness, leaving the water still and mirrorlike, while strange and magical pictures moved in its shimmering depths. Chryse could see the pictures, but he wasn't sure what they meant. He held his breath and watched the magic, while some of his mouse friends ran up his back and paused for a moment on his shoulders, their tiny whiskers trembling, ears alert.

"What is it?" he asked them.

He suddenly felt sure that the mice were giving him some sort of warning; then he saw that a small trickle of blood crept down from Cassandra's nose. The princess ignored it—her whole attention was fixed on what she saw in the water; but the mice stretched their snouts up toward Chryse's ears and he heard their thin, starlike voices speaking to him in the squeaky language that only he seemed to understand.

Chryse got up and started running back toward the temple, while a dark gray shadow made up of many tiny racing bodies swirled about his feet, for wherever he went his mice went, too. "Mother!" he shouted. "Mother, come! The princess needs you! The mice are telling me this—you must come."

Chryseis appeared in the archway at the side of the temple and ran quickly down the flight of stone steps, but when she saw the blood on Cassandra's gown she slowed down, making herself speak in a low, calm voice. "Princess," she whispered. "Princess, come back to us! It is not good for you to go where you have gone!"

She moved steadily toward her friend, but now every step was careful and measured. "Princess," she whispered, putting out her hands to gently touch Cassandra, ignoring the flow of blood that marked them both. "Dear friend, come back to us!"

At last Cassandra blinked and tore her eyes away from the pool; she spoke with agitation. "I have seen them!" she cried. "Iphigenia! Myrina and her young daughter! They are in terrible trouble . . . taken prisoner on a boat, their ankles roped, stripped of all weapons . . . Myrina's snake mirror gone . . . surrounded by dark waves."

"Who is doing this?" Chryseis asked, her voice low and fearful.

Cassandra shook her head. "Achaean ships! I know that black shape on their banners; it is Achilles' standard! The sign of the ant!"

Chryse looked scared. He had heard stories of Achilles, the dreaded warrior who'd fought for the Achaeans in the war against Troy.

"But Achilles is dead," Chryseis reminded her friend firmly.

Cassandra nodded. "It is his son—Neoptolemus!" She spoke with certainty now, but turned to her friend in deep distress. "What can we do?"

Chryseis shook her head and hugged her friend tightly, stroking her hair. "Nothing . . . there is nothing we can do—but watch and wait and have faith in those we love. Iphigenia is not the helpless child that you once knew; she is a priestess now and warrior trained. Myrina is the greatest survivor of us all; I swear they will rue the day they took our Snake Lady and her Moon Riders aboard their boat."

Part One

VOYAGE TO THE NORTH

CHAPTER ONE

The Last Salute

MYRINA GRITTED HER teeth; the rocking of the galley made her feel sick. All the captive women were in great discomfort, crammed into narrow corridors beneath the thwarts, stowed like baggage around the edges of the ship. Myrina's daughter Tamsin clung to her, white faced, but there was little that she could do to comfort the child in that confined space. They were roped together by the ankles, Iphigenia on one side of her and Coronilla on the other; only the young girls were free. Myrina hugged Tamsin tightly. Keeping her daughter safe must be her main purpose now, but she was concerned about Coronilla, who was suffering from a battered head and seemed to be falling into a deathlike sleep.

Despite everything, Myrina felt that she must make one last farewell. "I may never see this land again," she muttered. She twisted around so that she could look up through the oar holes, as the galley pulled away from the shore. Though her view was restricted, she managed to glimpse two grave markers standing out stark on the horizon. She had raised those markers herself—one for Hati, her grandmother, and the other for Atisha, the old leader of the Moon Riders. Both old women had died within a few days of each other in the Month of Falling Leaves. Myrina had taken their ashes from the pyre and buried them side by side above the River Thermodon.

"Good-bye, Hati, warrior grandmother," she whispered. "Good-bye, Atisha, wise old woman. Though I crouch here in shame I salute you both: you will always be here with me in my heart." Then she said fiercely, "I am glad you are not here to see what has become of the once-honored Moon Riders!"

As the two boats moved farther away from the shore, she craned her neck to see the other riverbank, searching for yet another marker. Myrina's horse Isatis had been her faithful companion since the blue-black foal was born into her arms when she was five. Myrina had seen only thirteen springs when she'd ridden away from her home tent on Isatis's back to join the Moon Riders, warrior priestesses of Earth Mother Maa.

But both horse and rider had suffered many years of hard struggle since then, and as they grew older together, Isatis had developed a breathing sickness that gradually made every movement difficult. When the sight of the suffering mare became too much, it was Myrina herself who'd hammered a sharpened spearpoint into Isatis's forehead, so that death came instantly. Her friends had offered to relieve her of the terrible job, but for no other Moon Rider would Isatis drop her head in perfect trust and stillness. So Myrina had forced herself to strike the one powerful blow. She had cremated the carcass and buried Isatis's ashes along with the fine snake-patterned harness that her father had made.

At last, as she craned her neck, she saw the hillock on the shore with the small cairn of stones piled up carefully to mark the spot. Her lips twisted with bitterness and it was hard to get the words out, but they had to be said: "Sleep well, my brave Isatis." She lifted her hand from Tamsin's head in salute.

Deep anger at what had happened kept her eyes dry. Two hundred and fifty women had lived with their children beside the River Thermodon; they were all that was left of the Moon Riders, who'd long been respected for their sacred dancing and warrior skills. Many of the women had once been slaves in the city of Troy, but they had escaped and regained their sense of worth and dignity by joining the ranks of the Moon Riders. Their Achaean enemies had feared these warrior women and called them Amazons, but they'd lived peacefully enough during these years, in harmony with the fisher folk who inhabited that shoreline by the Thermodon. Then, in the Month of New Leaves, news had come of a fleet of warships sailing northward through the Bosphorus into the Black Sea, bearing the much-feared symbol of the ant. Neoptolemus, son of Achilles, had recovered from the long struggle of the Trojan War and, being still an energetic man, he came raiding along the southern coast, looting all those who'd tried to defend the city of Troy and the Anatolian tribal lands.

Myrina had set up a system of beacons to give warning of their approach. When at last Neoptolemus arrived, it had been in a light, fast flagship, and though he'd sailed close to the land at the mouth of the Thermodon, he'd looked carefully at the landing places and then sailed on. There had been a day of uncertainty and then relief followed, for it seemed that they were not worth the trouble of an attack. But the following morning black dots appeared on the horizon and the sea soon darkened with the shapes of sails, while Myrina rushed to reorganize their defenses. Neoptolemus had sailed ahead of a huge navy, spying out the land, leaving the real dirty work to his followers.

When the battle came at last, both warrior priestesses and fisher folk fought bravely, but this new generation of Achaeans were huge in number. Jealous of their fathers' stories of the Trojan War, they burned with their own desire for adventure and riches. Moon Riders who did not die fighting were taken captive, their boy children slaughtered before their eyes. Among the young girls who had survived were Leti and Fara, but their mothers had died in the battle, and now the older Moon Riders tried hard to care for them and watch them with motherly concern.

The horses had been slaughtered, too, for the seafaring Achaeans had little use for the beasts. The captives were stripped of their weapons, their sheep and goats herded aboard the young Ant Man's ships, while the main fleet sailed onward to the west, still eager for more plunder, leaving two smaller vessels packed with prisoners to be taken they knew not where.

Myrina muttered angrily, reminding herself sternly that her tribe was nomadic and had always roamed from pasture to pasture. Home was a tent, family, and comrades; home could be wherever you made it. "I am Mazagardi born! What does it matter where I go?"

Tamsin had at last fallen asleep, exhausted, her arms wrapped tightly about her mother. Myrina gently wiped a smear of blood from the corner of her child's bruised mouth. Though she could feel nothing but anger, she forced herself to remember that some of those she loved remained; she must think fast to save what she could. She put one arm around Coronilla, trying to make her more comfortable. Others had survived the battle; though many, like Coronilla, were in a bad way. Myrina's own body was covered in cuts and bruises, but she considered herself lucky. Tamsin was a fair weight to support in these cramped conditions, but she took comfort from the heavy warmth of her daughter leaning on her shoulder—her seven-year-old lived, when so many others had been slaughtered. Then suddenly she looked about her in panic. Where was Phoebe? Her niece was the much-loved child of her sister Reseda, killed along with most of the Mazagardi tribe while the war for the city of Troy raged all about them.

"Phoebe! Phoebe!" Myrina shouted urgently.

"She is here—Akasya has her safe!" Iphigenia answered.

Myrina leaned across and saw them farther down the corridor. Phoebe's head was resting against Akasya's shoulder, though she looked bruised and pale. Myrina had ordered the young girl to stay inside the home tent, but Phoebe had crept out in the middle of the battle and wounded many an Achaean by raining down arrows from the hillside. Eventually one of them had crept up behind her and felled her with a heavy blow to the head.

"Will she live?" Myrina did not like the stillness of the young girl or the sight of dried blood among her matted curls.

"Her head is battered, but she breathes steadily," Akasya promised. "Do not fear, Snake Lady, I will take good care of her."

"If it were not for these two who call me Mother and this rope, by Maa, I swear I'd throw myself into the sea," Myrina said. "They cast my mirror into their melting pot—and all my power has melted with it! Father made it for me with such tenderness and care when I went with the Moon Riders."

Iphigenia shook her head. "You are mistaken, Snake Lady." She spoke with calm determination. "Your power does not lie in a mirror, beautiful and magical though it was. Your father's tenderness and care is always there in your heart. I still have the mirror that the Princess Cassandra gave me, hidden away inside my robe; it is yours to use whenever you wish. Close your eyes now and rest."

Myrina was calmed and touched by Iphigenia's generosity. A Moon Rider's mirror was her most precious possession, and Iphigenia treasured the gleaming black round of obsidian that Cassandra had given her long ago. The offer to share it showed the deepest love and trust.

"I must not give up all hope!" she agreed.

"No, you must not," Iphigenia said. "Have you noted the ship's figurehead?"

Myrina strained to see the prow of the ship, high above

the foredeck. For a moment she glimpsed the head and shoulders of a woman carved in wood, a crescent moon on her brow; then she quickly understood. "Artemis." It was to the Achaeans' huntress goddess that Iphigenia had been dedicated as a child. The crescent moon had long been the symbol of the Moon Riders, too.

Iphigenia nodded. "This ship is named for the Moon Lady."

"You think that bodes well for us?"

"Oh yes! We have often agreed that the Achaeans' Moon Lady is close to the moon aspect of Earth Mother Maa. And I saw that the other ship is named for her twin brother, the sun god."

"Apollo—the god of our friend Chryseis?"

"You see"—Iphigenia nodded again sleepily—"things are better than they seem. Let us trust that the Moon Lady and her brother will protect us while we are in their ships. You have not slept for two days and nights, so put your head on my shoulder and let sleep give us the strength that we need."

"I wish I felt as certain of this protection as you do!" Myrina grumbled, but she knew that she must acknowledge her own exhaustion and accept that at the moment she was helpless. At last she lowered her head like an obedient child to rest on her friend's slim shoulder, her eyelids so heavy that they would not stay open anymore.

They woke with the morning sun and for a moment Myrina could not think where she was. Her body ached in every part, and foul-tasting fluid rose in her throat; then terrible memories flooded back. She looked beside her at Coronilla, who murmured words that meant nothing, while Tamsin whimpered as she woke.

"It's all right, Young Lizard," Myrina murmured automatically. "Snake Mother's here!"

Iphigenia woke, blinking up at the sun as it shot over the bows, and groaned as she shuffled around in the confined space, trying to ease her cramping muscles.

"We've been in trouble before," Myrina said, "but I don't know how we're going to get out of this!"

She struggled hard to force back the despair again, gently smoothing Tamsin's hair away from her face. The child did not weep or wail as she woke and remembered what had happened, but stretched her limbs a little. "I am hungry, Snake Mother," she said. "When did we last eat?"

"That's my young lizard." Myrina smiled at her with fierce pride. "We must eat to survive."

CHAPTER TWO

While We Have Life

IPHIGENIA LEANED FORWARD to look farther down the narrow corridor space. "See what is happening . . ." She touched Myrina's arm. "They are allowing those at the end to creep out one by one onto the deck and get water—and something to eat! At least they are not planning to starve us."

"By Maa, it's kind of them!" said Myrina.

"They would have slaughtered us by now, if they were going to. You know what this means?"

Myrina frowned. "Aye!"

The thought had been there in her head, but she was reluctant to acknowledge it. She looked down the row of shackled women to Akasya, remembering how—along with many of the women—she'd once been a slave in the city of Troy. If Akasya survived she would understand well enough what was intended for them.

"Slavery!" She shuddered as she spoke the word. "We are taken as slaves!"

"Slaves?" Tamsin murmured.

Iphigenia nodded. "But . . . at least that means they want us alive and strong!"

Myrina looked at her fiercely. "Better dead!" she mouthed, so that Tamsin couldn't hear.

"No!" Iphigenia contradicted her. "While we have life, we have . . . a chance."

Myrina groaned, but she knew that Iphigenia was right. The terrified young girl who'd once been offered as a sacrifice by her own father had now acquired wisdom that would grace a crone.

Myrina must dredge up her old fighting spirit from the depths of her soul; she must find courage, observe their situation, and see if there was any possible way of escape. She looked up and shouted in the Luvvian language at the oarsman above her. "Hey, you! Speak Luvvian?"

"Shut your mouth!" he snarled back at her in the same tongue.

"Where are we going?"

"None of your business! Shut your mouth!"

Myrina bit her tongue with fury, sensing that there would be no help from that source. He would be the first to suffer if she was ever free to move again.

At last, as the sun moved up into the sky, shining sharp and low, they prepared to shuffle out, still roped together, onto the lower middle deck. The women ahead of them were moving slowly in a long chain when there was a sudden splash and a horrified, suppressed gasp from the captives.

"What is it?" Myrina whispered.

Akasya turned back to her, shuddering. "It was Ebba." Her mouth worked with bitterness. "They have thrown her overboard. They'll only feed those they think will live!"

Myrina turned back to Coronilla, who still lay white faced and crumpled beside her. "Wake up!" she hissed, bending over her fearfully. She shook her shoulders and then began frantically pinching her cheeks. "Wake up, fierce one, and open your eyes!"

Tamsin picked up her mother's concern. "Wake up, Coronilla!" she cried.

In desperation Myrina lifted her hand to slap her. But before the blow fell, Coronilla's eyes fluttered open and a faint tinge of rose touched her cheeks where she'd been pinched.

"Thank you, Maa!" Myrina gasped. "Come on, brave one! Force yourself to life again, or we shall lose you. Do you understand? Lean on me, but don't let them see it."

"Mmm," Coronilla murmured.

"Can you move? You must move!"

Coronilla lurched over onto her hands and knees.

"That's it, brave one! You must crawl and keep going."

She managed to struggle on as they were allowed out, one by one, onto the low middle deck, where they were given a little fetid water and a barley biscuit. They were watched eagle-eyed from the higher afterdeck by the captain of the *Artemis*. Myrina itched to leap up and put her strong hands around his fat neck. But for the rope that hobbled her, she could have done it and killed him there and then, for she knew how to snap a man's neck like a rabbit's—but where would such an action leave them? Instead she gave Tamsin some hard biscuit dipped in water, then took a little herself. Iphigenia unobtrusively propped up Coronilla, helping her to drink and eat. Akasya fed Phoebe, and Myrina was relieved to see that her niece was awake and seemed to be reviving.

The captain came down from his position on the afterdeck and inspected his goods. "Young ones"—his voice was thick and hoarse with pleasure as he gently touched Phoebe's curls—"pretty ones—sweet as honey."

He stretched out his hand and felt Leti's muscular shoulder. The young girl bared her teeth at him, but he laughed in her face. "Ha! They will fetch a good price!"

Myrina swore silently to herself that he would die, but she swallowed her pride and forced her voice to sound gentle, her face to look sad and sorrowful. "Not if they starve or sicken—there will be no price for them then. Release us from these bonds and we will feed and clean them. We have no weapons, and where can we go but into the sea?"

The captain sneered and laughed. "I thank you, madam, for your kind concern for my cargo." He climbed back up to the afterdeck. "Release those two bitches with the young ones," he ordered, indicating Myrina and Akasya. "Set them to work feeding the sickly ones and get them all cleaned up!"

The two ships turned, heading steadily west, still in sight of the shore. The *Apollo* pulled a little way ahead, but the wind blew against them and the oarsmen had a job to keep them on course. Myrina and Akasya moved dutifully about the deck of the *Artemis*, carrying water and slops, cleaning wounds as best they could. Myrina kept Tamsin, Leti, and Fara busy helping her, hoping to keep them out of the captain's way. Though Phoebe was recovering well, they made her lie still, hoping that she would not attract attention.

"Rest," they told her. "Keep quiet and still."

The captain would not be persuaded to release any more of his captives, and it was hard work for so few of them. Coronilla's bruising deepened in color, but Myrina was relieved to see that she seemed to be recovering and coming to her senses.

"Did you hit me, Snake Lady?" she asked.

"Would I dare to?" Myrina smiled, relieved to hear her speak so.

When the midday sun beat down on them, Myrina flopped down beside Iphigenia to have a brief rest. "I have been counting the sea pigs," she hissed. "There are fifty-five of them, while there are eighty-two of us. Were we free we could take them easily."

"But only you and Akasya and the girls are free!" Iphigenia answered.

Myrina grinned fiercely. "With one knife I could release you all very fast."

Iphigenia nodded, but her face was grim. "You'd be more likely to get that knife between your shoulder blades," she said. "And what of the other boat? I saw them drag Centaurea aboard the *Apollo*, along with some of the fishwives."

"Was she hurt?"

"I do not think so."

"Thank Maa for that." Myrina frowned. "They have taken fishwives, too?"

"Only those who are big and strong; I saw them slit the throats of those who were wounded!"

Myrina shook her head. "These sea pigs will die," she whispered. "I swear it! We must watch and wait but be

21

ready to pounce should any chance come to us. If the moment arrives and we bellow out our war cry, our friends on the other boat will hear and understand. Centaurea will know what it means well enough."

Iphigenia nodded. "The Moon Lady will be with us."

The day passed on the crowded deck beneath the hot sun, but during the night most of the women were herded back under the cramped thwarts. They slept as best they could, still roped together in that restricted space while the oarsmen rested above them. Myrina and Akasya were allowed to stay on deck with the girls, though they were roped together and fastened to the thwarts. The captain repeatedly prowled about through the hours of darkness and Myrina was terrified that he'd snatch Tamsin and Phoebe away from them.

At times a helpless knot of shame tied itself tight inside her. Playing the submissive woman was deep humiliation to her. It was against everything she'd been taught by her parents, her tribe, and as a Moon Rider. All through the night she and Akasya whispered desperately together.

"That fat pig of a captain who keeps leering at Phoebe has a sharp paring knife stuck in his belt! I want to snatch it and pare his guts with it!"

"Yes." Akasya scowled. "But his crew would be on you in an instant!"

Myrina ground her teeth in the shadows. "If he comes near Phoebe once again I shall have him! Whatever it costs!"

Phoebe was recovering from her head blow, but she seemed not to remember what had happened or where she was. The captain had offered her figs from a barrel he'd got stashed aboard, and she ate them and then was sick. Tamsin was fretful and miserable; in her early years she'd grown used to having a great deal of freedom.

Another day passed, and with careful tending some of the women seemed to be regaining their strength. As darkness fell on the second evening, the sea turned choppy and Myrina's spirits sank again, for she could see no way out of this terrible situation. "If somehow one of us could distract them, while the other snatched a knife . . ." She knew that it would lead to instant death.

"It is the very last resort," Akasya said. "It could go wrong and bring death to all of us!"

But fear of such an attempt going wrong was soon replaced by fear of a very different kind. As the *Artemis* swung farther out into the Black Sea, struggling to hold a course westward, the wind increased, raising the sea to great rolling waves so that the deck began to lurch violently up and down. It seemed they were heading into a storm.

Clouds covered the moon, and it began to rain heavily.

As the ship rolled and the deck turned slippery, neither captives nor crew could do anything but cling to the thwarts and gunwales; before long many aboard were spewing up their guts. The captain called for the helmsman to swing the steering oar around so that they could head back to land and take shelter in the lee of the coast.

"By Maa! We could do without this!" Myrina cursed, clasping Tamsin tightly in her arms.

Akasya held Phoebe, murmuring words of comfort as the girl clapped her hand over her mouth and vomited. But as the ship lurched again Myrina remembered what Iphigenia had said and turned to Akasya. "No—maybe I see the Moon Lady's hand in this! The sea pigs are struggling to stay afloat and cannot watch what we do. Maybe our moment will come."

CHAPTER THREE

The Moon Lady's Hand

AKASYA UNDERSTOOD MYRINA'S suggestion, but she laughed bitterly. "If this is the Moon Lady's hand, I would have chosen a gentler kind of help, not a filthy storm! But that goddess was never known for her gentleness!"

They both looked up to the afterdeck, where the captain and the helmsman struggled and argued over the steering oar. The captain skidded on the wet deck as they tried to haul the heavy oar about and control the ship's direction. The small knife that Myrina had coveted suddenly slipped from his belt and fell onto the lower deck, unnoticed by its owner.

Myrina saw it at once. "Blessings of Mother Maa," she whispered, "but I cannot reach it for this wretched rope!"

She looked back at her young niece, who was struggling not to vomit over Akasya. Phoebe was nimble and brave as a tiger, but this was not the best moment for her.

Tamsin was free to move, but how could she ask one so young to do something so dangerous? Leti and Fara were older and they were free, but should she ask them to carry out something that she feared to ask her own child to do?

Then, as they were hurled against the gunwales, Tamsin wriggled out of her mother's arms. There was no need to ask her—Tamsin was alert at once to the possibility of snatching the knife.

Myrina's guts clenched with fear when she saw what her daughter was about, and Akasya gasped. But Tamsin was a Moon Rider's daughter and already trained to hunt. Myrina gritted her teeth and nodded calmly. "Think lizard," she whispered.

Tamsin sank to the deck and slowly began to move forward on her hands and knees, her movements smooth and slinky. She crossed the small, slippery space while Myrina and Akasya held their breaths. Suddenly she darted fast and accurately toward the knife, snatching it carefully by the handle.

They breathed out with relief. "Little Lizard," Myrina whispered.

Within a moment Myrina had the knife in her hand and had cut her own rope, but then the ship lurched violently again so that her hand cracked against the gunwale, sending the knife sliding far away down to the other end of the middle deck.

"Fool!" Myrina said to herself. "Now get up from the floor and follow it!" She heaved herself to her feet, then skidded through water and vomit the length of the deck. She was kicked and bellowed at by the oarsmen as they struggled to gain control of their vessel. Eventually she banged her elbow so hard against the side of the foredeck that it felt as though the bone had splintered, but there beside her was the knife. Her hand closed over it. "Thank you, Maa!" she whispered.

As she felt the wooden haft inside her palm, the knot of shame burst open and fierce joy rose in her. Now she could fight. She looked up at the afterdeck for the captain. "You first," she muttered. "I will cut your throat!" But then she saw that Iphigenia was watching her every move; she was tied up at the fore end of the corridor, huddled beneath the thwarts. The sight of her friend brought better sense: revenge must wait; freedom must come first. She crawled over and cut the ankle rope that restricted Iphigenia. "You were right. The Moon Lady is with us!" she whispered. "Take the knife and pass it on. I shall wait till more of us are free, then attack!"

Myrina made slow, painful progress back along the lower deck as the ship rolled violently and water swilled and lashed against her. Some of the oarsmen saw and cursed her, but they still struggled to turn the ship around and were afraid to leave the oars. At last the knife appeared at the other end of the corridor, signaling that all the women on Iphigenia's side were free. Myrina snatched it, but the helmsman caught a brief glint of the metal and shouted a warning to the captain and crew. Myrina leaped across to the other side, passing the knife into the hands of her friends. Then she bellowed out the wild Moon Riders' war cry, and the women on Akasya's side answered her, rising as one, grabbing whichever oarsmen were nearest to them and snatching their knives. The men were too shocked to put up much of a fight. They swore and yelled orders at one another, while the oarsmen on the other side howled out curses, uncertain whether they should hang onto their oars or go to the aid of their fellows. Soon all the women were free of their bonds and rose as their sisters had done, snatching weapons and oars. The men were outnumbered, and before they had a chance to understand what was happening, they were sent flying into the ravening sea at the point of their own knives. Myrina leaped onto the afterdeck and sent the captain rolling overboard with a wild howl of glee.

Her heart was now racing with delight at their victory. She snatched Tamsin up into her arms. "Little Lizard, Little Lizard! Snake Mother is so very proud of you," she yelled. But as the boat tipped again and they were flung once more against the gunwales, the joy fled and fear swam back. Myrina's mind swirled with confusion. She knew nothing of boats or sailing, and the fierceness of this storm filled her with dread. She began to bellow orders that sounded confident, but within herself she had little certainty that she did right. "Grab the oars! Haul them in! Sit it out!"

The women obeyed her and after a struggle most of the oars were secured, but then it seemed there was little that they could do but hunker down to sit out the storm and brace themselves against the rolling of the ship. Myrina crouched beside Tamsin and Phoebe to wait until the sun rose or the wind abated, praying that Maa would calm the sea.

At last, as darkness lifted, the wind began to drop, and the waves subsided so that the terrible lurching swing of the *Artemis* ceased. The women clung around the decks more battered than ever, their skin sore and grazed, hair and clothing matted with a thick crusting of salt. As the sun warmed them, they began to stir, gaining confidence in their survival, murmuring and questioning, rubbing themselves down.

"What now?"

"How do we master this boat?"

"We should have kept some of the sea pigs and made them work for us."

Myrina bit her lip, thinking that they were right in

their murmuring. She wandered among them, still afraid to let go of Tamsin.

"Snake Lady?" They looked to her for direction. "What now?"

As her uncertainty and anxiety grew, she looked for Iphigenia, Akasya, and Coronilla, who she knew would always support her. She saw that they were right down at the other end of the ship, standing in the prow, with many of the women gathering about them. Myrina strode toward them, climbing onto the foredeck, the two girls following in her wake.

"Look!" Akasya cried fearfully, pointing into the distance. "The *Apollo* is turning back. Are they coming back to attack and make us slaves again?"

"No!" Iphigenia cried.

Myrina's hand went to the haft of her stolen knife and her heart sank at the thought of it. "We will have to fight again."

But Iphigenia and Akasya were both waving and smiling. "Look!" they cried. "Look at them—see how they row!"

Then Myrina saw it, too: the *Apollo* moved slowly but steadily through the water toward them, her oars rising and dipping as one. As the ship came close, Myrina heard a sound that sent her spirits soaring and warmed her like a fire. It was the ululating Moon Riders' joy cry coming to them from across the rolling waves, soon taken up by those around her.

Centaurea stood holding tightly onto the *Apollo*'s mast, while a plump fisherwoman stood at her side, beating out a steady rhythm on a drum. Each oar was manned by a Moon Rider and rose and fell in excellent time. The *Apollo* had been fortunate to have the fisherwoman aboard—one of those who'd spent their whole lives in and out of boats.

The two ships drew together and one of the fisher-women ran to the gunwales and threw a rope over to the *Artemis*. Soon the brother and sister ships were fastened together and the women swarmed from one to the other, greeting old friends and telling their own tales. Myrina struggled through them to the mast of the Apollo, where Centaurea still stood, but when she got there she was concerned for her friend. Centaurea clung to the mast for support; she had a deep knife wound in her chest. As Myrina took her in her arms, she sank slowly to the deck, the wound bleeding afresh, the seriousness of her hurt only too clear.

Water was brought and Myrina tore a strip from her own ragged smock to wash the wound and try to stanch the bleeding. The fisherwoman who'd been beating the drum bent to help.

"What happened?" Myrina asked her.

"We heard your war cry," she told Myrina, "and this fierce one rose at once, the chant on her lips, too. She snatched the oarsman above her and hauled him down from his perch."

"She was still roped?"

The woman nodded. "Aye, the fellow behind was quick to get out his knife and cut her down, but we'd all heard her cry and understood. We rose in her support and we had a bitter struggle. Three of your Moon Riders are dead and some wounded, but it was Centaurea who took up your cry and led us."

"Our victory is bought at a bitter price," Myrina murmured. She was not surprised at Centaurea's action. The older woman, who bore the body picture of a bear, was as fierce as her special symbol, and in her youth she'd been known for the way she growled as she fought. She had been the special friend of Penthesilea, the leader of the Moon Riders, who was killed fighting Achilles in the struggle for Troy.

"But you, too, have acted with courage," Myrina said. "It was your skills that set them to work on the oars. I did not know how to keep us all afloat on the *Artemis*. What is your name?"

"I am Kora and you honor me with your words," the fisherwoman told her. "The price of our rebellion was high, but it seemed to be a price that both Centaurea and the others were willing to pay."

Myrina's stomach churned, for in a way her action had brought about these deaths and might yet kill Centaurea. By rights the older woman might have claimed the leadership of the Moon Riders long ago and challenged Myrina's youth and suitability for the role, but despite her ferocity, Centaurea had given the Snake Lady nothing but loyalty and encouragement through the years. Since the two old women had died, Centaurea had spent much of her time training and teaching the younger Moon Riders, offering wise advice and help.

"You must get better," Myrina whispered in her ear. "I cannot manage without you."

But Centaurea's strength seemed to be ebbing fast, and she closed her eyes as they tried to make her comfortable on the deck.

The two ships drifted for a while, roped together, while the women ate and drank and rested, but there was little food aboard the two boats even though they shared out the figs that the captain had hoarded for himself. As the sun moved high above the yardarms, Kora made her way to Myrina, who still sat beside Centaurea, feeding her small sips of water.

"Snake Lady," she said to Myrina, "we cannot float here beneath the midday sun forever! What do we do next? Do we turn back to the mouth of the Thermodon?

Do we go home? I know naught of my man and three little ones."

Myrina was uncertain. "Of course you must go back, but as for us . . . ?"

She knew that the main body of Neoptolemus's fleet had gone farther to the east along the shoreline; at some point they must turn back and discover that two of their slave ships had gone astray. If only she'd had a strong army and weapons she would have lain in wait for him and taken a bitter revenge, but she knew that nothing could be gained from thinking in that way. Hati and Atisha had always praised her for leading the slave women out of Troy rather than staying to be slaughtered; she must think hard again—not to seek revenge but to see what could be saved. In this weakened state they must avoid another encounter with Neoptolemus at all costs. If they sailed east, back to the Thermodon, they might well clash with him again. If they sailed west toward the Bosphorus and the Sea of Marmara, they'd never know when he might appear behind them.

Kora saw her doubt. "You Moon Riders know naught of seafaring ways!"

Myrina's cheeks flushed red with the shame of it, and she shook her head. "You speak truth, though I wish I could deny it."

Kora cackled and thumped her shoulder in a friendly

way. "I wouldn't last long on horseback, I can tell you—but the sea is my steed and I know how to ride her. Though he'd deny it, I'd say I'm as good a sailor as my man. Tell me where we should go and I shall show you how to make these ships take us there."

CHAPTER FOUR

Lunardia

MYRINA WAS WARMED by Kora's cheerful confidence, but deciding where they should go was not easy. The whole southern coast of the Black Sea was in danger from the young Ant Man's raiding parties. Myrina frowned—but then almost instinctively she turned toward the north; it seemed there was nowhere else left for them to go. There was nothing to the north but miles and miles of dark blue waves and then, beyond that, the barbarian lands. She had sometimes heard terrifying stories of the bloodthirsty tribes who lived on the northern shores of the Black Sea in a land that was barren and cold. Dare they attempt such a thing?

Kora saw the way her mind was working and raised her eyebrows. "You'd not be thinking of going north, would you? There's naught up there but leagues and leagues of sea—like a wilderness of water; and then when you get there, there's naught but another wilderness of grassland. We can't turn about and set off in that direction—we'd soon run out of food and water."

Myrina nodded, but she still stared northward. Now that she'd taken such a bitter leave of the Thermodon, to return there and live in constant fear of attack seemed a bleak and hopeless prospect.

Kora's brow wrinkled as she racked her brains. "I know a place that would provide safety for a little while: a tiny island, just a little way past the mouth of the Thermodon. We call it Lunardia. There we could catch our breath and have time to think; the fisherfolk would feed us and help you to stock these boats for the longer journey, if you really want to venture north. I could stay for a few days to teach you how to handle the steering and the oars before I set off back to my home."

"I know it." Myrina smiled, warmly gripping Kora by the shoulders. "An island off the coast where the cherry trees grow. We Moon Riders call it the Nest of Maa. Yes—please show us how to get there."

Kora soon had them unfurling the mainsail of the *Artemis*, for the wind was still blowing from the west.

"The wind has blown against us all the way." Myrina laughed. "Maa and the Moon Lady must wish us to go back to Lunardia, I'm sure of it!"

* * *

After just one day of sailing they were back within sight of the coast. As they passed the smoking desolation of the Thermodon in the distance, they stood in silence and watched. Many of the women's cheeks were wet with tears, but their spirits rose when the small island of Lunardia came into view. Dusk fell as they beached the two boats with just a little difficulty and much shouting of instructions from Kora and her friends. The fishing families who lived on the island set aside their nets to greet them with warmth and concern. When they understood who they were and heard what had happened to them, they offered generous hospitality. Neoptolemus had passed their little island by, thinking it not worth the trouble of attacking.

They lit a fire on the beach and organized a good but simple meal of freshly made bread and spit-roasted mackerel.

That night all the Moon Riders who were not injured danced in thanksgiving, both to their kind hosts and to Mother Maa.

They made a strange sight on the beach, a great group of young women, their long hair matted with salt, their skin covered with cuts and bruises, dancing unaccompanied, dressed in rags. Some of them wept as they danced, reliving the terrible slaughter of their boy children, praying to Maa to look after their little ones. Myrina watched with tight lips and dry eyes, remembering the rich jewelery that had once adorned the dancers, the layers of beads and the tinkling bells and cymbals that had been their pride.

"We have nothing left to us," she whispered to Iphigenia.

But Iphigenia would not allow her to be miserable. "Look at them," she insisted. "Look at their spirit and energy; see how their body pictures ripple as they move. They have youth, they have their dances, and, most of all, they have life."

Coronilla lay resting beside them, not quite recovered enough to lead the dancing as she usually did. Now she laughed. "Your words sound strangely familiar, Princess," she said. "It is usually the Snake Lady who speaks with such crazy cheerfulness."

Iphigenia smiled. "It is from the Snake Lady that I have learned such determination," she said.

Myrina was cheered by their praise. Two fisher girls came over to them, carrying the battered drum they had taken from the *Apollo* and an old wooden pipe. Another girl pushed a bundle of wooden spoons into their hands.

"See!" Iphigenia said. "Maa heard your complaints and provided you with instruments."

"Give the pipe to Coronilla," Myrina told them. "She can make a simple pipe sound like the song of the goddess!"

Coronilla took the old chipped pipe and put it to her lips.

Myrina began to beat the drum in a familiar rhythm that made all the Moon Riders smile; they picked up their feet and danced with renewed energy. Iphigenia snatched the wooden spoons and quickly set them clacking in time with the rhythm, two in each hand. Those who were too badly injured to dance clapped and sang. Myrina's spirits soared. Everyone went to sleep feeling warm and exhausted and safe—for a little while at least.

In the cold light of the morning Myrina and Kora tried to explain to the islanders what they wished to do. When they heard Myrina's plans, they shook their heads. Fear gleamed in their eyes, their fingers flicking northward to ward off the evil they believed might come from that direction.

"No, no. It's a terrible journey. We call it the Inhospitable Sea!"

"It's a big voyage."

"The weather changes with a flick of Maa's fingers."

"The winds and waves rise like mountains—and they crash down onto a deck like knives!"

"They kill people there—kill strangers! They sacrifice them to their gods! They are barbarians!"

"Wild men, who drink the blood of horses!"

Myrina smiled. "When I went to Troy as a young girl, I discovered that my tribe, the Mazagardi, were thought to be barbarians by the well-fed city dwellers."

The fisherfolk still shook their heads. "The storms that rage in the northern parts of the Inhospitable Sea will tear a boat apart. We know—our men who have ventured too far do not come back!"

"Better to face storms and barbarians than live beneath the yoke of Achilles' whelp!" Myrina insisted fiercely.

Iphigenia touched her arm in a soothing gesture and began explaining to the islanders more gently. "The young Ant Man will demand tribute from you fisherfolk, which will be harsh enough; but from us he will demand our lives. We warrior women are a threat to him—he will never let us stay here in safety. To us, who love to ride and dance, it will be misery indeed if we are forced to live in hiding."

"We would keep you safe," the shout went up. "Stay here with us!"

"Moon Riders bring the blessings of Maa on our crops and our harvests from the sea!"

"We would guard you with our lives!"

Myrina and Iphigenia were both silenced by such loyalty.

Kora intervened. "Your honor to Maa is not in doubt," she told them, "but I have seen how fiercely these women fight against oppressors. They cannot thrive without their freedom! If they wish to go venturing across the dark sea, I say we should help them!"

There was disappointment but subdued agreement. Aid was offered and determined, practical advice, along with provisions for the voyage, but it was clear that the people of Lunardia were sad to lose their strange and magical visitors so soon.

They all set to work to prepare for the voyage. Kora helped tirelessly, instructing the younger, stronger Moon Riders in the work of hauling in the loose-footed brail sail and turning it to catch the wind. Akasya and Coronilla, now much recovered, learned how to direct the heavy steering oars. Two teams of oarswomen rowed the boats back and forth along the shoreline until they had regained much of their muscular strength and pulled on the oars in perfect harmony.

Phoebe recovered so well that she was soon beating all the fisher boys at races along the beach. She and Tamsin were sent off with their new friends to pick the dark red cherries that grew all around. They would return in the evening, their hands and faces stained with juice, weighed down with the sweet harvest they'd gathered. All the women set about gathering wood, to make new bows, and feathers for fletchings to make their arrows fly true.

Myrina was heartened by it all but worried about her

old friend Centaurea. One of the fisherwomen had made her comfortable in a clean and cozy cottage, hidden among the cherry groves, but though she was nursed with care, her wound was slow to heal and it was clear that her spirits were low.

"You'd best bang a spike through my head as you would a horse," Centaurea told Myrina gruffly when she went to see how she fared. "Or give me a sharp knife and I'll despatch myself."

"Don't you dare speak so," Myrina said, but at the same time her concern grew. How could she take so sick a woman off on a dangerous sea voyage, uncertain whether they would ever find safety at the end of it? To do such a thing might truly make her responsible for her friend's death. She had seen so much death lately that the thought of bringing about one more was terrible.

After seven days of hard work, the *Artemis* and the *Apollo* were ready to set sail, stocked well with grain, salt meat, goat cheese, and cherries. The islanders brought them two pairs of breeding goats and a pair of sheep so that if they could manage to struggle through the winter, they'd have the means to start new herds in the spring.

Kora and four of her friends who lived near the mouth of the Thermodon wished them well and set off in a fishing boat to sail back to their homes. Myrina missed the bossy, capable woman as soon as she had gone and quickly realized how much she had been depending on her sensible, down-to-earth advice.

The younger Moon Riders danced energetically on the shore, hoping to bring a steady southerly wind. Despite the hardships they had suffered, they were eager to be setting sail for the voyage northward across the unknown sea, ready for an adventure after the hopeless despair they'd felt as they faced slavery.

CHAPTER FIVE

A Southerly Wind

T PHIGENIA AND MYRINA sat by Centaurea's bedside,
watching her as she slept; her breathing was light
and shallow. Ida, the daughter of the house, hovered shyly in the doorway.

"May I speak?" she asked respectfully.

"Of course you may," Myrina told her. "We cannot say
how grateful we are for the tender care you've given our
friend."

The girl took a deep breath and began nervously: "We
have been talking, my parents and some of the others."

"Yes?" Myrina was a little impatient.

"Well . . . we have a suggestion to make and if you
answer yes, it would please us greatly."

Iphigenia and Myrina looked up at each other uncertainly.

Ida went on, "We wonder if you would think of leaving
the sick priestess here with us?"

Myrina shook her head at once, but the girl hurried to explain more fully. "I have always wanted so much to join the ranks of the Moon maidens," she whispered. "I wish to learn herb lore and the beautiful sacred dances. Were you to leave the priestess in our care, we would nurse her back to health and give her all the honor that is due to an aging Moon Rider."

Myrina and Iphigenia smiled sadly at each other, touched by the young girl's respect, but the thought of leaving one of their women behind was dreadful to them.

But now that she'd found the courage to speak, Ida was determined that they should understand her intention. "Were you to leave the priestess in our care, we would build a temple to Earth Mother Maa, hidden away high up in the mountain caves that have always been sacred to the goddess."

"You have been thinking carefully about this," Myrina said.

The girl rushed on, sensing that she was at least being listened to. "Should we be blessed with her recovery, the priestess Centaurea would be chief in our country. I would be her devoted servant, and if she judged me worthy, I would be her assistant, too."

Myrina still hesitated, but Centaurea, who they'd all thought was sleeping, murmured and stirred. She had heard and understood Ida's words and now, with

Iphigenia's help, she struggled to sit up.

"Snake Lady," she whispered hoarsely, "this is not for you to decide." She fought to get the words out, but it was clear to them all that they must let her speak. "My answer is . . . yes. I will stay here."

Myrina was deeply saddened at the thought of leaving her old friend behind. Centaurea's good sense had helped the Moon Riders through many a terrible situation, but she could not deny that she was worried about taking her with them. Ida's suggestion had instantly brought a glimmer of determination back into the sick woman's eyes.

"But you are my oldest friend," she whispered, kneeling down beside Centaurea and taking her hand. "You are the only one left of our little group that rode south to rescue Iphigenia."

Centaurea smiled and squeezed Myrina's hand. "What an adventure that was, eh?" She looked up at Iphigenia. "And worth every risk!"

Iphigenia smiled down at her.

Centaurea shook her head. "I don't know why I didn't think of it myself—it's a fine idea. Listen, Snake Lady . . . I may be getting older, but I am no fool—your sea voyage will finish me off, for sure. This way I may live, and live with honor. Ida will make a fine Moon maiden for me to train, and when I die she shall take my place, and in her turn she will train others. We cannot all live here on this tiny island—we would soon be discovered and destroyed—but a few of us, hidden away, may well manage. It will mean that our ways will live on here in secret."

Myrina was running out of arguments.

"I trust these islanders," Centaurea told her firmly. "I trust them completely. And you, Myrina, are quite capable of leading the Moon Riders without my help. You have Iphigenia and all your loyal friends."

Myrina saw how Centaurea's voice grew stronger as she spoke; her will to live was returning as every moment passed and the idea gripped her.

Myrina turned to Iphigenia. "What do you think?"

The serene face of Agamemnon's daughter brightened with amusement. "I think you have your answer clear enough," she said.

The following day a steady southerly wind blew down from the mountains; it blew across the island, making all the fishermen's sails flap and belly northward across the sea.

"This is your moment," Ida's father told them. "This is a blessed wind and you must set sail at once. Neoptolemus will soon be heading back this way and you will ensure your safety and ours by leaving now."

Myrina nodded and gave the signal to leave. Though the idea of sailing northward had been all her own, she was now very sorry to depart from this place of peace and safety. Centaurea was carried down to the beach on a litter, and Myrina saw that her color had already improved. Her voice was now strong and purposeful as she gave orders to the new devotees who crowded around her, running to obey her every command. She cheerfully hugged her departing friends and gave them the priestess's salute.

"Well, well," Myrina murmured. "Perhaps this was meant to be."

"Look at their faces." Iphigenia pointed out the satisfied smiles that appeared all about them. The islanders were well rewarded, now that they had their own priestess.

Myrina acknowledged that she was right. She touched Iphigenia's arm. "Thank goodness I still have you."

She strode aboard the *Apollo* with her crew, each Moon Rider well armed with a strong new bow, a full quiver at her side, a sharp gutting knife in a sheath at her belt. Iphigenia went aboard the *Artemis*, for the fishermen had insisted that each ship must have a captain: in the chaos that might come from fierce wind and waves, each crew must take orders from just one voice.

The teams of oarswomen rowed away from the land, while their friends began to unfurl the brail sail to catch the favorable wind. The *Artemis* moved ahead a little, for just as they were unfurling the sail aboard the *Apollo*, Myrina spied a small fishing boat rowing fast toward them from the west. A red scarf fluttered as though in warning and Myrina did not know whether to hasten away or wait to see what this might mean. Then, as she hesitated, she saw that it was Kora who was waving to her from beneath the red streamer.

"Wait!" she cried. "Hold the sail! Hold the oars! Drop anchor!"

While the *Artemis* headed steadily north, Myrina slipped a rope over the side and hauled Kora aboard the *Apollo*.

"Take me with you!" Kora demanded.

They saw that the strong woman was trembling.

"Of course you may come if you wish it," Myrina assured her. "But what of your man and your little ones?"

"Gone—all gone!" Kora whispered. "Slaughtered in the young Ant Man's wake. Our crops and huts are burned to the ground. I come with you and you must not wait!"

"With all your skills we will be ten times better off," Myrina told her. "There can be nobody more welcome than you. But . . . I am so sorry you have lost your family."

"Unfurl the sail! Get under way!" Kora told her, brushing away sympathy. "A horseman came riding fast down the coast, crying out a warning. The Ant Man's warships are returning from the east."

Myrina gave the order at once and the sail bellied out to catch the wind; only then did Kora allow her to take her into her arms and hug her tightly.

They sailed north for two days with a steady wind behind them. Myrina tried to be calm, but she had never been so far away from any sight of land and she found it frightening to sail on and on and see nothing but waves.

She longed to ask Kora's help, but once they were under way the fisherwoman had became very quiet and withdrawn. They all respected and understood her grief, and Myrina dared not allow her thoughts to be drawn away from the sight of the moon and stars at night, the direction of the wind and pathway of the sun each day.

On the fourth day the wind changed so that it began to blow from the north. They managed to furl their sails carefully and take up the oars, though it was hard work rowing into the wind. They battled onward, the *Artemis* still leading and the *Apollo* struggling on in her wake. The women's newly gained seamanship was tested and proved worthy, but on the evening of the fifth day the wind grew stronger and the waves sent the two vessels tipping fiercely up and down.

Myrina was so worried that, whether the woman was grieving or not, she went to Kora and begged her to get up from beneath the gunwales where she lay and help her.

"One captain only aboard," Kora told her sullenly.

"There may be only one captain, but this captain needs help!" Myrina bellowed.

"I told you that this sea was treacherous! This is the Inhospitable Sea!" Kora shouted back, but she got up with the faintest of smiles and marched to the prow. She pointed out a red streamer, just visible in the gloom, flying from the yardarm of the *Artemis*, still ahead of them.

"Look," she cried. "Iphigenia signals that she will lift the oars and try to sit it out. We should do the same!"

"Lift oars!" Myrina shouted. "Drop anchor!" At once the oarswomen obeyed her. Akasya and Coronilla prepared the heavy anchor to be dropped over the side, but just at that moment they heard a shocking crack that seemed to come from the direction of the *Artemis*. It was so loud that the sound carried over the heaving waves and reached their ears above the roaring of the wind.

"Maa defend us from these winds!" Even Kora could not maintain her confidence, as they saw that the mast of the *Artemis* had crashed down onto the deck, smashing a great gash across the gunwales.

"We must go to help them," Myrina cried. "Lower the oars! Kora—you are captain now—we need your skills!"

Coronilla and Akasya left the anchor and hauled with all their strength to swing the great steering oar around. The oars creaked and groaned as they battled once again with the furious waves. Kora bellowed orders, while Myrina stayed silent as she struggled down toward the prow, ready to help when they neared the stricken vessel. Iphigenia threw them a rope from the stern, and as soon as the two vessels were lashed together prow to stern, Myrina started pulling her friends aboard. The women from the *Artemis* swarmed over the gunwales, wildly grabbing the offered hands of their friends in the *Apollo*. Suddenly, another lurch of the damaged vessel sent the broken mast crashing through the thwarts so that the wild waves rushed in, and in no time the lower middle deck was filling up fast.

"Where is Iphigenia?" Myrina cried.

"There!" Kora yelled and pointed.

Myrina's heart sank when she saw that Iphigenia had gone back to the prow to check that there was nobody injured who might need help.

"Come down here now!" Myrina screamed at her. "Curse her dutiful ways! You must come now!"

But suddenly with another crash the heavy broken mast appeared to split the deck completely in two and Iphigenia was trapped on the far side and carried down into the dark swirling water.

"No! *No!*" Myrina howled.

Coronilla was at her side, the two of them still holding the rope that had lashed the broken *Artemis* to safety.

"We must let go!" Coronilla shouted at her.

"No! No!" Myrina cried. "I cannot lose her!"

The broken half of the *Artemis* that was still fastened to the *Apollo* filled with water fast, the weight of it dragging the *Apollo* over dangerously to the side. Myrina's hands were bleeding and torn, but still she clung to the rope that held the sinking, smashed stern of the *Artemis*. She stared out into the wild darkness after her friend.

Kora strode across the deck and put her own strong hands over Myrina's clenched fists. "You must let go, or we shall all be lost."

Coronilla let go of the rope and then at last Myrina opened her bloodied hands and let it tear through her palms into the sea.

CHAPTER SIX

The Inhospitable Sea

"COME, TAMSIN NEEDS her mother." Akasya took hold of Myrina and pulled her away from the gunwales, dragging her along toward the greased-felt tent they'd rigged up on the lower deck to give some small shelter. Tamsin was crouching there with Phoebe; both girls were silent, their eyes wide with fear. Myrina crumpled down between them as they both put their arms about her. She lay there, clinging tightly to them both for a few dreadful moments, but then she tried to struggle to her feet again. "I am captain, I must give the orders!"

"No," Akasya told her. "Kora is captain for now. You rest. Kora has seen that we are close to land!"

Myrina felt as if her head was full of wool. "Then we have crossed the sea?"

"So it seems! There's land on either side of us! We struggle through a narrow passageway and Kora will try to run for the shore."

The ferocity of the storm continued and the ship swung violently through the darkness. The decks were crowded now with those who'd been saved from the *Artemis*. The women crouched together, quietly gritting their teeth against the wind and rain, each one trying to hold onto the thwarts or the gunwales. To the west for a few moments they glimpsed the distant lights of a city, but the *Apollo* was soon carried violently away from that glimmer of hope on into the wild darkness beyond.

Kora's sharp orders kept them calm, but at last, as they struggled to hold a course, one huge wave sent the *Apollo* lurching sharply up and then down, shaking the mast loose from its base. There was another sickening crack, as the mast and yardarm crashed down through the deck, just as it had on the *Artemis*; it caught Myrina a sharp blow on the head. Black darkness flooded her mind as raging water swamped them, flinging women and girls wildly in all directions, sucking them down into its depths.

Myrina became aware that she was cold, numbingly cold; so cold that it did not seem worth even trying to open her eyes. Perhaps it was best to just slide slowly back into the numb, comforting blankness again. She lay there for what seemed a long while, all energy spent, strangely contented; perhaps she could just stay here and sleep forever.

Somewhere in the distance she could hear a young girl sobbing. The sound disturbed her enough to make her wonder why the girl's mother didn't soothe her; but then with a faint sense of alarm the thought pierced through to her brain that she knew that cry. She began to understand that she herself might be the mother of the girl, and painful though it was, she ought to get up and soothe her daughter.

At last with a huge effort she managed to open her eyes. Bright light sent a sharp pain shooting through her head, so that she quickly snapped her eyelids shut again. When she tried once more, the assault of the light was not quite as powerful, but she still could not focus properly. She blinked hard, shifting the gritty crust that had formed, and at last her eyes began to work again. She was covered in wet sand and seaweed, and there were other sandy, weed-strewn lumps around her that might be her companions. She still had her quiver strapped to her thigh and her knife in its sheath, stuck in her belt.

"Oh Maa!" she whispered. "Where have you brought us to now?"

The sobbing came again and she managed to lift her head, turning blearily in the direction the sounds came from. Tamsin was there and the hopeful thought came to her that if her daughter was sobbing, then she must be alive. Myrina pushed herself up on her palms for a moment, and before her arms gave way she managed to see that Tamsin was crouched farther up the beach, hunkered down beside a rock, her hair matted and wild but her lungs good and strong.

Tamsin was silent for a moment as her mother flopped down again into the gritty sand and seaweed, but then the young girl let out a long, lonely howl of distress that sent energy shooting through Myrina's veins. She pushed herself up again and this time she managed to struggle onto her hands and knees. "He—here," she gulped. "Snake Mother's here! Come to me . . . Little Lizard."

Tamsin scrambled to her feet at once at the sound of her mother's voice. She ran to her, arms spread wide. "Snake Mother," she cried. "I thought you'd gone!"

"No, no," Myrina gasped, hugging her so tightly that the wet sand that covered them both grazed their skin. "Where's Phoebe?"

"I don't know." Tamsin shouted it, as though her mother were stupid to ask.

The noise they made seemed to rouse those about them; almost at once the sound of groans and coughing filled the beach. Vague lumps of soggy sand moved and shuffled, women struggled to their feet and shook themselves, until familiar shapes appeared from the gray featureless grit, though some of the lumps did not move at all.

Myrina looked about her desperately. "Akasya, is that you? Where is Coronilla?"

Akasya looked about wildly. "Coronilla!" she cried.

Tamsin took up the cry. "Coronilla!"

A hump of sand farther up the beach moved a little, then Coronilla rose to her feet, shaking herself like a dog. "Don't worry," she growled. "You can't get rid of me."

Akasya ran to her, smiling.

Myrina spied a large sand lump down by the sea that moved and struggled, trying to roll over. She ran to help. "Kora—thank goodness! What happened?"

The fisherwoman sat up in a shower of damp sand. "What happened? What happened? We ran ashore!"

"Where's our ship?" Myrina asked.

Kora struggled to her feet. She shook her head and pointed to the wreckage that littered the beach and floated in the sea. "It broke up, you stupid woman! It could be worse—Maa has a rough way of dealing with folk."

Myrina might have smiled if her mouth had not been so stiff and numb. Kora's rugged words raised her spirits better than any soothing could have done.

"At least there are no warriors in sight." Myrina scanned the landward horizon for movement.

"Huh!" Kora huffed. "No one but us is crazy enough to claim this desolate spot!"

Kora tried to rouse the inert lump by her side. "Vita! Vita! Come—wake up, honey!"

There was no response.

Kora looked at Myrina and shook her head, her expression grim. "This girl is the same." She had tried to pull a young woman to her feet.

"Phoebe! Phoebe!" Myrina shouted, desperate now to see her niece safe.

A small figure emerged from behind a rock, dragging a broken ship's timber. "M-making a fire." Phoebe struggled to speak. "G-got to get warm! I found your drum, Snake Lady, and your bow!"

Myrina almost wanted to laugh as she hugged her. "Right idea, Young Tiger!" she told her. "A fire's what we need most, but wet wood's no good."

Only then did she really look around her to see what might be scavenged in this land. They were on a wide beach, and though it was covered with wreckage from the *Apollo*, none of it would burn until it was dry. Myrina swung around and put her hand up to shade her eyes. The land was low and featureless, a desolate marshy grassland, with no sign of habitation. A copse of plane trees in the distance might provide some dry fuel and shelter.

She pointed it out to Kora. "We must get ourselves warm or we've no chance."

Coronilla and Akasya had set to work at once to organize the survivors; now they pointed out two young women, waist high in the water. "Snake Lady!" Coronilla reported. "Leti and Fara are wading into the sea to fetch what they can from the wreckage, but we have women with smashed arms and legs and grit and water in their lungs—they must have rest and warmth. We must find some kindling somehow."

"Up there—where there's trees!" Myrina said. "And we must search for our weapons and gather together all we can."

Akasya nodded and held out her hands to Phoebe and Tamsin. "Come on, all the girls—we will walk fast to warm ourselves, then find dry sticks to turn until we make a flame."

Myrina let Akasya go ahead with the girls, then she dragged the two bodies that were closest to her away from the sea and laid them side by side beneath a small, stunted tree, thinking sorrowfully that they must find wood for a pyre as well as warmth. "But we must save the living first!" she muttered, as though giving herself instructions.

Then she went back to the water's edge to help those who were injured. "Go up to that copse," she ordered. "Huddle together! Give each other warmth! We will find kindling as soon as we can."

Wood was not plentiful in the marshy grassland, but among the group of windblown trees the girls managed to scavenge enough and at least what they found was dry. Akasya pointed out dry animal dung that would burn. A clear stream ran through the copse. Tamsin and Phoebe found dry sticks and shaved sharp points on them. They set them turning on dry logs, rolling them between their palms until their hands were sore. But their hard work was at last rewarded with a skein of smoldering, sweet-smelling smoke, then sparks and flames. They carefully fed the flames with dry kindling, and the freezing, soaked women who slowly gathered beneath the trees smiled with relief and held out their hands to the fire.

"Well done!" Coronilla approved. "Do not let this fire go out! It is your job to guard it! This fire will mean life or death to us!"

Phoebe nodded, taking her responsibility seriously, determined to do this job as well as she could. "Fetch those twigs!" she ordered Tamsin. "And more over there!"

Back at the beach Myrina saw the twirling smoke and smiled. Leti and Fara had managed to garner many items from the water, and so planks of wreckage now became crutches and litters to carry those who'd been injured up to the fireside. They hauled ashore the bodies of the four drowned goats, for Myrina swore that nothing must be wasted.

"That is our meal for tonight," she told them, without mercy. "So much for our hopes of breeding. What of the sheep?"

Fara shrugged wearily. "Drowned like the goats, I should think."

"We must find them," Myrina insisted. "If they have drowned, then we need their meat to sustain us and their skins to help us keep warm."

After a short search Fara gave a shout and dived into the deeper water. She emerged with one of the drowned sheep, its thick wool so heavy and drenched that its body could not float on the surface.

"Well done!" Myrina cried. "Meat and a skin—we must try to find the other one."

She made them drag the corpse of the sheep up to the camp. Only then could they give their minds to the best way of treating their own dead with respect. Six drowned Moon Riders were now laid out by the stunted tree, so Myrina organized a solemn procession of women to carry them up to the campfire.

Myrina walked behind them, distressed to have lost so many. As she followed in their wake her steps slowed and her thoughts fled back to the sight of Iphigenia disappearing into the dark and terrible sea. At least she had the bodies of these six Moon Riders and could perform the sacred rites that would send them safe into the arms of Maa.

Somehow she had managed to force Iphigenia out of her mind while it had been so vital to save Tamsin and Phoebe and help the others. Now that the immediate crisis had passed, the horror and terrible emptiness of losing her dear friend flooded back to her.

CHAPTER SEVEN

Where Magic Lies

THE PROCESSION MOVED ahead while Myrina stumbled and stopped, sinking down onto a rock beside a small pool. She dropped her head into her hands and sat, still and desolate, slowly growing cold again, her thoughts a wild muddle of sorrow and despair.

Her mind slipped back over the years. "We have lost too much," she murmured. "Too much!"

Over and over again the Moon Riders had fought back against all the odds. They had struggled on despite the loss of friends, lands, purpose, and power. The battle at the River Thermodon and the destruction of Myrina's magical mirror had been terrible, but the loss of Iphigenia, whom they had risked so much to save . . . this was more than she could bear.

At last she lifted her head, gazing down into the still water at her feet. "Princess—priestess," she whispered, her voice hoarse and breaking, "where have you gone?

Did we rescue you from the sacrificial knife only to let you die in this cold, dark sea?"

The water beneath her reflected a white-gray sky, with clouds that slowly shifted across her vision. The surface of the pool glinted with a touch of frosty light that struck right down through the water to the bottom, where the sand was patterned in waves. The tide had etched small diamond shapes there, creating a small but perfect world inside the pool. As Myrina stared down at it, she slowly drifted into a dreamy state of half sleep that was not unfamiliar to her. A tiny seed of comfort grew and began to spread through her body. She gazed at the reflection of the moving clouds and then through them to the mirrored image of the sky beyond.

Her shoulders drooped and her breathing slowed; this was almost like gazing into her mirror. Was it possible that she did not need a magical mirror to see loved ones far away?

"Iphigenia. . ." She murmured the name over and over again. "Iphigenia!"

She gasped as at last the pattern of shifting clouds slowly began to clear, showing her the recognizable shape of a coastline—very different from the one the sea had thrown them onto. An inlet of water with a narrow sea entrance was almost enclosed by towering cliffs. Inside was a small beach edged by buildings, some of them very large and grand. A city had been built into the steep hill-side, with the water lapping at its feet.

Her focus shifted to the flotsam and jetsam that had been thrown onto the beach in the wake of a storm. Could it be wreckage from the same storm that had smashed the *Apollo* and driven them ashore? Could this be the city whose lights they'd glimpsed? But there in her vision was a sight that made her heart beat faster. A young woman lay on the beach, thrown up onto the sand among the rubbish; it looked as though the woman clung to a solid wooden shape that she recognized: the carved figurehead of the Moon Lady—Artemis herself.

"Iphigenia. . ." Myrina's lips moved in wonder. "Can she be alive?"

She watched and saw that many people were running down to the beach, picking up bits of wreckage, curious to see what the tide had washed up. They gathered about the inert figure. Myrina watched with concern. Were they friendly? Could Iphigenia really be alive?

Then she saw with joy and gratitude that they were wrapping her in a warm cloak and giving her something to drink. "She must be alive!" Myrina murmured.

The figurehead was lifted high, and suddenly these strange people were dancing around the carved figure and bowing to the princess who'd been washed ashore in such a bedraggled state.

"She's alive, she's alive!" Myrina cried out loud with delight and clapped her hands.

The vision faded as she spoke, though she tried hard to grab it back again. At last she reluctantly gave up the struggle; she was too exhausted and cold to find the image again and she'd seen the most important thing. She sat on the rock for a moment, smiling and wondering. "My dear friend lives and . . . I do not need a magic mirror," she whispered. "The magic is in me—it is here in me!"

She did not know where Iphigenia was, but she had seen enough to trust that she was not dead and not in any immediate danger. This knowledge meant everything to her; now despair could be thrown aside. She and her companions must find a way of surviving in this unfamiliar, bare landscape. Perhaps, after all, the decision to travel north might still prove to have been a good one. She rose to her feet, stiff and cold again, but her spirits were higher than they had been all through the day. She set off at once, marching toward the Moon Riders' camp and the fire.

Coronilla, Akasya, and Kora had worked wonders. Barrels and baskets were stacked outside the copse, drying in the last rays of the setting sun. Even some of the cloaks and clothing had been retrieved and were now hanging out to dry on the lower branches of the trees.

"Here, see what we've found!" Tamsin leaped up at the sight of her mother. She held out a handful of hazelnuts.

"I can crack them with my teeth!"

Myrina smiled and then she suddenly laughed out loud at the sight of Leti chasing the other sheep. Somehow against all the odds the creature had managed to scramble ashore and find itself a bit of fresh grass to nibble. Pleased with its newfound freedom, it was determined not to be caught. The strong young woman chased it around the marshy ground with just the same determination, and at last she flung herself full length and wrestled it to the ground. The sheep gave up at last and allowed itself to be led back to the camp, bleating and protesting loudly, both animal and Moon Rider covered in sticky mud.

"Well done! Well done!" Myrina clapped her hands.

Then she looked down at the six bodies of her friends and her laughter fled. "Now, as darkness falls about us, we must build the fire up into a pyre," she said. "Then we will feast and dance to honor our dead—but I must tell you this: I believe Iphigenia lives! I have seen her in a strange watery vision. I cannot swear that what I have seen is true, but I believe it is."

Kora frowned and shook her head and murmurs of sorrow came from all around, but Coronilla touched her shoulder. "Snake Lady, if our lost priestess lives and could send a vision of hope, then she would surely send it to you."

Myrina smiled, glad that they did not pour scorn on her words.

The two drowned goats were roasted on hastily improvised spits and the mouthwatering scent of roasting meat drifted among the trees. Myrina hesitated for a moment, but then she remembered her vision of Iphigenia and decided that they should open a barrel of cherries stored in wine that had been saved from the sea.

Suddenly she was struck by uncertainty. "Maybe we should eke out our provisions," she said to Kora. "Do you think this right?"

"Yes," the practical woman agreed. "In the days to come we must save all we can, but tonight we are battered and bruised. Open the barrel and let them eat, for we must somehow get through this harsh night and honor the dead. Let us keep our self-respect and dignity."

Myrina nodded, grateful for this support. Roasted goat meat had never tasted so good and the cherries in wine cheered and warmed them all, but nobody begged for more, not even Tamsin, almost as though they sensed the need for restraint.

When they had eaten, they all stood up to dance. First they moved in a solemn circle around their comrades' pyre. Though the air was full of sadness, still it was good to move. Coronilla played her pipe, the slow notes rising and falling in a lament that had become all too familiar. Myrina beat out a rhythm on her drum, though tears poured down her cheeks as she thought of the missing clack of Iphigenia's castanets. Even those who were injured made their contribution, keeping up a steady clapping rhythm and lifting their voices in the slow thrumming songs that would see their lost sisters safely back into the earthy care of Mother Maa.

Later, as the flames licked high into the darkness, the atmosphere changed and the women began to catch each other's hands and form the long chain of crisscrossed arms; this was the dance that many of the women had invented when they were Trojan slaves. It expressed respect for the dead, just as much as the slow circle, but it was also a dance of life and survival. At first the young people stood back and watched their elders as each woman began chanting and singing in the language of her own long-lost homeland. But as the dance progressed, they all began to chant in the Luvvian tongue, symbolizing their unity, and moved together in perfect harmony.

Then at last the young ones leaped up to join them, smiling and laughing as they remembered the stories of their births. Most of the children had been conceived in slavery, their mothers used for comfort by the warriors who had traveled far from their homes to defend the city of Troy. The women had had no choice but to bear these children and they had suffered terribly, but the years of peace on the banks of the Thermodon had restored their pride and purpose. No Moon Rider had anything but total love for her child.

"We live! We live!" they sang. "We live and survive!"

As the flames burned low, sending smoke twisting high into the night sky, the rhythms of the dance quickened even more and wild songs of thanksgiving made their spirits soar, while blood went racing through their veins, making them warm and cheerful.

Then at last Myrina called for the gentle moon dance, fearful that they would exhaust themselves and anxious to settle them to a restful sleep, for they would certainly need all their energy to face the coming day.

Night watchers were appointed, and Myrina snuggled in between Tamsin and Phoebe, grateful for the warmth that they'd built up beneath the smoky, seaweed-smelling blankets that the fire had dried.

Coronilla shook Myrina awake as the first blurry rays of acacia-colored light touched the eastern horizon. "What now?" she growled.

But Coronilla would not be put off. "Open your eyes, Snake Lady," she insisted. "Akasya and I have seen such a sight that will make you howl for joy. Get up off your backside and come and see!"

The suppressed excitement in Coronilla's voice made Myrina snap into action, wide awake and ready for anything. She leaped to her feet, full of curiosity. "What is it?

Why do you have to make such a mystery of it?"

But Coronilla's eyes gleamed with mischief. "I'm not saying! I want to see your face!"

"Then take me to it—quickly, at once!"

Her friends grabbed her by the arms and pulled her along between them, away from the sea, away from the copse of trees, and up a gentle slope to some rocks, where Leti and Fara were crouched. They lay flat on their bellies, keeping their heads down, but Myrina could see that they watched something or someone down below them on the other side of the rocks. They both turned at her approach, huge grins on their faces. Leti lowered her palm in warning, then raised a finger to her lips for quiet.

Myrina sank like a cat, moving slowly forward, belly low. They made a space for her to creep between them, then at last she carefully stretched her neck out to see what it was that brought such excitement. They all turned to witness the wonderful look of surprise that lit her face. "Thank you, Maa," she whispered, closing her eyes for a moment. "Now we are safe! Now we can survive!"

A grassy valley rolled gently away from them, sloping down to a wide river that curved its way through the lowest ground; but, most wonderful of all, along the banks of the river, tossing their manes, nickering gently to one another, moved a herd of wild horses.

CHAPTER EIGHT

A Gift from Maa

T HE MOON RIDERS lay for a while just watching
the horses, still as statues, huge smiles on their
faces, eyes wide with delight.

The main herd grazed on the river-watered grass.
Their coats gleamed in the early morning sun, gray,
brown, black, and chestnut. One huge light-bay stallion
moved among the mares like a king or a great chieftain.
A little way upriver a smaller group of young males con-
gregated, expelled from their mothers' care as they
reached maturity. They were the hangers-on kept at a
safe distance from the mares by the stallion, who
patrolled the boundaries of his harem. All the beasts were
strong and healthy, well fed from the green grass.

"Mare's milk!" Myrina whispered. "Mare's milk, hide,
and steeds."

"Do you see the herd leader?" Coronilla pointed to a
beautiful blue-black mare who moved among the young

foals, giving them bossy nips if they got in her way. "She should do for you."

But the sight of the beast rung Myrina's heart, making her think of Isatis. "No"—she shook her head—"I could not have a blue-black mare again; you take her."

"With pleasure," Coronilla whispered, her voice full of reverence. "Do you think Maa placed them here just for us?"

"I don't know," Myrina replied, "but no other sight could bring such a warmth to my heart."

They stayed there for a little longer, but then Myrina backed away, keeping her head down until she was well out of sight of the herd. She struggled to her feet, trying to calm her excitement. "There is much to do. Leti, Fara, will you two stay here and keep watch? Fetch me if there is any sign of them moving away."

Leti and Fara were more than content with their role, while the older women crept back to the camp, full of plans.

News of the discovery flew fast through the camp. Though some of the younger women were eager to rush off to claim their chosen beast, Myrina insisted that they gather about her and talk through their plans.

"We cannot take a chance of startling them!" she said fiercely. "This must be done the Mazagardi way—you all know what that means. Any woman who disobeys can walk away and find her own way of living in this desolate place."

Some of the girls were shocked to hear her speaking so sternly, but Kora, Akasya, and Coronilla backed her every word. At last they settled down and listened carefully to her plan.

"Do you understand?" she demanded. "This time we cannot afford to make a mistake!"

They listened carefully and agreed.

That night the Moon Riders performed the horse dance about their fire. They pawed at the ground and stamped, tossing their heads this way and that, imitating the movements of trotting, cantering, and galloping. They remembered with great sadness and longing the steeds that had been so cruelly slaughtered by the Ant Men, but they also recalled the joyful swing of the hips that came to every rider as the horse got into its stride. They longed for the pleasant feeling of a cooling breeze swishing through their hair as the horse gathered speed. They yearned for the wonderful warm scent of horseflesh.

Next morning they rose before dawn and danced enthusiastically to welcome the sun. Coronilla's group set off first, for they had far to go, and they carried small bundles of food strapped to their backs. Akasya and her friend Nessa soon followed them, walking quietly through the woods. Leti and Fara also went, each in a different direction, Leti walking calmly away to the east and Fara to the west. All the women kept well out of hearing range or scent of the horses.

Myrina waited with Tamsin and Phoebe—they were the last to leave the camp. Kora stayed behind to tend the sick and feed the fire, with a few good bow-women ready to defend the meager stock of food they possessed. Though Kora understood the delight that the Moon Riders felt at the discovery of the herd, she swore that she would never go near one of those dangerous beasts.

Phoebe and Tamsin walked stealthily beside Myrina, moving like leopards. They approached the lookout spot and dropped to the ground without a word. Then they quietly set about making themselves comfortable on their bellies, keeping their heads low, for there would be a long wait ahead. They must be patient: their very lives might depend on the outcome of this venture.

They lay watching the horses with greedy eyes. The sight of them was so exhilarating that for the moment they could be content just to look.

"The golden mare with the sandy mane is mine," Phoebe whispered fiercely. "Sandmane I name her."

Tamsin frowned. "You're welcome. The black with white boots is mine!"

"White boots?" Phoebe protested. "Where? Oh—I see her; I want her, too!"

"Tough!" Tamsin grinned. "She is mine! I name her Snowboots. A horse once named is yours forever!"

Phoebe sighed, but then she smiled again. "See how Sandmane tosses her head! I will stick by her. Which will you name, Snake Mother?"

Myrina pressed her lips together in perplexity and shook her head. The delicate stepping, the rippling, muscular hides, many of them gleaming blue-black, made her heart bleed anew for Isatis. She was in no hurry to name another steed.

The sun moved slowly across the sky and at last, as it hovered above them, Myrina got to her knees and nodded. "Stand up now," she whispered.

The Moon Riders in the far distance rose smoothly to their feet as soon as they saw Myrina move. They spread out in a long encircling line, in full view of the horses but still far away from them. They stood watching but keeping very still and quiet, while a few of the horses raised their heads, sniffed the air, flared their nostrils, and looked at them. The calm stillness of the women was so unthreatening that they soon dipped their heads again to the river-watered grass.

"There." Myrina spoke with satisfaction, nodding into the distance. They could see that Coronilla's group had waded through the river out of sight of the herd and now emerged from behind some rocks on the far riverbank.

Myrina turned her head to the east and saw with satisfaction that Nessa and her friends stood beneath a clump of trees. Then they looked westward and saw that Akasya had staked out a spot on the gentle slope of a grassy hillside.

"Right!" Myrina gave the order in a low voice. "Six steps!"

Phoebe and Tamsin took six steps forward with her, counting carefully under their breaths.

Some of the horses looked up again, catching the movement, but again the stillness of the women soothed any fears and they were soon cropping grass again.

The other Moon Riders saw them move and followed their lead, each taking six steps forward, so that a wide loose circle was formed about the herd.

"Sit!" Myrina said.

They sank smoothly down to the ground and their friends in the distance did the same. They calmly took out their bundles and began to eat the flat grainy bread and small scraps of roast goat meat that they'd managed to save from the night before.

"Talk," Myrina ordered. "You can talk now, but do not shout."

At the sound of low voices the horses put back their ears and a few tossed their heads, rolling their eyes at the intruders; but as the murmur of voices continued, they lost interest and went back to their grazing.

Myrina gave the order to move twice more as the sun traveled across the sky, so that as it began to sink in the west a thin line of Moon Riders stretched all around the herd. There was no singing or dancing that evening; the women settled quietly to sleep wherever they were, taking turns to watch through the night.

They woke early next morning and rose to their feet at Myrina's signal. Once again they stood very still for a while, then began to move around and chat to each other. Their backs were sore and muscles stiff, still suffering from the bruising of the waves. When Myrina signaled again, some of the women began walking steadily down to the water, pitchers in their hands. The nearest horses skittered away nervously; the stallion snorted at the disturbance, shaking his head from side to side. The blue-black mare came forward, snapping her teeth, but the Moon Riders simply ignored her, unhurriedly filling their pitchers with the clean water, then walked slowly back up the riverbank to join their friends. The beasts settled quickly as they saw the women calmly retreating again.

That evening there was still no dancing, but they lit small fires. The Moon Riders moved about a little more freely and ate the rest of their food, then stood solemnly in their wide circle while Myrina raised her drinking horn. "We share water with you, four legs," she said in a deep, singsong voice. "Now we will sing to you."

The women began a gentle rhythmic humming that rose and fell in pleasant, soothing tones, almost like a lullaby. The horses raised their heads and pricked up their ears. A few of them cantered about for a while, but the strange music continued and when they saw that no threat came with it, those who'd been disturbed soon settled.

The low singing continued as darkness fell; gradually it ceased as the women wrapped themselves up as best they could and settled to sleep again.

"I will get you, Snowboots," Tamsin promised sleepily. "I will get you and it won't be long now!"

As pink fingers of dawn stretched across the sky, the women rose and wandered down to the water, yawning and stretching, ignoring the beasts that stamped about the shallows. This time there was little disturbance among the horses. Kora and the others who had stayed behind at the old camp arrived during the morning, carrying their barrels and precious supplies up through the trees. All those who'd been hurt had recovered enough to walk a little, and Myrina was satisfied that their horse gentling was going well and a sense of order and purpose had returned to the Moon Riders. The one precious sheep was settled in a small corral, well away from the horses.

Kora stared in wonder at the sight of the powerful beasts calmly cropping grass as the women wandered among them. She watched them, eyes wide, but nervously kept her distance.

"I made a net from scraps of salvaged rigging," she told Myrina, ever practical. "I have caught a basketful of mackerel. We may cook them tonight, but then we have little left but one barrel of cherries. Up here there's nothing but grass. I see very well that you lot can live like horses, but that is taking it too far for me!"

Myrina laughed. "You have all the skills we lack; together we'll do well!"

She was grateful for Kora's determined humor, but she knew that there was a worrying truth behind the jokes. "There are a few mares still in milk and their foals are old enough to be weaned. Once we have their trust, we will be able to milk them, but that will not be until after the next full moon."

Kora was not impressed. "It is going to take more than a pitcher of mare's milk to feed this lot," she insisted. "Don't you eat horseflesh? I thought you Moon Riders made your body armor from horsehide!"

Myrina shrugged uncomfortably. The possibility of being forced to do just that had already been in her thoughts. "We bring merciful death to a horse that grows old or suffers, and then, yes, we use the skin and hair, for we believe the wearer of horse skin is endowed with the beast's courage. As for eating horseflesh—if it comes to that or starvation, yes, we will do it, but it is not the best way to gain their trust!"

"Don't you arch your neck like that at me, Snake Lady!" Kora folded her arms and stood her ground.

Myrina relented and smiled ruefully, knowing that she'd been unfairly sharp. "You raise fears that I don't want to face—not just yet. But you are wise to think ahead. Get your net and take some of the girls fishing again!"

Kora imitated the Moon Riders' salute and went away smiling.

Myrina sighed. They should go out hunting, but the horses were not ready for it; and to rush them could mean losing everything. It was suddenly very hard to be patient.

CHAPTER NINE

Mazagardi Skills

K ORA, AND THOSE who were not fit enough for
the horse gentling, busied themselves keeping
fires and gathering wood. All who felt that they
could do it spent the morning wandering back and forth
to the river, appearing to ignore the horses, but secretly
moving closer to them all the time. When the sun
reached its highest point in the sky, Myrina lifted her
hand, and at this signal some of the women retreated to
the camp. They all understood what it meant: the time
for gentling was over; now the real work of taming must
begin.

Myrina backed off a little so that she could watch carefully, for this was the most important moment of all. If
the horses began to accept their names and riders, they
had won the herd; if the beasts took fright and dashed
away, everything would be lost.

The small group who had stayed were the most skilled

and experienced horsewomen, and now they strode toward their chosen steeds, a determined advance guard but patience still the most important of their weapons. Each woman picked out her favored mare and in a deep, firm voice spoke the name that she had chosen, fixing her beast eye to eye with a direct gaze.

"Boss Lady, you are mine!" Coronilla named the blue-black leader of the mares. The newly named Boss Lady backed away for a moment, but then advanced, fiercely snapping her teeth. Coronilla stood her ground and snapped back, so that the mare hesitated, pawing the ground uncertainly.

"Silversnow . . ." Akasya claimed a beautiful silver-white mare, who seemed to accept her willingly.

Each woman stayed close to her chosen one, moving at the beast's side, repeatedly speaking the magical name that she had given, but still no attempt was made to touch. Myrina watched them, her eyes searching among the mares for the one that she would choose. "When I see her, I will know," she told herself.

Tamsin was anxious. "Can I go now? Someone else may choose Snowboots! And a horse once named—"

Phoebe flared her nostrils and ground her teeth. "You've made it clear enough to us all!" she said. "None of us would dare!"

"Patience is everything, Little Lizard!" Myrina told her.

Tamsin sighed and tried to settle down to keep a watch on Snowboots.

Myrina sighed, envying her child such certainty. Still she searched among the pricked ears and flashing manes, but none of the horses seemed to be quite the right one for a weary snake lady. After the powerful bond that she'd had with Isatis, it was going to be difficult to give her heart to another horse. Well, she would set Tamsin a good example by waiting calmly and allowing the others to go forward and make their choices first.

For a while the horse taming went well: the mares seemed to be accepting the strange two-legged creatures who fixed them with determined stares, then strode at their sides. But as the sun began to sink, the big bay stallion became unsettled. He stamped angrily as he sensed this crafty, uninvited intrusion among his mares. He began to canter around the edges, snorting, so that some of the mares backed away from their Moon Rider, aware of his agitation.

Myrina watched him uneasily and rose to her feet. She swore under her breath as the thought came into her head that perhaps her choice was about to be made for her—and what a choice! They might well lose all the mares if the stallion could not be mastered. A dangerous situation was developing and something must be done to stop it.

"Wait until I call you," she ordered Phoebe and Tamsin.

They watched her, wide-eyed and anxious, as she set out to face the snorting bay, racking her brain for the right name.

The huge horse screamed, baring his teeth at her approach. All the Moon Riders saw what Myrina was doing and stood still, holding their breaths. She strode toward him, fixing his gleaming dark eyes with an angry stare. He reared threateningly, his hooves trampling the air high above her head.

"Dear Snake Lady!" Akasya whispered. "Please Maa she knows what she does!"

Myrina stormed on until she stood right in front of him. She pulled herself up to her full height, stretching up on tiptoe, stiff and straight as a rod; they stood head to head, both breathing heavily.

Tamsin bit her lip, clutching Phoebe's hand. None of the women dared move or make a sound; everything depended on this.

Suddenly the stallion reared again so that Myrina was forced to flinch back a little or get one of those heavy hooves in her face. As he reared, he screamed again, a ter-rifying, warlike bellow, mouth wide open, baring his great teeth.

But as his hooves thumped down onto the grass in front of her, Myrina was ready for him. She strode forward again, slapping him sharply across the muzzle and baring her own teeth. She answered him with a wild beastlike bellow. "*Aaaagh!*" she roared. "I can do that, too!"

The stallion's ears shot back in surprise and his eyes rolled wildly.

"*Aaagh!*" she roared again, at the top of her lungs. "I name you Big Chief. You are Big Chief and nothing else will do!"

There was silence for a moment as the two stood head to head again, both very still but eyeing each other fiercely. The stallion stamped again, but did not rear this time.

"Big Chief!" Myrina spoke his name again in a gentler tone. "I name you Big Chief and I shall be your rider!"

There was another tense moment, but then the huge stallion stretched out his muzzle and sniffed all around Myrina's hair with unexpected delicacy. He blew warm horse breath over her face and shoulders. The scent of it warmed her and brought back happy memories.

"We will be friends," she told him firmly, putting out her hand to stroke his nose. "See—I can touch you like this! I will not hurt you again."

Big Chief gave a low, gentle whicker.

The watching women breathed out in relief and turned their attention once more to their own chosen beasts. Myrina smiled shakily and stroked the horse's nose again;

she knew that she had won, but it had drained her of energy, leaving her feeling weak. As she withdrew her hand, the great bay lowered his head to crop peacefully at the grass at her feet; Big Chief had accepted both his name and his rider.

Myrina turned to where Phoebe and Tamsin stood watching and beckoned to them. They strode down to her with confidence, anxious to give Snowboots and Sandmane their names before the last rays of sun left the plain in darkness.

That night, as the women moved back to the circle of campfires, some of the horses raised their heads, almost as if they regretted that their new friends were leaving them so soon. They watched carefully to see which path their chosen Moon Rider took.

Later that night, as Myrina sat eating the roasted mackerel that Kora had provided, Fara and some of her friends walked to her. Myrina looked up, concerned that they had left their side of the circle unguarded.

"Snake Lady, there is something we think you should know!" Fara spoke quickly. "We watch the horses—but we ourselves are watched!"

Myrina looked about in alarm. "Where? Who?"

Fara pointed over to the north on the far side of the river. "There beneath those rocks that we think have the shape of an eagle. There is a small camp of men with horses," she whispered. "Not many, I think—they seem to do nothing but watch."

Myrina swore. This was something they could really do without, but she knew that they couldn't expect to turn up in a strange land and find it empty of inhabitants.

"We have heard that bloodthirsty warriors ride in this land." Fara made a fierce face. "But we are no cowards; we can fight!"

Myrina was irritated; she really did not want to hear such news, just as things were going so well. "Yes, we will fight if we have to, but"—she shrugged—"I know what it is to have your traveling lands invaded by strangers. These men cannot know who we are or what we want."

Coronilla, who was usually the first to leap into a fight, supported her. "I have never forgotten the fear we felt when strangers came raiding our home. I would not rush to attack them. If they were going to expel us, why have they not done so already?"

Fara shuffled her feet and huffed impatiently.

"If they do attack, we will defend ourselves," Myrina assured her. "But I do not wish to interrupt our horse taming at the moment. If we have to stop and fight, we may lose the whole herd. It will not be long now before we have steeds to carry us. With these we may defend ourselves from a much stronger position."

Fara nodded. This couldn't be denied. "Can't we speed up the horse taming?"

"No!" Myrina snapped.

Fara flinched.

Myrina saw at once that she'd been ungrateful. "Do not look so hurt," she begged. "You have done well to tell me. But while they hide in rocks and peek at us, let us ignore them. Pass the message around that they are there. We must keep an eye on them and have our bows ready at all times."

Fara nodded and went off obediently, but it was clear from their resentful whispering that she and her friends were keen to take action.

The next morning the women returned to mingle with the herd, each Moon Rider following her chosen beast. By the late afternoon handfuls of fresh grass were being offered and accepted; firm but gentle hands stretched out to soothe a nose or fetlock. When darkness fell and the women walked away, faint whinnies of disappointment followed them. They smiled at one another, well content to hear the friendly sounds.

"The men still hide out in the rocks and watch us," Fara told Myrina.

"Yes," she said. "I have seen them myself."

* * *

The following morning they were delighted to see that a few of the horses had wandered up the slope toward their camp and were waiting patiently for their special friends to come and feed them grass. Big Chief trotted away from the waterside and up the bank, looking for Myrina, ready to fix her with his fine black eyes. The morning was spent again in friendly feeding and grooming; blankets were slipped onto the horses' backs so that they could get used to the feeling of weight.

Days passed and both women and horses fell into a contented pattern of companionship. Each night the Moon Riders sang and danced while the herd listened, twitching their ears, reassured now by the sounds. As the days passed, little by little, bundles of sand and soil were placed on the horses' backs. Then, the morning after the full moon, they agreed that the time had come for them to teach their chosen ones what real closeness between horse and rider was all about.

The women strode confidently down the bank toward the herd. This was the most important day of all—this friendly battle would finally be won or lost. As the sun rose to the highest point in the sky, Myrina raised her hands, and with one accord each woman leaped lightly onto the back of her steed. A few horses skidded in panic, but the women held on tight with their strong thighs that remembered well the warm feel of horseflesh. Soothing hands on necks and flanks reassured the beasts and soon each rider had her chosen one trotting obediently in whichever direction she wished.

Tamsin laughed out loud as Snowboots turned obediently at her command.

"Steady, Little Lizard," Myrina warned. "Do not gallop before you can trot!"

The women struggled to maintain their tranquility, but they could not help but send beaming smiles at one another, rejoicing in this achievement. On horseback their spirits lifted, so that the humiliation of their capture and slavery faded far into the past. If they could live in partnership with these spirited steeds, then they were truly Moon Riders once again, half-wild, magic women, full of strength and confidence.

Myrina could not help but crow. "Mazagardi horse skills, once learned, are never forgotten!"

CHAPTER TEN

Leti

FARA POINTED OUT to Myrina the glint of metal
that she'd caught in the moonlight, over beyond
the rocks and trees. "Now we have our steeds
should we not charge over and rout them out?"

But Myrina shrugged. "Let them play at peek and
hide." She laughed. "They do not seem eager to advance."

The horses whinnied contentedly in the bright moonlight as the Moon Riders danced and sang. That night
everyone went to sleep exhausted but content.

Startling wild cries from the horses woke them just as
the first fingers of light crept across the sky. The Moon
Riders struggled to their feet, snatching up their bows at
once. As they emerged from their shelters the sight that
met their eyes filled them with fury. A small group of men
rode fast among the horses, roping whichever beasts they
could reach, sending terror racing through the herd that
they had worked so hard and so patiently to win.

"Maa take them!"

"Curse their hides!"

"Who was on watch?"

Myrina strode down toward the river, whipping an arrow from her quiver and bending her bow. She was furious with the thieves and furious with herself. She'd been so pleased with their achievements, so exhausted at the end of the day, that she'd forgotten to set a watch. The women followed in her wake, swearing beneath their breaths, unwilling to scream out their rage for fear of sending the horses into further panic. But though they were at a disadvantage, still bleary eyed from sleep, they nocked their arrows and sent them flying fast toward the now fleeing men. Leti managed to catch her chosen horse running wild and distressed toward the camp. She leaped astride and raced after them, screaming abuse.

"No!" Myrina bellowed after her. "Come back. They are not worth the risk!"

But Leti's fury made her deaf to all commands and, as she hurtled after them, her anger grew. She loosed her arrows and brought two of the men down. But the thieves were also armed with bows and they turned easily on horseback to swat this bothersome fly that would not be shaken off.

"Ah . . . Leti!" the women gasped. They saw her fall, two arrows in her chest.

"Vermin!" Fara cried, wildly looking for her own chosen horse among the panicking herd. "I will kill them! They shall feel my darts!"

"No!" Myrina shouted, racing after her. "I forbid it!"

"Stupid, ignorant ones," Fara went on, venting her rage. "Such cowards! They raid us like wicked children and run away!" She vaulted up onto the back of her chosen one, but saw that the women were looking again into the distance.

The men had turned their horses back and dismounted close to where Leti lay. It seemed they were stooping to examine her body.

Phoebe was fearful. "What will they do to her?"

"Oh Leti!" Tamsin trembled.

"Whatever they do, Leti will not know," Akasya told them, putting her arms about both girls. "She could not take two arrows in the chest like that and live. Ah Leti . . . why? They were not worth it."

Fara's spitting rage turned to desperate sorrow, so that she raised her head and howled like a wild dog, making her new, nervous steed skitter dangerously. Myrina's heart was heavy as she went to her. "Come to me, Fara!" she ordered. "Dismount!"

The young girl fell forward and slipped down from the beast's back. Myrina caught her and held her tightly, rocking her, as Fara sobbed wildly in her arms.

* * *

Kora watched it all from the higher hillside. She muttered fearfully at the sight of the mares galloping frantically in and out of the stream, crying wildly and rearing up and down. At last she gathered the courage to come down to join her friends.

"I told you so! You cannot tame such wild ones!" she insisted. "I told you so!"

"Yes we can!" Myrina answered, letting go of Fara, who was now a little calmer. "They are terrified now, but we must start again—almost at the beginning, but we will start again."

Coronilla agreed, shaking her head with bitter resignation. "We must not lose them, but we will need all our gentling skills to soothe them after this attack."

Myrina shrugged her shoulders. "And . . . we must start at once."

"What if they come back?" Kora asked.

Myrina glanced furiously in the direction of Eagle Rocks. "We will be ready for them!" she hissed.

A watch was set to give good warning should the horse thieves try to return. Wearily the women wandered back down to the river, burning with quiet anger but determined not to lose all that they'd gained. They began by making soothing noises and clicking sounds, pursuing their chosen one. There would be no riding, not that day—nor the next. There was much ground to be made up if the horses were to trust them again.

It was a day of hard work and the riders struggled to be patient, but by sunset the herd were once again quietly cropping the grass and only a few stragglers had wandered away.

That night Myrina and Coronilla agreed to perform the Ring of Fire, the most warlike of their dances. The women circled the fire, bellowing out their anger, teeth gritted, muscles tense, their movements mimicking the attack on an enemy. They swung their sticks, making them swish through the air as they howled out their rage. Their body pictures gleamed in the leaping firelight so that the strong young women made a terrifying sight.

Down by the river the horses raised their heads and flattened their ears.

Suddenly a cry rang out. "Watch out! They attack!" Fara had been a lookout on the hillside above.

Myrina whirled about and led the angry Moon Riders out to meet their opponents, sticks and bows at the ready.

It was hard to see clearly in the darkness, but it seemed that the small group of men who had raided them that morning were riding slowly out toward them, carrying torches and leading the few horses that they'd managed to rope and steal away.

The women growled furiously at the sight of them.

"Well—do we let them have it now?"

"Let's have our revenge!"

"What are we waiting for?"

Myrina was full of energy after the exertion of the dancing and ready to fight, but something about the slow progress the men made told her that they were not threatening them this time. Myrina had never seen a war party like it; it seemed to be more of a deputation.

As they came closer, they could see the men's faces in the light of their torches. They appeared to have ridden out without weapons or bows. Were they returning the stolen beasts?

"Fools! They are unarmed!" Fara snarled.

"Brave fools!" Coronilla said.

"What is it that they drag behind them?" Fara asked.

"I fear it is our Leti!" Myrina told her.

The men reached the sloping bank of the river, close to where the horses grazed, but this time they made no attempt to steal. The horses moved nervously away, but when they saw that they were not pursued, they fell to eating and drinking again. Some of the men dismounted, moving purposefully in the torchlight.

"What are they doing? We have them in our sights," Fara cried.

"Wait!" Myrina commanded. "We do not attack unarmed men, however angry we may be. We are not barbarians!"

The men bowed their heads in the direction of the Moon Riders' camp and then remounted their horses. They backed away toward their own camp, leaving behind the long, low sled and four roped horses fastened to a peg in the ground.

"Are we letting them go?" Fara was appalled.

"Yes," Myrina told her firmly. "Light brands from the fire! Let us see what they have left there."

The women moved forward cautiously as the men cantered away in the direction of Eagle Rocks. As the thud of the horses' hooves faded into the distance, the women lowered their weapons. At last they came close and saw that it was indeed the body of Leti. She'd been carefully laid out on a wooden sled.

"Aah, Leti!" they cried in pity.

A necklace of amber beads had been set around her neck and flower petals sprinkled over her body.

"What is this?" they murmured, their anger fading to sorrow and wonder.

They touched the beads, speaking quietly with surprise and puzzlement. This was not the way a Moon Rider would be prepared for the pyre, but still they could see that Leti had been laid out with respect. At her feet were two large horsehide bags. Kora bravely reached out and opened one of them, gasping at what she found.

"What is it?" Myrina demanded.

"Grain." Kora plunged her hand inside the sack and scooped up a handful of the golden seeds, letting them run through her fingers.

"And the other?"

"More grain." Kora's voice was warm with approval.

"What is this?" Coronilla almost laughed. "An apology?"

"Well," said Kora, with practical good sense, "if it is, it's an apology that we can eat and we need to eat. This is a funeral feast that's been provided and we should not turn it down. I feared that tomorrow we would be eating grass like the horses."

Myrina sighed. She suddenly felt very tired, but she saw that Kora was right. "We will build a pyre and tomorrow we will dance for Leti and enjoy the strange feast that she has brought for her friends."

Fara nodded and wept again.

They worked hard the next day, gentling the horses and grinding grain. Kora pounded dough and made flat bread and served up the last of the cherries. They built a pyre and danced and sang the songs of the dead. As the flames died down they sat around the embers drinking mare's milk. Tamsin and Phoebe and the younger girls stood up to do the Dance of the Foals. They pranced and kicked and tossed their heads, their own youth and awkwardness touching the older women who watched. This was the

Moon Riders' way of giving thanks to the leggy foals who had been separated from their mothers that same day and settled to live on grass, while the newcomers stole their milk. The faint glimmer of another fire in the distance told them that the men were still camped by Eagle Rocks but didn't try to interfere in any way.

Though they were desperately sad to lose Leti, the taste of the grainy bread made them long for more. They wrapped themselves up in their meager clothing and settled to sleep, but despite the warm glow from Leti's pyre, the night air was chill. Myrina found it hard to sleep, for the cold brought discomfort and also troubling fears; winter was fast arriving. They must find food and skins and better shelter or they would not survive. Perhaps Kora was right about slaughtering some of the horses.

CHAPTER ELEVEN

Rebellion

T HE FOLLOWING DAYS were difficult, and the
Moon Riders had to dredge up all the patience
they could. However, by the next full moon
they were up on the backs of their chosen steeds and cantering off into the wide grasslands to hunt deer, gazelle,
and boar.

The meat they brought back kept them fed, but they
could not prepare enough skins to keep everyone warm
through the freezing nights. Then one night another
unarmed deputation came from the watchers who
camped by Eagle Rocks.

Three young men came riding out toward them,
warily leaving more bundles just above the riverbank.
The women waited curiously until they had gone, then
went to examine what seemed to be gifts. Kora was
delighted to find more grain, and the others opened up
bundles that turned out to be thick felted-woolen cloaks.

The women could not help but be pleased and curious.

"See here—feel the warmth of this!"

"Do they keep sheep up there by the rocks?"

"How have they made this felt so smooth and soft?"

They feasted on bread and meat and slept warm through the night.

Fara was very quiet and refused to allow them to cover her with one of the cloaks, but as the nights grew colder still, at last she crept inside and snuggled beneath the covers with the rest.

As the days passed, it became a common sight to see the young men riding out from their rocks, leading goats and sheep and carrying more bundles of fine felt, bone needles, and strong horsehair thread. The women quickly sliced the felt and stitched it into warm tunics and trousers.

Some of the younger Moon Riders began to look out for the strange visitors, eager to see what they might bring next. Fara overcame her reluctance and soon she was there with the others, watching for them every day.

Once they left some pitchers of a strong grainy drink that set the women's tongues loose and laughing.

"Did the tall one come today?" Fara asked.

Phoebe nodded and giggled. "And the smaller one who limps a little!"

"Why did they have to come when I was off hunting?" Fara growled.

"The smaller one limps, but he rides like a centaur . . ." Phoebe's voice trailed off dreamily.

Myrina listened to it all uneasily. "They killed our Leti," she reminded them sharply. Something about the girls' chatter made her hurt deep inside.

"But you stopped me riding after them and punishing them." Fara was resentful.

"It would have done no good," Myrina told her.

Kora grinned. "Don't worry"—she nudged Myrina— "they are just young girls, released from the shame and fear of slavery, so they do what healthy, happy young girls always do—they admire the muscles in a young man's thigh."

Myrina nodded, remembering that just this kind of talk went on around the Mazagardi campfires when she was young; but sadness came with the memory.

She sighed. "You are right."

"I thought you Moon Riders released a girl after seven years of riding and let her choose a husband," Kora said.

"The ancient ways of the Moon Riders are lost to us," Myrina answered quickly.

Kora cackled. "When ancient ways are lost, then new ways must be tried."

"What do you mean by that?"

Kora shrugged and laughed again. "Look at them," she said. "Many of them are old enough to be wed."

The faces and eyes of the young girls were bright and happy, reflecting the flames. Myrina understood very well what Kora meant, but she did not want to hear this earthy talk. They still had to face a bitter winter in this alien land. Survival was what mattered. Had they struggled across that terrible sea and lost her dear Iphigenia just to send these girls off as hearth wives to the first boys who sent them a gift? For her no man could ever be considered after her brave Tomi.

"Mazagardi men were the fiercest warriors," she told them. "But still they would gently nurse a sick child all night and never move for fear of disturbing the little one."

Kora smiled sadly, nodding her head. "Mazagardi men were famous all through Anatolia, and any girl would consider herself honored to get herself a husband from your tribe, but . . . we have no Mazagardi here. You cannot deny they are fine, strong young men who camp by Eagle Rocks, and their riding skills are second to none."

Myrina caught her breath and shook her head, but she couldn't in fairness disagree. The young men rode like the wind. "When I thought of turning the prows of our ships to the north," she said, "I feared many hazards, but I never thought that we were going in search of husbands for this lot! I do not like the thought of it at all."

Coronilla had been listening to it all quietly. "Huh!

You can keep your spindly horse boys—they would not do for me—but I do remember that Hati and Atisha used to say, 'The old ways have to change if we are to survive.'"

The gifts kept coming and soon became the highlight of the day, so that the women looked out for the young men and waited in anticipation, guessing excitedly what might next appear. The weather had grown bitterly cold, but at the same time enough felt and skins had arrived to make tents and dress all the women in soft warm tunics, trousers, and boots.

"Where are they getting it all from?"

"They cannot have these goods stacked up behind the rocks!"

Curiosity grew on both sides. The young men had long dark hair that they wore loose to their shoulders, and the older ones sported thick neat beards. They wore tunics and trousers of horsehide and deerhide, their arms and necks ornamented with fine gold bands. As the days passed, they did not rush away as they had at their first encounter but stayed to smile and wave from a distance, watching with pleasure as the women admired the gifts they'd brought. Sometimes they called out words that the women couldn't understand, but once or twice Myrina thought she'd heard that tongue somewhere before. Sometimes the young men would race around them on horseback, so that the Moon Riders stared and cheered at the speed they achieved.

"What riders!" they murmured.

Myrina had seen such riding before and watched it all with growing unease, but how could she make the Moon Riders refuse these precious gifts? There was now a corral full of sheep and winter shelters built for them. She was honest enough to acknowledge that she couldn't see how they'd all have survived so far without this unlikely help.

Tamsin and Phoebe looked forward to the gifts, just like the other girls. If the brave young rider who limped a little did not appear on his fast horse, Phoebe would mope all day.

Late one evening, when they were dozing around the fire, Coronilla and Akasya came to sit by Myrina and Kora. "I don't know if you have noticed it," Coronilla said quietly, "but one of our girls is missing."

Myrina looked at her, alarmed.

Kora shook her head, chuckling a little. "It is nothing fearful, for I have noticed this one missing before and seen that she turns up safe and cheerful in the morning."

Myrina frowned. Why was she the last to notice such a thing? She looked about her, checking first Tamsin and Phoebe, then Fara. Where was Fara?

Suddenly Myrina understood. Of late she had noticed

that Fara was quieter than ever, but she'd seen with relief that the girl no longer watched the young men with calves' eyes, giggling and gossiping about them after they'd gone. How could she have been so stupid not to realize what had happened? Fara didn't need to giggle at the boys when they came with their gifts because something much more real and exciting was happening for her.

She turned to Kora, troubled. "She's meeting them in secret! I should have realized. How long have you known?"

Kora shrugged. Akasya leaned forward and touched Myrina's shoulder. "I knew this would happen. Once they started bringing gifts and we accepted them, it was bound to happen sooner or later. We should have traveled on, if we didn't want it."

"Yes, we should have known. We've made a big mistake . . . we know nothing about them!"

Kora laughed. "We know that they have fed and clothed us."

"That is true." Myrina forced herself to be just, but her heart was beating fast and her chest felt suddenly tight and uncomfortable. "But . . . to have a Moon Rider creeping away from her friends like that. Where is Fara's loyalty?" She clenched her fist, anger shooting up to the surface. How could Kora be so tolerant of this? "Has Fara forgotten that they killed her dearest friend?" she cried.

"Have you all forgotten Leti?"

Her raised voice was bringing sleepy women from their tents, a look of concern in their eyes.

Coronilla frowned and nudged her arm. "Don't be so angry, Snake Lady! We just thought that you should know. I shall be wishing I'd never told you. Look at it this way—perhaps Leti's death was a terrible mistake. Those young men have tried hard since then to make it up to us. They cannot speak our tongue to beg forgiveness, but every day their actions seem to beg forgiveness for them."

Myrina knew that this was reasonable, but deep inside her anger grew. She even seemed to be at odds with Coronilla, the Moon Riders' most devoted supporter. She was angry that all the others seemed to know what was going on but not her. This giving and taking of gifts was draining away their power and freedom. Perhaps they should have made a fight of it after all.

She spat out her concern. "I can't believe that you are gone so soft, Coronilla! Have we struggled so hard to free ourselves from Neoptolemus, only to be soothed and cajoled into another kind of slavery?" She leaped to her feet. "We must leave at once!"

"What?" Kora was angry now; she got up, too, and stood her ground, hands on hips. "You must be mad! We have all we need here and just as the Bitter Months begin you say we leave! Who knows where we can find a safe and sheltered place in that freezing wilderness out there?" She waved her arm toward the north.

Phoebe emerged from her tent, tousled and resentful; she had overheard what was being said. "I like it here, Snake Lady," she said.

Tamsin appeared behind her, sleepy and anxious at the sound of argument. "Snake Mother?" she murmured.

Coronilla frowned. "There is no need for all this fuss," she said. "Perhaps we should try to speak to the men!"

Myrina's mind was racing—why was she so frightened by this suggestion?

Kora was in full flow. "If we pack up now and move on, we may not survive. This time I cannot understand you, Snake Lady, and I for one will not be following you. I stay here close to the sea!"

"Well, I think we should have gone long ago!" Akasya said.

Myrina was not sure whether that was support or challenge.

"Snake Mother!" Tamsin cried, distressed.

"Go back and sleep!" Myrina told her daughter sharply.

"I like the boys," Phoebe insisted.

Myrina looked up. "You have not been sneaking off to meet them?" she asked.

"No, I have not!" Phoebe spat back at her.

Kora wagged a finger at Myrina. "Our girls have been given many useful gifts, but a young man's admiration is also a gift and one that brings joy. You should know that and understand. You have experienced such joy; it brought you Tamsin."

It was too much. "How dare you speak of that unbidden!"

The Snake Lady leaped to her feet and marched off down to the water, leaving her friends looking alarmed, while many of the other women came out to join them, whispering in worried voices.

CHAPTER TWELVE

Fara

D OWN BY THE waterside Myrina whistled up
Big Chief who, though he had been resting,
came to her willingly, just snorting a little
and shaking the sleep from his long sand-colored mane.
Did his new friend really wish to go riding in the dark?
His fine animal senses quickly told him that she was upset
and his nose might sting again if he didn't obey.

Myrina leaped onto his back and rode away from the
camp in the moonlight, her mind buzzing with troubling
questions. It seemed that there were no satisfactory
answers, and she was desperate to get away from the others, to have a good think.

Once they'd left the camp behind, she allowed the
horse to wander where he willed; she was too exhausted
to direct him. Big Chief slowed and stopped in the shelter of a rock that gave good protection from the cold
wind. Myrina heaved a huge sigh and sat there on his

back, her eyelids drooping. She needed this distance and quietness. Never had her friends argued with her so determinedly. Yes, they often spoke up honestly and gave their opinion, but never had they challenged her wisdom like this.

Myrina felt weary to the bone; she longed for peace. A hard, bitter lump seemed to be growing in her throat. It was a choking lump of misery that she knew could only be shifted by a great outpouring of tears. But Myrina did not weep for herself these days. Quiet anger had spurred her on through this hard struggle; she could not afford the luxury of self-pity.

She lifted her head and gazed across the bleak landscape, suddenly realizing how much she missed the lush green valleys of the Mazagardi traveling lands. She longed for the sight of the spring flowers that grew on the lower slopes of Mount Ida, and even for the sea of marsh-watered fennel stalks that reared their heads across the plain of Troy.

As Myrina sat stock-still on Big Chief's back, a slight movement in the bushes to her right caught her eye. Instantly alert, she instinctively reached for her bow; if it was a deer or a wild boar she must take her chance to shoot it. They still needed every bit of meat they could find, and up on the Big Chief's back she had a fine vantage point.

As she raised her bow and narrowed her eyes to take aim, she gasped, catching a gleam of gold. It was the glitter of a golden wristband. She slowly lowered her weapon, understanding with a rush of irritation that it must be one of the young horsemen. She could see the dark shape of his shoulders and thought that it must be the tall one that Fara admired. Then she saw that he was not alone—Fara was with him.

Myrina slipped down from Big Chief's back and crept forward, keeping herself well covered by the rocks and undergrowth. She held her breath, watching to see what they were about. There was no mistaking it: the young man's companion was Fara; her long fair hair blew in the breeze, touched with silver in the moonlight.

The two young people seemed to be sitting side by side in the darkness, not touching, though their faces were close. Then slowly, as Myrina watched, Fara held up her hand, the palm flat and open. The young man hesitantly raised his own hand, his thick wristband gleaming again; he pressed it against the girl's palm.

"Hand," Fara said, her voice firm and clear.

"Ha-and." The young man tried to copy her, but his sounds came out awkwardly. Then suddenly his voice took on a clear, confident tone as he spoke again. "*Dala.*"

"*Dala.*" Fara repeated the word with ease.

Myrina watched and listened.

"Turxu." The young man pulled his hand away to tap his own chest.

"Turxu," Fara repeated, stretching her hand out to touch him. Then she tapped her own chest and spoke her name. "Fara."

The young man touched her hair and Myrina could see that his fingers trembled. "Fa-ara." His voice shook, too. Then he murmured, "*Leipo!*"

Fara's voice was warm with amusement. "No—Fara!" she corrected.

"Fara, *leipo*," he insisted.

"Very well . . . Fara *leipo*," she said. They sat together in silence.

As she watched and waited, Myrina's anger fled. Why had she been so furious? She recognized the word for hand that the boy had used. It was similar to a tongue that she had heard long ago among the brave Scythian warriors who had gone like her and Penthesilea to defend the city of Troy. She recognized the word *leipo*, too—it meant "beloved." It was a respectful word that a Scythian warrior might use for his god, his child, or his wife.

She backed away quietly and returned to Big Chief. There was something very private and intimate in those simple gestures of trust and she'd suddenly felt that she was intruding.

"Fool!" she muttered to herself. "What have you come

to? Spying on young lovers!"

The images that had filled her mind when she first heard of Fara's absences were lurid and earthy compared to the gentle, trusting exchange she had witnessed. Quietly she led Big Chief away, her own thoughts flying back to a time long ago when she'd made her own first awkward admissions of love to Tamsin's father.

Tomi was a courageous young Mazagardi who'd been killed as the Moon Riders escaped from the stricken city of Troy. He'd given up his life to see Myrina and her friends safely away. Throughout her childhood she'd traveled with her tribe from place to place, Tomi always at her side. They'd learned to ride together, learned to shoot together, and in the evenings by the campfire she'd leaned against his strong, muscular back for warmth. There in the darkness she began to understand the bitter anger that had suddenly blazed out at her friends. She longed desperately for Tomi's strong back to lean on now.

How could she be angry with Fara? The truth was, the young men who brought them gifts reminded her of Tomi and his friends and therein lay the hurt and pain.

Big Chief stopped by a clump of well-watered grass. She let him drop his head to crop at it, while loneliness swept over her. She remembered the last time she'd heard Tomi's voice. "Ride!" he'd shouted. "Ride for your lives!" She hadn't looked back—she'd done as he said and led the slave women to freedom. Since then she had been so busy trying to keep everyone safe, when had she truly grieved for Tomi? Now, with raw, heart-wrenching pain, she felt his loss again. She knew just how lonely she'd been for that special kind of companionship. It had been all too brief; their marriage had only lasted for a few days.

"It wasn't fair," she cried out loud. A great rush of grief and pain made her fall to her knees and crouch there on the dark hillside, sobbing wildly.

Big Chief stopped feeding for a moment and whickered with concern, but as her weeping began to subside he returned to his search for grass.

As she dried her eyes she saw a glint of water close by. "Iphigenia," she murmured, "I wish that you were here with me."

She moved toward the moonlit pool and the bright reflection of the moon. It would be difficult in this cold, rocky place to find the ease of body and mind that she would need to let her eyes gaze through and beyond the water's inky blackness.

"I need you, dear friend," she whispered, and at last her shoulders eased and her eyelids drooped. Her breathing slowed and as she looked through the darkness, she saw that there were tiny pinpricks of light; reflections of the stars shimmering in the water's black gleam.

"Iphigenia," she whispered. Then the tiny lights

seemed to move about the dark surface and gather together, forming strange, blurry shapes that suddenly clarified into something recognizable. "Iphigenia—dear friend!"

She spoke her name and she was there. Deep in the dark silver depths of the pool she saw the shape of the Achaean princess. Iphigenia's long dark hair was loose and she wore a silver crown above her brow. Servants bowed low before her, offering her fruits on a silver plate.

"Princess!" Myrina murmured. "You are a princess once again!"

She watched her friend for a few moments, cheered to see her well and cared for. Then the cold and weariness cut through her vision and brought her back to the dark, grassy hills and Big Chief waiting patiently for her.

She gave a great sigh of relief. This place was good— she would come up here again when she needed a bit of peace. Why was she making a hard life even more difficult? She must think carefully and kindly about the future of the young women in her care. She had lost much, but they still had their lives to live.

The camp was quiet when she returned, apart from the movement of the animals and the distant snorting of resting horses down by the stream. Two lookouts saluted her as she passed them, but they said nothing. Then Myrina saw that her closest friends still sat together, shoulders hunched and tense, talking quietly. They turned at the sound of Big Chief's hooves and got up.

Myrina slid down from the horse's back and sent him to join his many wives with a gentle slap on his hindquarters. She went straight to the Moon Riders with her arms open wide; they cried out with joy and hugged her tightly in turn.

"I could not sleep." Kora's voice was warm with affection. "I am so sorry—I should never have said what I did."

"No." Myrina smiled. "You were right, but I could not see it. You have spoken the truth, though it hurt; sometimes that is what a true friend has to do. Where is Tamsin?"

"Tamsin is fast asleep; Phoebe settled her down," Akasya told her.

Myrina took Coronilla by the arm. "I have been remembering things that I should never have forgotten. Tomorrow we will take council and all the women shall have their say and everyone will be listened to."

"Well done, Snake Lady!" Coronilla said.

They all went to their beds and slept a deep, peaceful sleep that healed their hurts and restored their energy.

CHAPTER THIRTEEN

The River People

As DAWN LIGHT crept in through the opening of her tent, Myrina stirred and woke with a sense of purpose. For a moment she wondered why, then she remembered what had happened last night. Her heart was heavy for a moment as she remembered the argument; but then as she rose and stretched, she recognized that she felt more lighthearted than she had for a long, long time.

She stooped to tickle Tamsin's nose, which was the only part of her daughter that stuck out of a warm felt blanket bag, another gift from strangers. "They will be strangers no longer," she whispered. "Come on, Little Lizard. Rise and greet the sun—today is a new day and there is much to be done."

Tamsin emerged from the cozy wrappings, instantly awake like a cat, a wide smile on her face. "You sound happy, Snake Mother. Last night you bared your teeth so that I feared you were going to eat fat Kora!"

"I am happy today," Myrina said. "And because of that I will only eat you!" She stooped and kissed her daughter as she slipped giggling from her arms.

Phoebe pushed back her cover. "Are we friends?" she asked sleepily.

"Of course we are, Young Tiger! We are always friends!" Myrina reached out and kissed her, too.

The Moon Riders danced to greet the sun, and as they danced Myrina could sense that a ripple of excitement was passing among their ranks. Last night's arguments had troubled them all, but Myrina and her friends' cheerful smiles told them that some agreement had been reached. A meeting was called as soon as they'd eaten and been down to see their horses—whatever other troubles they might have, the close bond between horse and rider must not be lost.

Myrina opened the meeting by announcing that she was aware that a certain Moon Rider was secretly meeting one of the horsemen. She was pleased at the bold way in which Fara rose at once to her feet, ready to argue her case and openly admit that it was she. But when Nessa and Donna also stood up, then Agnis and Molla joined them, she could not help but whistle under her breath. "How little I have seen," she murmured.

Kora could barely contain herself as she stifled a guf-faw. Myrina was annoyed for a moment and the thought came to her that this was a Moon Riders' meeting and she'd be well within her rights to tell Kora to leave. However, her sense of justice soon quashed the unworthy thought and a wicked idea crept into her mind and made her smile. She would set Kora right!

"Well," she murmured, as she looked from one guilty face to another.

"I did not tell you," Fara explained, "for I feared that you'd see me as disloyal. But I have wished to speak up about it for a long time. I meet one of them and we try to talk together. I cannot understand much of what he says, but I learn fast and I believe these men wish us well!"

Molla backed her up. "We take their gifts," she insisted. "They are fine riders and warriors. They could have warred with us and made our lives a misery, but they have taken careful note of what we need and been gener-ous. Why shouldn't we be friends with them?"

"Of course we should!" Kora folded her arms in her usual determined pose.

"This is a Moon Riders' meeting." Myrina was grim faced and spoke firmly. "Only Moon Riders may speak!"

Kora stared at her with disbelief and anger. She rose to her feet, her face flushed, ready to do battle. Everyone else gasped in shocked silence.

Myrina could not hold back her smile any longer. "Therefore," she went on quickly, winking at Coronilla, "my first suggestion is that Kora the fisherwoman be fully instated as an honored Moon Rider."

There were many smiles and sighs and laughter, as Kora's outraged expression changed to one of astonishment and then delight. "You've taken the wind right out of my sails," she murmured.

"Yes!" Akasya cried. "I will support that!"

"Yes!" they all shouted.

"That's agreed then." Myrina grinned wickedly. "The daughters of Maa welcome you to their ranks, Kora!"

"Me—an honored Moon Rider!"

"The honor is ours." Myrina opened her arms to hug her.

There were wild, ululating joy cries—they leaped to their feet, twirling around, as the tense atmosphere that had hung over the camp exploded into one of delight. This was more like the old, crafty Snake Lady they'd known; the resilient one who'd led them out through the gates of Troy and given them their freedom.

But as they settled down again, Fara remained on her feet, her brow drawn into a frown, her jaw set in determination. "But what of the young men who bring us gifts?" she insisted. "I have spoken out with honesty. I swear by Maa that we owe these warriors our lives and I for one will not agree to give up my meetings. I am glad they are secret no longer!"

Myrina smiled at her courage. "Sit down, Fara," she said. "You speak like a true Moon Rider and I have come to see that you are right. We should treat these people who have helped us with more respect and courtesy. Ask your young man to come to see me; we will invite them to eat with us."

"What?" It was Fara's turn to be surprised, her face flushed with pleasure.

"There is much that I would like to know about them," Myrina said. "Where are their women? Where did they gain such wealth? We are not likely to find the answers to these and many other questions unless we change our ways and greet them as friends."

Fara nodded. "I . . . I will do my best to invite them, but their tongue is difficult and I struggle to make him understand me."

Myrina grinned. "Bring him to me."

That evening, after they had eaten, Fara went off to her usual meeting place, hidden among the rocks, but this time she quickly emerged from the stony cover with Turxu following sheepishly behind her.

Myrina beckoned him toward her. *"Hosu Gelden!"* She spoke warmly the only Scythian words of welcome known to her.

"Aah! *Hosu Boldum!"* he answered, giving her the polite reply that would be expected, surprise and relief on his face.

Fara looked quite taken aback, but then she smiled, too, wagging a finger at Myrina. "Snake Lady!" she murmured reprovingly. "I should have known! You can speak their language."

"No." Myrina shook her head. "I recognize some of the words. They speak a Scythian tongue, but I do not know it well."

The Moon Riders crowded around the young man, full of curiosity to see one of their benefactors close up. They smiled approval of his dark, weather-beaten skin, his long black hair, and deep-set brown eyes. They stretched out their fingers to touch the muscular arms that gleamed with gold. Tamsin settled herself at his feet, smiling admiringly into his face. Only Phoebe hovered outside the circle, looking out toward Eagle Rocks, as though she hoped that more of them would come.

One or two more tentative hands strayed out to touch Turxu's hair and pat his hands, but they pulled back quickly as Fara gave them a sharp warning look. Myrina tolerated this curiosity for a few moments, but then she sent them away to their tents, keeping back only Coronilla, Kora, and Akasya. Fara remained determinedly at Turxu's side, for he clung tightly to her hand. The others went reluctantly, but Myrina insisted. "Poor boy!" she said. "This must be more of a trial to him than having to face a pack of wolves."

She knew that their conversation would be difficult enough without such a huge admiring audience. As soon as they had gone, Myrina struggled to ask Turxu about his people. For a moment he looked puzzled, but then he replied, "Sinta!"

"Aah"—Myrina was pleased with both his understanding and his response—"Sinta; the people of the river. His tribe call themselves Sinta, the River People."

The long-forgotten words that she'd heard spoken in Troy came back to her with halting slowness, but with enthusiastic signing and many encouraging smiles, at last she thought she'd made Turxu understand that he should bring the other men and eat with the Moon Riders the following night. The young man kept glancing across at the beautiful body painting of a snake that rippled down Myrina's forearm.

Fara noticed this and pointed to Myrina. "Snake Lady," she told him. "Like my gazelle," she said, referring to the delicate leaping gazelle on her own forearm.

As the fires burned low, Turxu got to his feet to leave,

glad that nothing too terrible had happened to him while in the Moon Riders' camp. "Kuspada?" he said as he turned to go.

Myrina frowned for a moment, unsure. "Kuspada?" Then she nodded in agreement. "Yes, Kuspada!"

Turxu smiled, held out his open palm to her, and after a moment of hesitation she pressed her own against it in a hand-to-hand salute.

CHAPTER FOURTEEN

Kuspada

TARA WENT WITH Turxu to retrieve his horse; then she sent him on his way, kissing him as they parted. She stood watching him ride away toward the glimmer of the fire in the distance by Eagle Rocks. A huge smile lit her face.

Back in Myrina's tent her friends could not contain their curiosity. "What does it all mean? What is this Kuspada he's so concerned about?"

Myrina shook her head and frowned. "*Pada* means leader and I think *kus* is the Scythian word for iron. Kuspada seems to mean Iron Leader."

"Ha!" Kora smiled knowingly. "Top dog! He means to bring their leader to meet you."

"Iron Leader." Coronilla laughed. "If we have the meaning right, he sounds like a tough fellow!"

Myrina's confidence waned. "I hope we have done right in giving this invitation."

"Of course we have!" Kora told her warmly. "Get to bed now. You have done very well, Snake Lady, but you must organize a hunting party early in the morning; then I will make ready a fine feast. Get to bed! Now that I am a Moon Rider I shall tell you what to do!"

"Didn't you always?" Myrina laughed.

As she drew back the tent flap, she smiled to herself at the low, excited whispers she heard.

"A feast," Tamsin murmured.

"Young men and a feast!" Phoebe replied. "They must bring the one I like!"

"If they don't, I'll go and get him for you," Tamsin told her sleepily.

Myrina woke up full of doubts again, but the pleasure and excitement on all the women's faces as they danced to greet the morning sun told her that there could be no going back.

The best hunters rode all morning and returned to the camp with an ibex, a pair of hares, a fallow deer, and a wild boar. Kora worked hard grinding grain and pounding dough to make her delicious flat bread. Water was carried up from the river, and a good smell of roasting meat drifted into all the tents. They saw no sign of the young men all day; for once they seemed to have deserted their camp beneath Eagle Rocks and Myrina could not help but be anxious again. Had she given the wrong impression? Had she given offense?

As darkness began to fall the excitement grew. Animal bones were hastily cut and used as combs, clothing was brushed down and straightened, herbs were chewed to freshen the breath. The few late flowers that could be found were picked carefully and plaited into hair. Cushions and rugs, nearly all of them gifts from their Sinta guests, were dragged out from the tents and arranged in a circle around the fire.

Then a tense quietness fell and for a while the women sat very still, waiting and watching.

Myrina was filled with self-doubt. Had Turxu understood her? Would they come? The meat would be burned if they didn't come soon, but worse than that, they would feel foolish and disappointed.

Then in the distance they picked out tiny, starry glimmers of light that moved toward them. While they watched and waited the lights grew, and they could see that the men carried brushwood torches as they rode toward them.

"Here they come! Look at them!" the whisper went around.

There were many impressed gasps as the Sinta men approached, for in the light of the torches their gold bangles and neck torques gleamed. They came to the feast decked in gold and beads, their hair combed, their beards neat, and their skin clean and glossy. It seemed that they, too, had prepared very carefully for this meeting. They wore clean trousers and smocks, not the strong and rugged horsehide hunting gear that they rode in every day. As they moved closer, the Moon Riders saw that even the horses were adorned with gleaming gold bits and harnesses, delicately crafted into intricate coils, whirls, and animal patterns.

Turxu led the train, along with an older man with a full neat beard. He was not as richly adorned as the younger men; but something about the confident ease with which he controlled his huge black stallion told them that this must be the Kuspada that Turxu had spoken of.

Kora stared in admiration. "Now that's what I call a man," she whispered.

Myrina watched with interest as he leaped lightly down from his horse; he was well muscled and strong, not the aged chieftain she'd somehow expected.

Turxu brought him straight to Myrina. The man bowed, then looked directly at her, as though calmly sizing her up.

"Kuspada," Turxu introduced him. "S-snake Lady!"

She took a deep breath and held out her palm to him, inviting a hand-to-hand salute. He pressed his own palm firmly on hers, looking sharply at the snake picture on her extended forearm. He gave a sudden warm smile of approval. "Snake Lady!" he said in the Luvvian language. "Now I understand. Turxu told us, 'The Snake Lady has come.'"

"You speak Luvvian!" Myrina gasped.

He bowed his head. "I do!"

Myrina was hugely relieved to find that she could talk to him in the language that her grandmother had taught her as a child. Many of the Moon Riders who'd once been slaves in the city of Troy could also speak and understand the language.

"Welcome," she told him. "Please come and sit down."

But Kuspada hesitated. "First, there is something that I must say."

There was silence then as both men and women held their breath.

"We beg forgiveness for the death we caused. We had no idea that you were . . . women. Such riders and horse tamers as you are we believed must be warriors, come to steal our horses and our river lands."

"You . . . you thought us men?" Myrina allowed herself a little smile.

He nodded. "We have never seen women who ride and shoot like you."

Myrina felt a little uncomfortable. Though the strangers were mistaken in thinking them men, it was true that they had come looking for land, and perhaps it would be true to say that they had stolen the horses.

"We are Moon Riders," she told him. "Warrior priestesses from the far side of the Inhospitable Sea. Our ship was washed into the Little Sea and we were shipwrecked on your shore. We came here seeking refuge and new lands. In a way you were right, we did come to steal horses . . . but you have treated us with great generosity. We forgive you for the death of our friend Leti, but we, too, must beg forgiveness of you for our intrusion into your lands."

Kuspada bowed his head in agreement. "All is forgiven."

"Now please sit down and eat with us," Myrina begged.

The Sinta men had brought fermented mare's milk, which they shared around. The camp was soon full of young people smiling and nodding at each other. As bellies grew full, they began to look and touch with shy interest. Phoebe crept around the circle to sit close to the brave rider she admired.

"His name is Leni," Tamsin bent to whisper in her ear. "I found it out for you." Then she went around asking them all their names.

Myrina felt strangely awkward and shy but couldn't hold back her curiosity. She hoped that her questions wouldn't give offense. "Kuspada . . . does that mean chief?"

Kuspada gave a hearty laugh and shook his head. "Chief—no, no. We Sinta people do not have a chief. Kuspada means Iron Man. I smelt iron, bronze, and gold."

"Aah." Coronilla spoke with frank approval. "You are the blacksmith."

"I believe that is the name some give for the hot and sooty work that I do."

"Important work," Coronilla insisted.

Myrina looked around at the beautiful gold jewelery that adorned the arms and necks of all the young men. "Is this your work?" she asked.

He bowed his head modestly. "Much of it is mine."

"And you adorn your horses with the precious stuff!" Myrina was fascinated. "Though we Moon Riders value our steeds above gold, we have never managed to make such wonderful trappings for them."

Kuspada looked thoughtful then. "There is much that we could do to help each other."

"You have already helped us beyond any of our expectations," Myrina said.

"Well . . ." The blacksmith hesitated. "We wish very much to know the magic of your horse taming. We Sinta can ride like the wind and rope a wild horse and force it to obey us, but you women from the sea . . . you walk among the wild mares and set them following in your wake. This is priestesses' magic, isn't it?"

Myrina laughed and took another sip of fermented milk. "I was born a Mazagardi," she said with pride, then her face clouded over with sadness. "The Mazagardi are no more, but their horse-training secrets live on with the Moon Riders."

Kuspada was solemn now and respectful. "Such magic would be very precious to us."

Myrina smiled. "The magic is not mine alone to give," she told him. "I will speak with the women and see what they think. Maybe there are skills that we may exchange, for the women admire the light metal bits and harnesses that you use to direct your steeds."

"The exchange of these skills would be our pleasure," he said.

"Now"—Myrina wanted time to think—"you are our guests and we wish to entertain you. Would you like to see dancing? We Moon Riders are trained to perform sacred dances in honor of Mother Maa, but sometimes we dance simply to celebrate."

Kuspada did not have to give a reply; his smile told her that such a thing would be a delight.

Myrina called the Moon Riders together and set them dancing. They did not perform the sacred dances of the moon but instead threw themselves into the cheerful, swinging dances in which they flung their sticks high into the air, catching them again as though a tiny thread tied hand and stick together. These dances were full of glee, but they also demonstrated the strength of these young women: they could turn a simple stick into a weapon with a flick of their fingers.

The young Sinta warriors clapped and cheered, and as the fermented milk was passed around again, the dancing grew faster and wilder and the men got up to perform a powerful horse-roping dance.

CHAPTER FIFTEEN

Argimpasa

AT LAST, AS the fires burned low, Fara led Big
Chief up from the waterside and begged
Myrina to perform the special dance that only
she had perfected.

"But I haven't taught Big Chief to do it properly," she
protested. "He's not quite ready yet."

"That beast will do anything for you." Coronilla would
not tolerate her excuses.

"Come on," Kora bullied. "It will honor our guests."

Myrina felt that she couldn't refuse, so at last she got
up and leaped onto Big Chief's back. She set him pacing
steadily around the fire while both Moon Riders and their
guests shuffled hastily back, sensing that this performance might be safer watched from a distance. Once she
felt that the horse was giving her his trust, Myrina rose
gracefully to her feet and with perfect balance began to
turn and twist in time to the beating of Coronilla's drum.

The Moon Riders clapped lightly to the rhythm, and as Myrina's confidence grew, she sprang up and down on Big Chief's back. She was applauded with wild cheers, but then she seemed to sense a new hush in her audience.

"Argimpasa!" The mysterious word passed from mouth to mouth, whispered by the Sinta men. "Just like Argimpasa!"

Myrina slowed Big Chief, fearful that the performance had somehow given offense. As she slipped down from the horse's back, new applause greeted her, but the atmosphere had changed. The Sinta men were quieter and watched her with a look of wonder.

The Moon Riders looked at one another, puzzled. Myrina turned to catch Kuspada's reaction and was a little shaken to see that he watched her with intense joy, as though he'd glimpsed a vision. She went to him, concerned.

"Argimpasa," he murmured. "You are Argimpasa, our snake lady."

Myrina smiled uncertainly. "I am just a very tired Moon Rider who fled across the sea to find freedom, and I am very glad to have made new friends."

The strange expression of rapture quickly left him and Kuspada rose to his feet, holding out his palm. "We will be friends," he agreed.

The other Sinta men took his lead, getting up from their

cushions, bowing and smiling, courteously taking their leave. Myrina realized that they were going and she still hadn't asked the question that she really wanted to ask.

She pressed her palm firmly against Kuspada's and asked it. "Will you bring your women to visit us? We would like to meet them, too."

A fleeting expression of anxiety seemed to touch his eyes, but it passed quickly and he smiled again. "Will you come with us to visit our home camp? That way you will meet the women of our tribe."

Slightly puzzled, Myrina glanced without thinking over at the dark silhouette of Eagle Rocks in the distance, black against the starry sky.

"No, no." Kuspada put the misunderstanding right at once. "Our home camp is half a day's journey to the west, but it will seem nothing to a fine horsewoman like you."

The thought flitted through Myrina's mind that this might be some kind of a trap. Kuspada waited patiently for her reply, not trying to persuade or rush her judgment, and a deep instinct told her that this was a man whom she could trust.

"We will come," she agreed.

"At sunrise?"

She was a little startled at his urgency, but she could not think of a good reason to refuse. "Yes. I will bring a few of my friends along with me," she agreed.

Kuspada seemed satisfied with that and bowed low before her, then went to spring lightly onto his horse. Myrina watched him ride away—almost like a Mazagardi warrior, she thought.

After the men had gone, the Moon Riders joined together to do the gentle, soothing moon dance. They honored the silver disk that lit the night sky and went calm and sleepy to their beds, but they were up before sunrise, ready to perform the important sun-welcoming dance that warmed their muscles and set their minds busy for the day ahead.

Myrina gathered her friends together, telling them to wrap up well and prepare for a short journey. They obeyed eagerly and went to seek out their horses.

"I'm coming, too," Kora insisted. "Now that I'm a true warrior priestess, I can climb up onto your stallion's back and ride along with you."

"No." Myrina shook her head.

Kora folded her arms and dug her heels stubbornly into the earth.

Myrina smiled and sighed. "You must stay here and keep the camp safe for me. I think we can trust these men, but just in case, there must be somebody to stay here who can make sensible decisions and take the lead."

"Me?" Kora was surprised and pleased.

"Yes. I leave Tamsin and Phoebe in your care. We

expect to return after one night, but just in case . . ."

Kora nodded her head, then looked up and saw the Sinta men approaching again, Kuspada at their head. "Here's your man," she said.

"Not *my* man," Myrina said.

"Is he not?" Kora smiled knowingly. "I would not say no to him!"

Kuspada led them off to the west, past the camp at Eagle Rocks. Myrina was impressed to see that the young men had made a neat and cozy arrangement of tents. Rugs were hanging out to air and dry in the morning sun.

"Your men keep themselves clean and comfortable," she approved. "We call this Eagle Rocks, for they seem to us to take the shape of the bird."

Kuspada nodded. "You women would do better to camp here beside us," he told her. "We call this place Levas Rocks, which to us means 'sheltering rocks.' Your eagle's half-furled wings keep away the bitter north wind."

She was a little disconcerted at the suggestion, but then she saw what he meant and understood. The warm south-facing rocks that the men had backed themselves up against made a much warmer winter base than the exposed spot by the river that they had chosen. Perhaps they did have much to learn from the River People, who had spent many winters in this alien climate.

"What name did you choose for your fine horse?" Myrina asked, admiring the blue-black stallion.

"Dorag," he told her. "In our language it means Thunderer. He serves me well."

"A good name," she affirmed. "Last night you called me by a name that is strange to me."

He smiled. "Argimpasa." He spoke the word with reverence, as though it were full of magic.

"Who is this Argimpasa?" Myrina asked.

"She is the mother of all Sintas," he said. "More than that, she is the mother of all the Scythian tribes."

"Aah!" Myrina began to understand. "Perhaps she is like our goddess Maa! The mother of all things alive on this earth."

He nodded his head. "It is our belief that Argimpasa was married to Targitos, the sky god; these two were the parents of the Scythian tribes. Once we were all one family." He sighed. "Now, sadly, we often war with each other!"

Myrina nodded. It was a familiar story.

Then Kuspada smiled as though she might think him foolish. "The story that every young Scythian knows is that Argimpasa comes from the sky, standing on the back of a golden stallion, so you see . . ."

"Aah!" Myrina smiled. "I am honored that my performance made you think of such a wonderful goddess."

Kuspada laughed and shook his head. "Not only did you look like Argimpasa standing on a stallion, but you see, our goddess is half woman, half snake." He shrugged his shoulders, still amused. "Just for a moment I thought I had seen the goddess herself."

They smiled at each other with warmth and understanding and rode on over dry grassland that stretched for miles and miles. Though they saw gazelles and antelopes in the distance they ignored the chance to hunt, intent on the main purpose of their journey. At last, as the sun reached its zenith, they saw ahead of them a sprawling cluster of tents made of thick, warm felt, with spirals of smoke rising up from holes in the roofs. Corrals of healthy sheep and horses surrounded the encampment. As they approached, a small group of children ran out to meet them. They surrounded them, waving and shouting with wild excitement. *"Aruna! Aruna!"*

"What is it that they shout?" Fara asked.

Myrina looked puzzled. "I think the word they use is "mothers"! They are calling us mothers!"

"No, no!" Coronilla laughed. "It must be their word for women."

Kuspada said nothing and Myrina thought that he seemed a little uneasy once again. Her hand touched the feathered flights of her arrows, which she carried in a quiver strapped to her thigh. Was her instinct to trust him true? Her hand moved on to check the bow that she'd slung across her shoulder.

The children seemed wild with delight to have visitors, and soon some older men and a few women came out from the tents, making beckoning signs of welcome with their hands. A girl came running out of her tent shouting wildly, reaching up to Kuspada.

"Zimapo!" he called her as he hauled her up to sit in front of him on Dorag's back. He hugged her tightly.

Myrina saw at once that she was his daughter. For a moment she found herself struggling with an unexpected sense of disappointment. Of course a man of his age and standing would have a daughter, and of course that meant he would have a wife. Why should that surprise or bother her? Perhaps Kora's earthy suggestion that he might admire her had somehow sunk unbidden into her mind. She pushed such thoughts away, feeling foolish again, and swung down from Big Chief to greet Kuspada's daughter with a friendly hand salute.

Another very confident young woman came over to greet them, a baby in her arms and a toddler at her skirts. "This is Tabi," Kuspada introduced her.

Myrina wondered if Tabi was his wife, but he did not say that she was.

The Moon Riders were invited to sit down and offered some warming herb tea. The Sinta women greeted them with huge smiles, but didn't sit down to join them until all the guests were served.

Zimapo and Tabi marched about giving orders. Turxu brought a very old woman out from one of the tents; she greeted them all with smiles and much nodding of her head, seeming especially delighted with Fara. Kuspada introduced her as Turxu's grandmother Sere, the Gray One. Myrina thought she heard the young Sinta warrior use the Scythian word for wife.

Soon they were being fed with freshly roasted wild boar, stuffed with delicious herbs. They could not fault the hospitality, but Myrina was not the only Moon Rider who turned her head this way and that to see if there were other women hiding shyly in the tents.

After they had eaten and sipped at the flask of fermented mare's milk that was passed around, at last Myrina got up her courage.

"We would like to meet the other women!"

There was an awkward moment as the Sinta men fell silent, understanding enough to know what she asked.

Kuspada paused for a moment and then he sighed. He looked up at the other men, as though asking them a question, and they nodded.

"It is time," he said, turning to face Myrina and her friends. "Time that I told you of the great sorrow that has cursed our tribe."

CHAPTER SIXTEEN

The Shame of the Sinta Warriors

Turxu came to sit down in the fire-lit circle. Quietness and attention spread through all those present, and Kuspada and his daughter exchanged a look of deep sadness.

Myrina saw it and suddenly her heart was very heavy; she knew that she would not like what she was about to hear. But the Moon Riders were no strangers to sorrow, and if they were to live beside these unhappy, gold-decked strangers they must try to understand what it was that troubled them so. She regretted the pain, but they must know the truth.

"Our children called you 'mothers,'" Kuspada began. "That is because they long to have mothers. You cannot meet the other wives, for they were stolen away and many of them have gone up into the sky to live with Argimpasa."

Myrina looked around at the sad faces of the few

women who were left to them. The men looked down at the ground, their faces miserable and full of shame.

The Moon Riders looked at one another uneasily and waited. "What happened?" Coronilla asked.

Kuspada shuffled his feet uncomfortably. "They are lost through our own stupidity!" His voice was low, so that they struggled to hear him clearly. "I will tell you, but the telling will not come easily, for it is great shame to us. Great shame and sorrow."

"We will try to listen patiently," Myrina assured him.

"We remember it as the Bitter Winter." Kuspada spoke with reluctance, as though each word were dragged from his throat. "It was the winter that my daughter Zimapo was born. All through the summer we men, who call ourselves the gold smelters, had been away from the home camp seeking gold in the mountains to the east. We left the women and children and the old men behind in the northern pastures to watch over the sheep, for the grass grows green and lush up there in the summertime. This is how we Sinta live— How we used to live," he corrected himself. He stopped for a moment, his face lined with sorrow.

Coronilla and Akasya listened with concern, for they knew enough of the Luvvian language to understand most of his words. The Sinta women and men sat in silence, their faces sad even though they did not know the language in which the blacksmith spoke to their visitors; they knew the story only too well.

"Another group of Sinta men left the home tents and traveled northward," Kuspada continued. "They were the horse ropers who went seeking out herds of wild horses. As winter approached we should all have returned to move the camp south to this sheltered place, but we had found gold of a quality and quantity that we had never before seen. Each day we promised ourselves that we would return, but then we would swear that one more day would make no difference; we were hauling out from the mountainside more gold than we had ever seen."

The faces of the listening women were heavy with sadness, and many quietly wiped away a tear.

Myrina tried to give sympathy. "I can see that it must have been a great temptation for you," she said. "You must have thought that you were making your tribe very rich!"

Kuspada nodded. "We have bitterly regretted it ever since. You see, we thought that the horse ropers would have returned to the home camp, but their hunt for new steeds had taken them farther north than usual.

"I told you that the Scythian tribes were once all one family, but some of the tribes have become our enemies. That summer, unknown to us, the Hullalli tribe who live up on the plains to the northwest had sent raiding parties south, stealing our women and our herds."

"Aah! We have suffered from Achaean raiding gangs!" Coronilla growled in sympathy. "Many of us Moon Riders have lost our families like this!"

Kuspada nodded, glad of this rough understanding. "When the onset of severe weather brought us gold smelters to our senses," he continued, "we did at last set out to return, laden as never before, but snow fell and thick ice set in, so that our horses could not move. We had no choice but to make camp and stay where we were, far from our wives and little ones. There on the slopes of the mountains we struggled through the harshest winter we have ever known, living meagerly on the beasts that we managed to kill, telling ourselves that at least the horse ropers would have got back to look after the tribe."

The Moon Riders' faces were grim. They knew what was coming.

Kuspada gave a great sigh, heavy with misery and guilt. "When at last the thaw came," he told them, "we struggled back, our sleds piled high with the precious gold, to find a terrible sight of desolation. The horse ropers had been caught in the ice, just as we had. Many of the old people had died of cold and starvation, having lost all the sheep and goats; and worst of all, our wives had been stolen away by the Hullalli or had died in the struggle. My brave wife, Aplia, was one of them."

Tears filled Myrina's eyes and she wondered if she should stop Kuspada, for it was clear that his words gave great pain. But he seemed determined to go on; the story had to be told, however terrible. They must listen with patience, for nothing in the telling should be rushed.

Kuspada struggled with his feelings for a moment, but then he swallowed hard and went on. "We arrived home dripping with gold, rich beyond our dreams, but we'd lost all that we truly held dear, sacrificed it to gold . . . and greed."

Myrina had seen a great deal of sorrow in her life, but she understood that the terrible guilt of the Sinta warriors must be beyond anything.

Kuspada pointed out the young woman who'd come boldly to greet them; she sat listening quietly with two children on her lap, another at her feet. "Tabi was a young girl of twelve winters and she turned huntress, with her little group of warriors. She and her young team did their best to take the place of the men and they did well. We honor her greatly. Sere looked after Zimapo and the other motherless children and fed them, denying herself so that she almost died; now all the children call her grandmother. So when you ask to see our wives . . ." Kuspada broke down at last and it seemed he couldn't go on.

"We are truly sorry for you," Myrina told him.

He sighed. "We have gold to buy whatever we need.

We can buy sheep and goats and have captured many horses, but . . . we do not have many wives. Since the Bitter Winter we older men rarely travel far from the home tents; only the young warriors go off to hunt. That is how our young men first saw you when you struggled ashore and claimed the herd by the river. They made camp by the sheltering rocks and kept watch on you."

Myrina quickly perceived that the discovery of a camp full of young women must hold great significance for these lonely warriors. "We understand now," she said. "That is why the children called us 'mothers.'"

Kuspada nodded. "Those children are the ones that Sere saved; they long for new mothers. I will tell the truth, though I am shamed by it. When we came to understand that you were not men but women, our first wild thought was to raid your camp and snatch away as many young women as we could. But Turxu pointed out that you were fierce and deadly warriors; such a raid might well bring death to us all. So we decided to wait and watch and try a gentler way. We would make sure that you didn't die for want of food or warmth and hope that in time you would come to see us as friends. Our young men need wives—we cannot deny it. No women would be more precious and treasured than those who came to join the Sinta tribe; we would look to their every need and never, never leave them alone again."

Tabi suddenly spoke up in the Scythian tongue, holding both her hands out to Myrina in a pleading gesture. Myrina understood that she was begging the Moon Riders to join them and take the place of the lost Sinta wives.

Akasya and Coronilla both looked up with concern, raising their eyebrows and shaking their heads.

"We cannot offer our young women against their will." Coronilla was firm about that.

Akasya shrugged. "To be treasured and spoiled is not the way of Moon Riders!" Having spent many years as a slave in Troy she was often fearful that she'd lose her freedom again.

Myrina turned to Kuspada, choosing her words carefully. "We are a very different people and we have different ways. We Moon Riders choose ourselves a husband; nobody may wed a Moon Rider against her will."

Kuspada's face immediately clouded over with disappointment, so that Myrina hastened to say more. "We are full of sorrow for your terrible loss and grateful to you beyond words for the help that you have given us. Between the Sinta people and the Moon Riders there shall always be friendship."

The blacksmith looked up with renewed interest and began translating her words, so that the listening Sintas could understand.

"We came to these shores seeking new land and safety," Myrina went on, "for we have suffered at the hands of raiders and were taken into captivity. We are grateful that you did not attack us, as you had every right to do. You decided to wait and watch; that was most honorable. Let us continue to wait and watch. We all fear the winter that is coming soon, so let us live side by side and help each other in every way we can; then, in the Month of New Leaves, each Moon Rider will make up her own mind. Each woman shall choose for herself—until then, we shall be friends."

"Well said, Snake Lady!" Coronilla agreed. "Buy us time! We do not want to fight with them."

Kuspada respectfully rose to his feet, nodding his head at Myrina's answer and holding out the palm of his hand to her. "That is more than fair," he said. "Will you Moon Riders move your camp and set up your tents beside the sheltering rocks? You will be warmer there and you will get to know us better."

"Yes," Myrina agreed. Since she had seen the camp beneath Eagle Rocks, something of the kind had been in her own mind.

Kuspada repeated their agreement in Scythian to the listening Sinta people, and though their reaction was not one of wild joy, there was much thoughtful nodding and acceptance.

Tabi got up, the youngest child in her arms, and held out her palm to Myrina. "This is right," she agreed, smiling.

"Thank you." Myrina smiled back: she could see that this brave young woman would have made a fine Moon Rider.

Tabi spoke to Kuspada in the Scythian language—her words came out so fast and insistently that Myrina could not follow them, but she was pleased when Kuspada turned to her to explain. "Tabi insists that all our women and children move their camp to Levas Rocks. There we may all live side by side and keep each other warm and safe."

Myrina nodded at Tabi. "We would be honored."

The Sinta women were very excited at the idea, and at once they began to strip the felt from their tent frames and roll up their belongings.

Myrina looked around and saw that Fara's face was downcast. Turxu sat a little way off, his dark eyes full of concern, for Fara had moved away from him. What did this mean? Myrina thought that perhaps she understood and gently bent to touch Fara's arm. "Why do you look so sad?" she asked, wanting to be sure that she had not misunderstood.

Fara struggled to her feet and forced her shoulders back, reasserting the proud spirit of the warrior priestess.

"It's nothing," she said, quickly knuckling tears from her cheeks. "It is just that I see now why he wanted me. What has happened to these people is more bitter than anything, but because of their need—any wife would do!"

Myrina sighed; it was as she thought. But she remembered with a touch of guilt how she'd sat on Big Chief's back, secretly watching the two young people in the moonlight. Their intimacy had touched her to her very core and forced her to acknowledge her own loneliness.

She smiled and spoke again. "I understand your doubts," she said. "And you will have time enough to make your final choice, but I can tell you this—the expression that I see in Turxu's eyes when he looks at you is not just the admiration of a young man who needs a mate."

"Is it not?" Fara was listening.

Myrina shook her head. "It took me a long time to recognize that look in my own young warrior's eyes, and when at last I did, the time we had together was all too short. I would not want you to have so short a time. You must know that I would give anything now to see my Tomi ride over the hill. Do not let doubt and pride stand in the way. Look at Turxu and listen to what your heart tells you."

Just for a moment Fara glimpsed the pain that Myrina hid behind a burnished mask of courage, her fist clenched tightly to her chest. She looked from the Snake Lady to Turxu and saw that he followed her every move with his dark, worried gaze.

She smiled and hugged Myrina tightly. "Thank you, Snake Lady," she said. "Your words are as wise as an old woman's, though you yourself are still young."

Myrina shook her head, feeling very old indeed, while Fara went at once to Turxu and took him by the hand.

CHAPTER SEVENTEEN

The Great Camp

THAT NIGHT THE small group of Moon Riders
danced by the Sinta campfire. They even performed the sacred moon dance, while their
hosts watched in quiet awe. In the morning they set out
on their return journey, Kuspada insisting on escorting
them back.

Myrina felt more comfortable than ever in his company
and now, as they traveled, she told him much of the troubled history of the Moon Riders. His eyes gleamed with
admiration as she recounted the escape from the city of
Troy, for even as far north as the Sinta lands they knew
much of that long and bitter fight. His mouth became a
tight, grim line as she told of the battle of the Thermodon
and their enslavement at the hands of Achilles' son. There
was just one thing that Myrina left out: she didn't mention
Tomi or his brave and tragic death; somehow the right
words for that wouldn't come to her.

When at last they'd passed Eagle Rocks and were almost back at the Moon Riders' camp, Tamsin and Phoebe came galloping bravely out to meet them.

"Who is the mother of these lovely children?" Kuspada asked.

Myrina smiled with pride. "Phoebe, the older one, is the child of my sister, who was killed by Achilles' men. Tamsin is my own daughter."

"You have a husband?" Kuspada asked, with a touch of regret.

"No!" Myrina shook her head. She still could not bring herself to tell him of Tomi's death.

But he was quick to understand the expression of pain that suddenly clouded her face. "You have lost your dearest one," he said. "You are like me!"

That night, as the Moon Riders sat around their fire, the dreadful story of the lost wives of the Sinta warriors was retold. Everyone listened in silence; some of the women were touched with excitement, others were uneasy.

"We are wearing dead women's clothes," they said, pulling uncomfortably at the warm felt trousers and smocks the warriors had brought as gifts.

"Better dead women's clothes than freezing to death," Kora told them roundly.

"We cannot afford to fuss over that," Myrina agreed.

But then another concern was voiced. "Is this what we rode away from Troy to find?"

"We were slaves, but then we found freedom and honor as warrior priestesses. Are we now to sit like tame cats at a man's hearthside?"

"And men who are careless with their wives by the sound of it!"

Myrina told them all of the arrangement that she'd made with the Sintas. "In the Month of New Leaves you shall decide. I swear that none shall be forced—you shall all make your own free choice—but tomorrow we will move our tents and set up camp beneath Eagle Rocks, alongside them."

Those who were doubtful agreed reluctantly, and in the morning there was much grumbling at the extra work of having to move camp, but some of the young Sinta men arrived with horse-drawn sleds to help.

Big Chief and his mares watched them nervously, flurries of skittish movement passing through their ranks, but when the women started to erect their tents on the other side of the river, they lowered their heads to search for fresh grass again.

As soon as the Moon Riders arrived at Eagle Rocks, smiles of pleasure and understanding passed between them. "Warm!" they whispered. "So much warmer here."

Three camps were established side by side. There was

shyness for a day or two, but it wasn't long before barriers broke down, so that Tabi was soon to be found among the Moon Riders, while Tamsin and Phoebe sparred with the Sinta boys. Zimapo watched for a few days, then went to join them.

The Sinta boys tried to shoo her away, but she stood her ground, swinging a strong, straight stick at them.

"If they can fight you, so can I!"

"Sinta women do not fight!" the young boys told her, their faces marked with disapproval. "Go back to the cooking pot!"

Tamsin and Phoebe strode to Zimapo's defense, setting themselves one on either side of her. "She fights with us!" they said.

The Sinta boys gave in.

Kora enjoyed herself, flirting with the men and bossing the cooks about. Myrina had a few moments of doubt when arguments broke out, but these were quickly dispelled when she realized that they had moved just in time. Within days of the establishment of the great camp, snow began to fall. Some of the Moon Riders had never seen snow before; none of them had ever seen snow like this. Large flat flakes fell steadily, carpeting the ground so that it was hard to tell where the rocks stood out from the grass.

The hiss of bellows and the sound of hammering

issued from Kuspada's tent. Due to his hard work and generosity, the steeds of the warrior priestesses soon sported the dainty gold bits they'd admired so much. They set about learning this new way of steering their horses, skillfully directing their beasts by using gentle pressure on the sensitive parts of the mouth, rather than with the thighs as they had always done before.

The young Sinta warriors were eager to learn Mazagardi horse skills and it wasn't long before they walked among the skittish foals, stroking and touching their withers and flanks, just like the Moon Riders. They worked hard to master the clicks and cries, so that without ever using whips or ropes they could make a horse turn and follow them, obedient to their every command.

There was much laughter as the two groups tried to learn each other's way of speaking. The women swore that they were quicker to pick up the Scythian tongue.

In the evenings the Moon Riders sang and danced, and at first the Sintas watched them respectfully, but gradually they found the confidence to get up and perform the ancient horse dances of their tribe. Men and women danced together, gaining warmth and strength from the vigorous exercise, and as friendships grew and flourished, many couples enjoyed the warmth and comfort of sharing their tents through the freezing nights. Fara and Turxu were never apart; it seemed there would be little doubt about the choice that Fara would make when the Month of New Leaves came.

Sometimes Myrina would wrap herself up well and wander away from the camp, searching out a small pool of water to sit beside, letting her water visions bring her reassurance that her distant friends fared well. One freezing night she confided to Coronilla that though she had searched all evening, she couldn't find a pool anywhere that wasn't frozen solid.

"We had to break the ice this morning to let the horses drink," Coronilla told her. "You miss your mirror more than most, Snake Lady. Are we Moon Riders losing the skills that we had?"

"I think we are gaining new ones," Myrina said.

"Mmm . . ." Coronilla acknowledged uncertainly.

Coronilla and Akasya, who had always been close, now seemed to be inseparable. They gathered a little group around them who adhered strictly to the Moon Riders' ways. They competed with the Sinta men at riding, shooting, and hunting and seemed to enjoy their company, but it was clear that they would not be looking for a mate in the spring. It did not go unnoticed by them that their Snake Lady sat with the blacksmith most nights, and they saw how content she was in his company.

The Bitter Months came, and as the coldest days approached they planned a feast. "This is the Sinta way,"

Kuspada told them. "The feast gives us strength, and after that our hearts lift, for we know that we will soon greet the returning spring."

Myrina smiled, again reminded of the old Mazagardi ways.

At the winter feast small gifts changed hands and Myrina was a little disconcerted when Kuspada gave her a present wrapped in a scarf of soft felt, dyed purple.

"What is this?" she asked, dismayed that she hadn't thought to find a gift for him.

He smiled shyly. "For our snake lady."

She opened the soft wrapping, and there inside lay a gleaming mirror of solid gold, a finely crafted snake coiled daintily around the edge. It was so beautifully wrought that every tiny scale on the snake's skin was marked and the mirror shiny and polished so that she could see her reflection clearly.

"Aah!" She snatched it up and, neglecting to say thank you, fled away from the feasting circle, clutching the mirror to her chest.

Kuspada watched her go, dismayed, but Coronilla caught his sleeve. "No, no"—she wagged a finger in his face—"the gift is so wonderful that she cannot wait to use it. That mirror is perfect and in time you will understand why."

Just as Coronilla had promised, Myrina soon emerged

from her tent, a huge smile on her face. She went straight to Kuspada. "Thank you, thank you," she whispered. "You could not have given me anything more precious and beautiful."

Kuspada smiled, relieved. "Coronilla told me how the Ant Man's warriors melted down your father's careful work," he said. "I hope I do not presume too much in making something to take its place."

Myrina reached up and kissed him on the lips. They stood there for a long while smiling at each other, and Kuspada had no more worries about his gift.

At last the snow and ice began to retreat; the men and women who camped beneath Eagle Rocks were joyful with relief. A new energy seemed to buzz in the air. Lambs were born, and it was clear that many of the mares were pregnant. Fara also realized that she was pregnant and when she came to tell Myrina, the Snake Lady could not help but be happy for her.

"You must know what my choice will be," Fara whispered.

"You will stay with Turxu?"

Fara nodded.

But when the girl had gone, a touch of sadness came to Myrina. The incident had been a sharp reminder that the Month of New Leaves was not very far away, and she must honor her promise to let each young woman make her choice freely. Fara had always been so brave and bold, she'd made the perfect Moon Rider. Must they lose her now?

Kuspada came to her tent one cold bright day in the Month of Sheep's Milk to tell her that he planned to take some of the young Sinta warriors with him and travel west to a city where neighboring tribes gathered for spring markets and horse dealing. "I still have a wealth of gold to sell," he told her. "And we need more sheep and goats to provide for our great camp of people."

Myrina nodded. He seemed to be touched with renewed confidence and vigor; the old flinching look of shame was rarely to be seen in his eyes.

"Will you come with us?" he asked.

Myrina smiled. The thought of riding with him through the sun-wakening grasslands was very pleasant, but she shook her head.

CHAPTER EIGHTEEN

The Month of New Leaves

K USPADA LEFT THE next morning and Myrina
followed his progress almost daily in her beautiful new mirror, missing his warmth and good-
humored conversation by the fire each night. But while
he was away she took the opportunity to spend each
evening listening to the Moon Riders voicing their hopes
and fears.

Coronilla insisted that she would not be looking for a
husband among the Sinta tribe. "They're fine men, every
one of them," she said. "But I am far too old and wise to
take pleasure in such a life."

Akasya agreed. "You'll not catch me sitting in a home
tent when I can be galloping through the sea of grass, a
warm wind in my face."

The two women shared a tent and were rarely apart;
Myrina could see that together they were complete and
needed no husbands to make them happy, but the thought

of evenings without Kuspada brought sadness to her heart.

Her mirror told her that Iphigenia was still safe and living in comfort, waited on by servants and dressed in the finest gowns. Just once or twice she thought she saw a shadow of loneliness cross the young priestess's face. As for Cassandra, the once sorrowful princess of Troy seemed to be always laughing and smiling, young Chryse at her side. Myrina could not help but smile when she glimpsed them. "You would almost think that she was his mother, rather than Chryseis," she murmured.

She watched them with love, longing to see them in the flesh once again. She had lost so many friends—was she soon to lose more? Could she not find a way to keep all the Moon Riders together and happy? She wandered back to the camp from her mirror gazing, deep in thought. A new idea was coming into her head.

Kuspada returned with his men just as the Month of New Leaves began. His beautifully wrought gold work had bought them a fine collection of new stock. Myrina admired the healthy beasts and complimented him on choosing good breeding animals. If we Moon Riders ride away, we will leave all this behind, she thought.

It was almost as though Kuspada saw her thoughtfulness and knew the way that her mind was working. "Whatever is decided," he told her, "half this stock is yours!"

Myrina smiled at him with gratitude; he was a very fair and decent man.

Kuspada was welcomed back to the camp with a feast and dancing, but that night he whispered to Myrina that the Month of New Leaves was here and if they were to feed their new stock they must soon move north, looking for fresh pastures.

"The grass grows fresh and lush to the north across the river," he said. "We must move on and come south again to Eagle Rocks when the frosts return."

She looked at him seriously, understanding well what must come next.

"The time has come for choices to be made," he said. "Even the most slippery Snake Lady cannot slither out of this one." Suddenly his teasing words turned solemn and he reached for her hand. "Will you stay with the Sinta tribe and be my Argimpasa?" he begged. "Argimpasa is the mother of our race. You and I can put our sadness behind us and start again. We can have fine children together and heal each other's wounds."

Myrina wanted to put her arms about him and say, "Yes, yes, yes!" But there were others to whom she owed loyalty. She shook her head sadly, and he turned away.

She could not go on like this—the decision could not be put off any longer.

* * *

That night, after they had eaten, Myrina rose to her feet and began to walk slowly around the fire with such an expression of solemn importance that it made the others quickly take notice and understand that she wished to speak. Silence fell, filled with anticipation—they all knew that this moment must come.

"Now is the Month of New Leaves," she said. "And I must keep my promises both to the River People and to the Moon Riders."

A rustle of uncertainty passed all around the camp; uncertain glances flew from person to person, woman to woman, and Sinta warrior to his loved one.

"You all have the right to decide. But before you make your choices I want to put another possibility to you."

There were many glances of surprise, but Myrina continued quickly before she lost her nerve. "Why should we not all stay together, whether we wish to have Sinta husbands or not? We have weathered this winter in harmony, taking care of young and old. We have been hunters, men and women, riding out side by side to feed those who are too young or too sick."

There were frowns and glances of suspicion, but Kuspada looked up at her, his face touched once more with hope. Coronilla turned to Akasya and shrugged; they whispered together, concern on both their faces.

Myrina went on. "There is something that I must say

to the River People and they must try to understand. We Moon Riders are priestesses and wherever we are, whatever we do, we will dance for Maa and we will never cease to be warriors."

"More like it, Snake Lady!" Coronilla cheered.

Myrina smiled, grateful for her support. "If you Sinta can accept wives who ride and fight, then why should we Moon Riders not live with you? We would hunt side by side as we have through the winter."

Uncomfortable looks and nudges passed among the young Sinta warriors. They clearly thought little of this idea. Turxu got to his feet, looking worried. "It is not the Sinta way to have a wife who rides and fights."

Fara was on her feet at once; the roundness of her belly did not impede her. She faced him angrily. "Why not?"

When he saw that her question was a serious one, he folded his arms, frowning and troubled. "It is just not the Sinta way!"

"But to crouch by the hearth is not the Moon Riders' way!" Fara insisted. "You River People must think carefully—do you want wives or not?"

Turxu sat down again, still unhappy. Some of his friends jeered, but others looked thoughtful. A tense silence followed, and then Coronilla got up. Myrina bit her lips; she was desperate not to lose her oldest friend.

"Well," Coronilla said roundly, "you all know what I

think of sitting by hearths!" Suddenly there were smiles and laughter, and the tension seemed to break a little. "There is no way you'll catch me doing that!" she continued.

"And no way that we'd ask you to!" a young and cheeky Sinta boy replied.

Kuspada looked at him sharply, but Coronilla had not taken offense. Now she turned to Fara and her friends. "My gang have been planning to ride away, should you decide to turn into 'hearth huggers.'" They smiled at her uncertainly, wondering whether she was still teasing them, but Coronilla's face was touched by sadness. "But we dread to do it." She spoke low, so that everyone became quiet, straining to hear. "The sisterhood of the Moon Riders is very precious to us; it is something we do not want to lose."

There was silence from all sides.

Coronilla smiled at Myrina and her tone lightened again. "But now our crafty Snake Lady has thought up another way, and I for one can see that it has merit. If these Sinta men that you like so much will accept wives who are bound to ride and fight, then we could stay with you, too. You younger women will need us older ones. When your bellies and arms are full of children, who will train the young warrior priestesses? We women who do not wish to take a husband will be the aunts and grand-mothers of your tribe!"

172

Myrina smiled at her with gratitude. But now Kuspada rose to his feet and the young Sinta warriors turned to him, waiting respectfully to hear what he would say; he could carry the Sinta tribe or split them all apart.

He paused, choosing his words carefully. When he did begin, he spoke slowly. "Turxu spoke the truth," he acknowledged. "Sinta wives have always been hearth keepers, but now, River People—I have to ask you this simple but painful question. Did living the Sinta way save our wives?"

It was a harsh question and there was a terrible silence. Many of the River People hung their heads and all was still.

Kuspada continued, and Myrina felt her heart wrung by the sorrow of the old wounds that the blacksmith bravely set bleeding. "I say that we should listen to the Snake Lady," he said. "Had our lost wives been trained to ride and fight as these Moon Riders are, I believe they would be here with us now. We have lived side by side with the warrior priestesses and survived a hard winter; not one of us has died. Why should we not agree to live side by side with them as we move to new pastures and together make a new way of living?"

"I will do it!" Turxu shouted out.

Fara turned to him, smiling. "Side by side," she shouted.

"Side by side," they all roared their approval.

The decision was made. Myrina and Kuspada turned to face each other, wide smiles on both their faces.

That night Kuspada came to Myrina's tent and they slept together, their arms tightly locked about each other. "Will you be my Argimpasa?" he whispered. "Will you bear new children to strengthen the bond that grows between the River People and the Moon Riders?"

Myrina laughed sleepily. "I am too old," she chuckled.

"No." His voice was warm. "Neither of us is too old. Will you be my Argimpasa?"

"Yes, I will," she agreed.

In the morning they began the slow and careful job of packing up the tents, ready to move north across the river to look for fresh pastureland. The herd was unsettled, sensing that there was something different in the air. Myrina smiled to see the young Sinta girls now riding with confidence; it was often difficult to tell the girls from the boys. Tabi rode with ease, a toddler in front and a baby strapped tightly at her back.

"Just like the Mazagardi," Myrina whispered.

By the evening they were almost ready; only the tents, empty of all their goods, were still in place. They all agreed that there was no point in waiting and that they should move off early next morning as soon as the sun peeped over the horizon. Myrina left them singing and dancing together, honoring the warm fold of rocks that had protected them through the Bitter Months. She wandered away, her mirror in her hand, feeling light and happy; all she needed now was to know that her distant friends were safe and well.

She found a sheltered spot and sat down, the reflection of the sky gray and pink in her mirror where the sun had just gone down. First she looked for Cassandra and was deeply saddened when she saw the priestess and the Mouse Boy hand in hand beside the still figure of Chryseis. What did this mean? Was Chryseis sleeping or sick? But as she watched she understood that the priestess had died. There behind them she could see a pyre. They had laid her out in her beautiful golden robe and sat beside her still and silent, mourning and keeping watch.

Myrina wept a little, wishing that she could be there with them, but she could see that Cassandra and Chryse were close, each comforting the other in their sorrow. She remembered how Cassandra had mothered little Chryse when he was a tiny babe and Chryseis too sick and hurt to look after him. Now it seemed she must mother him for good.

Myrina turned away from the sorrowful vision, feeling guilty that she should be so happy. Then she turned her thoughts toward Iphigenia. When she saw her friend she was filled with horror. "What is this?" she cried out loud.

Iphigenia was weeping bitterly in her elegant room. Her clothes were as beautiful as before, but when a servant approached her with food, Iphigenia turned around and knocked the elaborate tray to the floor. The angry gesture shocked Myrina. Iphigenia had never raised her hand in anger.

Myrina watched, so upset by what she saw that she could no longer hold the vision in her sight. Despite her efforts, the pathetic weeping figure faded and she could not manage to bring her back. Myrina was alone on the bleak hillside, afraid. How could she ride happily northward with the River People knowing that Iphigenia was in distress?

CHAPTER NINETEEN

A Friend in Trouble

K USPADA WAS COMING to look for her as she
wandered back, white faced and grim, her
knuckles white where she gripped the mirror
tightly. "What is it?" he asked, worried by the distraught
look in her eyes.

The sinuous strength of the Snake Lady slipped away,
leaving her weary with the struggle that her life had
become. "What has happened?" Kuspada asked.

"Can't come with you," she mumbled. "Can't come."

"Why not?" he demanded, a gleam of anger in his eyes.
"What has changed? You were warm and loving to me
last night! You promised to be—" Then he saw the pain
that distorted her face and stopped, afraid to press her
further.

They stood together in silence for a moment, he in disbelief, she in despair, then suddenly Myrina tossed back
her hair and lifted her chin.

"A dear friend has need of me and I must go at once to her aid!"

Kuspada was perplexed at Myrina's sudden change of mind. "What friend is this? How can you know that she's in trouble?"

Myrina sighed. How could she explain it to him? "I told you once how long ago we Moon Riders rode to Aulis and rescued the little Princess Iphigenia from being sacrificed to the goddess Artemis."

He nodded, frowning hard, trying to remember what she'd said. The history of the Moon Riders had been long, and there had been many rescues and threatened lives.

"Well," she went on, "then I also told you how we thought Iphigenia lost when the storm smashed our ship as we crossed the Inhospitable Sea. But . . . the princess was not lost—I cannot explain how I know, but you must believe me . . . I *do* know. It is the magic hidden in the beautiful mirror that you made that tells me so. She is in desperate trouble now and I must go to her."

Kuspada raked his fingers through his hair, trying hard to understand. "But where is she?"

Myrina sighed and her lips twisted into a wry and bitter smile. "That I don't know."

"Then how can you find her?"

Myrina shook her head. "You must think me mad and

perhaps I am, but I must do this. Iphigenia was washed away somewhere to the west of the river lands. What I do know is that she lives high above a city built on a steep hillside, where a narrow inlet from the sea makes a harbor. I will ride west and trust that I find her."

Kuspada started a little and looked thoughtful, then he took her by the shoulders. "I will come with you."

Myrina shook her head again with regret, for his steady, powerful presence at her side would indeed be a huge comfort. "No," she insisted. "If the Moon Riders are to ride north with the Sinta, then I need to know that you go with them. Only you can see them safe and united."

"But . . . to be parted so soon, when we just—!"

Myrina put up her hands and cupped his face. "Believe me," she whispered, "this is not what I want to do."

Kuspada pulled away from her. "What a fool," he muttered angrily. "What a stupid old fool, to give my heart to a slippery snake lady."

"Do not disappoint me so!" she told him, suddenly fierce, grasping his arm in a grip of iron. "Kuspada, you are a bigger man than that. I could not feel as I do for any man that were less than you."

He was silent for a moment, then he turned to her again and his face was full of quiet dignity. "I think . . . I may know where your princess landed."

Myrina loosed her grip and slid her palm down to clasp his hand, waiting for him to say more.

He spoke reluctantly. "When we traveled west selling our gold, in many of the small towns there was talk of a strange and beautiful young woman who was washed ashore at Tauris. That place is built on a steep hillside, high above an inlet. They call this young woman Hepsuash, which means 'the Girl from the Sea.' They said that King Thoas dismissed the old priestess of Artemis at Tauris and made this young girl priestess in her place."

"Yes, yes . . . ?" Myrina was eager to hear more. This fitted well with her visions of Iphigenia. "Where is this Tauris? Is it far?"

"A city to the west where the land dips out into the sea. If you follow the coast you will reach it, but . . . it is a long way and the people there are feared, for they sacrifice strangers who are shipwrecked—sacrifice them to Artemis. It is a wonder indeed that this Hepsuash was not sacrificed herself. If this is your Iphigenia, she may well be in great danger and if you go riding to her rescue again, you will be in peril, too."

But Myrina was not the Snake Lady for nothing. As she listened to his words her spirits rose and though she was so sorry to leave him, a faint tingling of excitement came to her at the thought of riding west.

She smiled fiercely and pulled him down toward her, kissing him on the lips. "Thank you," she whispered. "What you have told me is of great help—forewarned is forearmed. Now that I know where to look I may come back sooner than you think. If I live I will follow your trail and return to you. Do not fear for me—ask Coronilla; they all call me the great survivor."

Kuspada sighed. "I will wait," he said. "I will wait, however long it takes."

They walked back together hand in hand. "When will you tell them?" Kuspada asked.

Myrina looked sadly at the circle of eager, dancing warriors. "In the morning," she said.

The Moon Riders emerged from their tents to welcome the sun, but as the first pink fingers of light went streaking across the grasslands, Myrina took Tamsin and Phoebe by the hand and drew them away from the dance. "I have something important to tell you both and something to ask. I have made a difficult choice; now you, too, must make a choice and it may be very hard for you!"

They looked at each other, hushed by her serious words.

"I will not be going with the Moon Riders or the River People," she said. "My mirror visions have told me that Iphigenia is in great trouble and I believe that she is living many days' journey to the west of here. I must go to help her—do you understand this?"

They stared at her, frowning for a moment, but then they both nodded. "Yes," they answered firmly.

"What is the choice that we must make?" Phoebe asked uncomfortably.

"Do you want to come with me or do you wish to go with Coronilla and Akasya and make a new life with the River People?"

Tamsin was silent and Phoebe looked troubled. "You are not going away forever, are you?" she asked.

"No," Myrina told her. "But there is danger where I go. I cannot be sure what will be the outcome. You would both be safer traveling with the others and waiting until I return to you with Iphigenia."

Tamsin looked at her mother with astonishment. "I am only safe with you," she said.

Myrina could not help but be pleased at the fearlessness in her words. "Are you sure, Little Lizard?"

"Quite sure," Tamsin told her.

"And what is your choice, Young Tiger?" she asked Phoebe.

The girl who never hesitated did hesitate now, and Myrina saw at once that it was not the guardianship of Coronilla or Akasya that brought this about. She held out her arms to Phoebe and hugged her tightly. "The time comes for all young tigers to leave their mother," she whispered. "I will be happy thinking of you riding through the rolling grasslands, with Leni at your side."

"Thank you, Snake Lady." Phoebe smiled, but then she turned to Tamsin. "You and I have never been parted," she said.

Myrina watched them hug each other solemnly and she felt that her heart would break.

When they returned to their friends they found them ready on horseback, waiting only for Myrina to give the word to move. Kuspada stood awkwardly by Dorag, looking unhappy, knowing what must now be said.

"Come on, Snake Lady," Coronilla said. "We all wait for you!"

"You must wait a little longer, dear friend," Myrina told her.

When she spoke to them of her plan there was uproar, as she'd expected. "We'll come, too," Coronilla insisted. "How dare you think you can go riding off to fight the king of Tauris without us at your back!"

Myrina took a deep breath; she knew that she must be resolute. "I go to fight nobody—I go in stealth; you know that is my way. The rescue of Iphigenia from Aulis taught us that. You must head north and stick together if we are to make this plan of ours work. You all have skills to contribute if we are to unite with the River People and make a new and better life."

"By Maa, I should have suspected something like this—you crafty snake!" Coronilla hissed.

"But how will you live?" Akasya was concerned with the practicalities of such a plan.

"I have thought it all out." Myrina tried hard to sound confident. "I take only Tamsin with me and six of the best mares. I am a widowed Sinta horse dealer, traveling with my daughter. If I need money I sell a horse. Nobody will be suspicious of me because that is exactly who I am."

"Huh! That and a whole lot more," Coronilla protested.

But it was hard for them to argue, for it was true that a mother and daughter traveling together would raise little suspicion, and nobody would be likely to think that they were not all they said they were.

Coronilla turned to Kuspada. "Are you going to let her ride out of your life?" she cried.

Kuspada looked back at Coronilla, amazed, and then he suddenly laughed. "I never thought to hear you telling me that I should order the Snake Lady to do anything! If Myrina is determined, then nothing I can do will change her mind."

Coronilla frowned. "By Maa . . . I suppose you are right! Well, remember, Snake Lady," she said at last.

"Kuspada has made me a new mirror, too! I shall be watching you!"

Myrina smiled and went to them, her arms outstretched. Kuspada brought out six of the sturdiest mares, caparisoned with the finest gold bits and bridles, roped together so that Myrina would look like the Sinta widow she claimed to be. He also gave her a pouch of gold coins that she hid inside her smock.

Then reluctantly the great caravan of travelers set off, picking their way through the rocks on the hillside, heading northward across the rolling grassy plains.

"I will wait," Kuspada whispered; then he swung himself up onto Dorag's back and rode away.

Myrina and Tamsin sat watching them, their lips pressed tightly together in a brave line.

Big Chief tossed his head and snorted in protest at the sight of his many wives heading northward away from him. Myrina gentled him and whispered in his ears, so that he turned obediently at her bidding, but as they moved off they heard the sound of hooves behind them. Myrina stopped. What was this? She could not face more sad farewells.

"Snake Mother!" Phoebe came galloping after them on Sandmane.

Tamsin frowned as Phoebe caught up, a wide, confident smile on her face. "Leni will have to wait a while," she told them. "Snake Mother, you have two daughters once again!"

Both Myrina and Tamsin smiled. Then Big Chief moved off, leading his six new wives toward the marshes, heading westward as the sun rose in the sky.

Part Two

AGAMEMNON'S INHERITANCE

CHAPTER TWENTY

Tauris

YRINA MADE THE two girls ride all day across the marshy plain toward the southwest, where Kuspada had told her she would pick up the coastline, avoiding the populated curve of land that divided the Inhospitable Sea from the Little Sea. She knew that she was trying to put as great a distance as she could between herself and the Moon Riders; it was almost as though she feared she might change her mind and canter back to them if the distance were not too great. She kept up a steady flow of conversation, though her heart was heavy as iron. Tamsin and Phoebe had gone quiet, making little response to her cheerful comments, but they rode at a steady speed without groans or complaints.

It was a long time since they had ridden all day like this and covered so much ground. Myrina feared that they were missing the busy camp beneath Eagle Rocks and the companionship they had enjoyed all through the winter. Had she done wrong to bring them away with her on a mission that could put them all in danger?

At last the long, low horizon of the sea came into view and both the girls cheered at the sight of it. Big Chief snorted and snuffed the sea air; he at least seemed to be enjoying the adventure of such a long ride across new territory, with no turning back. They covered the last bit of marshy land fast, careless of the spattering mud, and rode westward beneath a bright sun, the sea washing at the horses' fetlocks.

As the sun began to sink Myrina called a halt. She knew that the girls must be exhausted and she herself felt too weary to try to make a fire. As soon as they'd eaten their cold supper of smoked venison, Tamsin fell asleep, wrapped in her felt rug.

Phoebe sat up for a while, staring gloomily out at the sea. "Regrets?" Myrina asked.

Phoebe nodded, but then she smiled. "So quiet without the others," she acknowledged.

"I miss them, too," Myrina admitted. "But I'm glad that you are here with me."

Phoebe reached over to kiss her and then yawned hugely.

"Go to sleep," Myrina told her.

Phoebe settled down beside Tamsin and soon they

were both snoring gently. A strange and empty feeling came to Myrina; a sensation that she recognized as loneliness, though it was something she'd rarely experienced. Her life had been so very full and busy that she usually enjoyed her moments of solitude. She often wandered away from the camp for a bit of peace, loving the brief respite from laughter and argument.

Now, beside an unknown coastline, the sleeping girls beside her, she longed for adult company. "I should have let Coronilla come," she murmured and then smiled. "Or the blacksmith."

The thought of Kuspada made her remember her mirror and she pulled it from the horsehide sheath that protected it and fixed it safely to her belt. Of course—this was what a mirror was for; she would never be lonely with her magical snaky mirror, wrought with such tender care.

She stared into the mirrored darkness, lit only by the moon, and at first all she could see was the dark round of her own face, surrounded by faint gleams of starlight and edged by the twisting glints of the golden snakes. As she watched, the stars seemed to pick up the gold of the snakes and swim together until they formed the flickering, flaming heart of a fire. Then she began to see the great camp of tents, set up in the lee of a low hillside. The Moon Riders were dancing, even though they must be as weary as she was. She saw Kuspada sitting a little away from the

191

others, his face sad and his thoughts distant. She smiled—his thoughts were with her, she had no doubt of that.

She watched him sadly for a while, then she rose to her feet, the mirror in her hand, and she too began to dance, still holding the vision, moving in time with the Moon Riders. She stepped quietly around the sleeping girls, the regular beat of the drum in her head as she performed the gentle, sleep-inducing moon dance.

"I must not forget that I'm a Moon Rider," she told herself. She watched the Moon Riders go to their beds; Kuspada got up and wandered sleepily into his tent.

"And I must not forget why I am here," she whispered, thinking of Iphigenia. She let her eyelids droop again as she gazed into the smoke that rose in curls and twists from the Moon Riders' fire. At last the smoke cleared a little to reveal the pale oval of Iphigenia's face. She was alone in the beautiful room that Myrina had seen before, but sleeping, and she looked for the moment as though she was at peace.

"Not long," Myrina whispered. "Not long and I will see you in the flesh," she promised. Then she settled down beside the girls, grateful for the warmth and comfort they gave.

Myrina woke them at dawn for the sun-welcoming dance.

"Just the three of us?" Tamsin asked.

"Of course," Myrina insisted. "We are Moon Riders."

Both girls smiled and laughed as they danced together; then, having breakfasted, they leaped up onto their horses with renewed energy. This formed the pattern of their days as they journeyed on. They grew used to the routine and Myrina was relieved to see that their spirits lifted, so that for much of the time they chattered together, excited at all they saw. They kept their distance from towns, but stopped in the villages, where fishing families made them welcome and sold them good fish, either smoked or fresh, and wholesome flat-baked bread. Myrina's knowledge of the Scythian tongue was now so good that nobody doubted that she was the Sinta horse-dealing widow that she claimed to be. Sometimes the villagers stared a little at the arrow pictures that decorated her cheeks, but she explained with a smile that it was a new custom in the lands east of the river, where her tribe came from.

The days grew warm and as they traveled on, flowers bloomed all about them; lizards sunning themselves scuttered away to hide at the sound of hooves.

"Lizards everywhere!" Tamsin laughed, pleased at the idea. "This is lizard country!"

The harsh winter was forgotten, and they rejoiced to find the land so warm and fertile. They saw hares and deer but did not stop to hunt, for Myrina was still borne onward by a deep sense of urgency.

Each night she took a little time to mirror gaze and found that it helped to stave off the loneliness that had descended on that first night. She saw that the Moon Riders and River People thrived and that Iphigenia did not seem to be in immediate danger. One night she watched as a tall man, richly dressed, came to visit her. She sensed that the princess was troubled by his presence and could see that she shook her head at him with determination. Another night she saw her friend holding up a familiar round, black, glassy stone and she understood that Iphigenia, too, was mirror gazing. Her mirror was not a beautifully crafted thing like the one in Myrina's hand; it was a rough-shaped circle of obsidian given to her long ago by Cassandra. Then, as she watched, Myrina saw Iphigenia look up and raise her hand to her forehead in the Moon Riders' salute.

"She knows," Myrina whispered, awed. "She knows that I am coming and that I watch her."

At once her own hand went involuntarily to her brow in an answering salute and then something happened that she'd never experienced before in all her years of mirror gazing. Without her willing it, the vision of Iphigenia faded a little and Myrina glimpsed the image of Cassandra, there beside Agamemnon's daughter. It was almost as though the Trojan princess were sitting beside her old friend in the elegant room.

"You will never be alone!" Myrina murmured, remembering the words that Cassandra had used so long ago to the young Iphigenia when they'd parted as children. The promise had proved true, for all through the terrible ordeal of being prepared as a sacrifice, Iphigenia swore that she'd felt Cassandra at her side.

Myrina's eyes grew wide as she saw that both princesses raised their hands in an answering salute. "They can both see me," she whispered. This astonishing three-way vision linked them all together.

"Deep magic!" Myrina murmured. "It is Cassandra who has sent me! It is she who has made me come riding so urgently to Tauris!" This thought brought with it a better understanding of the great sense of haste that she felt. "What else could make me leave Kuspada just as I was beginning to love him?" she murmured. "And Iphigenia—she knows that I am on my way."

Then the shapes faded into smoke and Myrina saw only her own pale, tired face in the mirror again. She gasped with exhaustion; this vision had drained her of energy, but it had also left her with a strong feeling of purpose and certainty.

Over the next two days they rode with renewed urgency, Myrina anxious that the pace was too fast for the girls. But when she related her mysterious mirror vision to them, they both urged her to hurry, impressed by the ancient magic that she described.

"How can Cassandra send her shade to sit with Iphigenia?" Tamsin asked.

"I wish I had known the Trojan princess." Phoebe spoke wistfully.

"You did know her!" Myrina told her at once, regretful that she had never thought to tell her so before. "She held you in her arms and called you the tiger's child when you were a tiny babe!"

"Did she? Is that why you have always called me Young Tiger?"

Myrina nodded.

"I never knew that!" Phoebe gazed in wonder at the tiger picture that Myrina had pricked onto her forearm when they lived in peace on the banks of the Thermodon. "I was given my own special symbol by a magical princess."

Myrina smiled; she, too, could only marvel at the power of the Trojan princess that could project, not just her image but her care and concern, so far from her island home.

"But Iphigenia must have this magic, too," Tamsin insisted.

"Yes," Myrina agreed. "Iphigenia has a gleaming black obsidian mirror that Cassandra gave her long ago; it is made of stone from a fire mountain. Atisha told us that it contained the most powerful magic of all."

"You promised to teach us far-seeing and mirror magic," Tamsin reminded her mother.

"I swear that I will, Sweet Lizard," Myrina promised again. "And you, too, Young Tiger, as soon as we see Iphigenia safe!"

They rode all through the next day and night, nodding briefly off to sleep as they rode, trusting themselves to their steeds, the mares they'd brought to sell following obediently in their wake but growing leaner by the day.

The following morning they arrived at a place where the far coastline seemed to split dramatically into two levels as it curved off to the northwest. The lower level was bathed in sun and sheltered by the huge cliffs that rose behind it. A small fishing village was situated in the middle of this strange junction and a great ship lay at anchor in the bay.

At first sight of the ship, Myrina felt a touch of apprehension. What was such a galley doing here? They rode slowly down toward the village and learned that the place was named Yalushta. Suddenly, as she looked again at the ship, Myrina called the girls urgently back to her side.

"What is it?" they asked.

"That ship . . ." Myrina spoke in a whisper, her voice shaking. "It bears the symbol of a swan. I know what that means and it is named the *Castor and Pollux!*"

CHAPTER TWENTY-ONE

The Land of the Taurians

T HEY ALL STARED down at the great Achaean
ship that was anchored in the small bay.

Phoebe was alert to danger at once but
puzzled by Myrina's concern. "This is not the Ant Man's
son that anchors in the bay?"

"No." Myrina frowned. "But that symbol of the swan
fills me with dread—I remember seeing it on many of the
Achaean ships drawn up in the Bay of Troy and also at
Aulis. It is the symbol that Agamemnon made his own
when he took Clytemnestra as his wife and claimed the
kingdom of Mycenae."

Tamsin asked, "Agamemnon? The cruel father of
Iphigenia?"

"But. . ." Phoebe struggled to understand. "Did you
not tell us that he was dead?"

Myrina shook her head, puzzled herself. "I saw him die
in one of my visions. Iphigenia was with me and she saw

it, too. It happened long ago and I believed it, for my visions have never let me down," she said, trying to calm her own fears. "It cannot be Agamemnon, so it must be somebody who has stolen one of his ships."

"It looks battered and worn," Phoebe pointed out.

Myrina could see that she was right. The ship looked as though it had limped into this place after a very long sea journey, its paint peeling and its wide brail sail in need of repair.

"I'd say it has battled through a storm, just as we did," Myrina guessed. "It doesn't look too threatening now. We will ignore it and go on our way, but we must be wary."

She stopped for a while, looking uncertainly ahead at the way the cliffs split so sharply into two at Yalushta. "Which path do we take?" she murmured.

The lower path led through small coastal villages, hung with flowers and vines. Cats slept in the sun and the scent of cooking filled the streets, while seagulls soared and mewed. The other pathway wound steeply up to the top of the cliffs; all they could see up there was grass and a few stunted trees.

Tamsin had no hesitation. "I would stay down by the sea."

Myrina shook her head. "It looks more hospitable down there," she agreed. "But we are not here to sun ourselves. I think we could approach this city of Tauris from a stronger position if we were up on those high cliffs."

Tamsin sighed, but obediently she turned Snowboots's head, and they all set off to struggle up the steep cliff pathway.

That night they camped on the bleak grassy cliff tops, where there was little shelter. They caught glimpses of fallow deer and partridges waddling in the distance, while eagles soared above their heads. Stoats and hamsters scampered around them as the sun went down and the evening turned cool.

"I like it up here," Tamsin decided after all. "I can see the whole world below me."

They moved on next morning, keeping close to the cliff edge, the sunny seaside villages beneath them on the lower level. It wasn't long before the open rolling plains around them became dotted with small clumps of habitation. They moved away from the cliffs to skirt an ornate, palatial building, topped with turrets and towers, perched precariously on high rocks. It was heavily guarded.

"Is that the king's palace?" Tamsin asked. "Shall we ask the guards?"

Myrina shook her head, strangely reluctant. She had never seen a palace in such an inhospitable spot. Though there was a steep road leading up to it, a cart would struggle to reach the top.

"Why so many guards?" Phoebe wondered.

"Why indeed?" Myrina murmured. "What is it that they guard so carefully? Or who?"

As she looked at the highest tower, topped with the shape of a stag's antlers wrought in gold, a slow sense of unease grew in her mind. A stag's antlers usually symbolized Artemis. Was this her temple? Iphigenia had always called Artemis the Moon Lady and swore that the goddess was close to Maa. Why then should the sight of these curling majestic antlers bring such disquiet? Myrina forced herself to urge the girls on, giving the strange building a wide berth.

It was not long before huts and houses merged into a great sprawl that must form the outskirts of a city. Could this be the city of Tauris?

At last her suspicions were confirmed as they saw down below them the inlet that formed a perfect safe harbor. The cliffs curved around on either side so that they almost met, leaving just a narrow passageway for a ship to pass through into safety.

"Is this it?" Phoebe asked. "A city built into a steep hillside?"

Myrina nodded. "I think so."

They stopped to ask a woman who passed them. "Is this the city they call Tauris?"

"Yes," she answered sharply. "Of course this is Tauris. Where else could it be?"

After the friendliness they'd found in the seaside villages, this response was something of a shock, but Myrina reminded herself that Kuspada had told her that strangers were unwelcome in Tauris. He'd even spoken of them sacrificing those who were shipwrecked and washed ashore in the harbor. Could this be the trouble that threatened Iphigenia? But in her mirror vision Myrina had seen her being saved from the sea and welcomed, or so it had seemed. Did the Taurians keep a victim in comfort for a while and then sacrifice her in the spring? Myrina had heard of such things and that explanation would fit the picture, but how much more terrible such a threat would be to Iphigenia. To be threatened with sacrifice once was bad enough, but twice would be too much for anyone to bear! She could not speak this dread out loud for fear of terrifying the girls. Why had she not brought Coronilla, she berated herself, and left Tamsin and Phoebe safe with the River People?

Hesitantly she asked a man if he could suggest a safe place for them to camp, but he swore at her and went on his way. Myrina could easily have knocked the fellow to the ground, but she knew that wouldn't help. She realized with growing apprehension that it would be easy to make a dangerous move in the wrong direction and lose all chance of helping Iphigenia. The coolness that she sensed in the Taurians made her feel more friendless than ever before. What a fool she'd been! The girls were so vulnerable here, even though they were both as brave as bears and trusted her completely.

But Myrina was not allowed to dwell on this. "What now?" Tamsin questioned her mother with simple practicality.

Myrina forced herself to stay calm and act sensibly. Her eyes swept the surrounding landscape. "Over there, where a copse of trees shelters the mouth of a cave, there's good grass for grazing. I don't see why we should not set up our camp."

The mares deserved a rest and feed; nobody would want to buy them if they didn't give them time to fatten themselves after such a journey. As they moved toward the spot, Phoebe raised her hand to her ear, her tiger senses all alert. "I can hear running water," she said.

They discovered a clear stream that rippled out from the mouth of a cave. "This is a wonderful place to make camp," said Tamsin.

Myrina agreed. She looked around again, surprised that others were not of the same mind. The spot had everything that anyone could want: shelter, trees, fresh grass, and clear water. In the distance they could see tents and huts open to the rain, wind, and dust. Why didn't those people camp here? Was it sacred ground? A momentary doubt troubled her, but then she shook her head, swung down from Big Chief's back, and led him to the stream. The water was sweet, and both horses and riders drank their fill.

They noticed an old woman sitting in the mouth of the cave with a girl who looked just a little older than Phoebe. The cave dwellers did not smile or raise a hand in welcome, but at least they did not drive them away. They merely watched with quiet curiosity. Myrina sighed; such behavior seemed to be the way around here.

Tamsin led Snowboots away from the water, but all the while she smiled and glanced toward the cave. "We'll make friends with them." She spoke with perfect confidence.

Phoebe was more cautious. "But do they wish to be friends?" she asked.

They set up their tent and made a roped corral for the horses, more to mark them as their property than to keep them from straying. They built a small fire and ate some of the flat bread, smoked fish, and goat's cheese that they had managed to buy the day before. Nobody came near them, but the old woman and the young girl continued to watch them warily. Though Myrina kept glancing in their direction, she saw no sign of the cave dwellers eating their own evening meal.

"No dancing tonight," Myrina told the girls. They both nodded, understanding that they'd be wise not to draw attention to themselves.

Myrina quashed the urge to take some sort of urgent action, for good sense told her that what she needed first was information. She needed to hear the latest gossip—to know what was going on in the place. But as nobody seemed to want to come anywhere near them, she realized that gathering information was going to be difficult.

She glanced thoughtfully over toward the cave mouth and at last she smiled at Tamsin. "I think you had the right idea, Little Lizard—let's go and see if we can make friends. Let's take the cave dwellers a bit of bread and cheese."

Tamsin rose to her feet with confidence. She was excellent at making friends; she'd had the Sinta girls and boys eating out of the palm of her hand in minutes. Phoebe also got up, giving Myrina a nervous smile. "I'm sure you are right, Snake Lady, but they do not look the most welcoming of strangers."

Myrina nodded and touched her shoulder. "It's good to be wary, Young Tiger."

They walked over toward the two women, Tamsin marching boldly ahead, but the older woman got up and, with a swift angry glance at the intruders, slid back into the dark shadowy interior of the cave mouth.

Myrina and Phoebe stopped for a moment, disconcerted, but Tamsin strode on, determinedly holding out a hunk of bread and cheese. She shouted out loud in the Sinta tongue that she'd been learning all winter. "For you! This food is for you!"

The cave girl leaped quickly to her feet, heading for the darkness as though she would follow the old woman inside, but when she saw the flat bread she hesitated, paused, and licked her lips. She seemed to understand Tamsin's invitation and there was no doubt that she wanted the food.

"For you!" Tamsin cried again.

The cave girl took a nervous step toward them. It seemed that Tamsin's instincts were working well, for the girl snatched the bread and began to eat it hungrily.

Myrina caught Phoebe by the arm and pulled her down to sit on the grass beside her at a little distance, making it clear that they did not wish to intrude further.

The girl, too, dropped to her haunches, whimpering a little as she continued to eat hungrily. Tamsin stood over her, hands on hips, a huge smile of triumph on her face. She insisted on making encouraging noises as the girl ate, patting her belly and smacking her lips, using the Scythian words that she'd learned from her Sinta friends. "Good food, eh! Fill up the belly! You are welcome!"

The girl ate like a savage animal, but every now and then she nodded at them, making her gratitude clear. When at last she'd finished eating she dusted down her clothes with surprising delicacy, then turning to them she spoke in the Scythian language. "I thank you," she said, her voice surprisingly clear and refined.

"Ha!" Tamsin turned to her mother with delight. "I knew we could make friends!"

"You were very hungry." Myrina spoke to the girl with warm sympathy as she and Phoebe at last moved a little closer. "Here is more food for the old one," she said, putting another small parcel of bread and cheese down on the rock. Now they could see that the girl was dressed in clothes that had once been beautiful, but were fast becoming filthy rags. Her legs were bruised and covered in sores.

Then suddenly Phoebe moved forward, smiling and clicking her fingers. She pointed to a worn set of silver finger cymbals that dangled from the girl's belt. The girl looked puzzled, but Phoebe raised her hands above her head as though she were dancing, clicking her fingers in a fast rhythm and twirling.

"Ahh!" Myrina saw the cymbals and understood. "She is a dancer!"

"A dancer, like us!" Tamsin turned to Myrina with surprise. "You were wrong about that, Snake Mother; we should have danced tonight."

Without another word Tamsin and Phoebe launched themselves into one of the energetic horse dances that they knew so well, full of stamping feet and tossing heads.

The girl's mouth dropped open in surprise, but she recovered quickly, pulling the finger cymbals from her belt. She set them clattering at once in time to the rhythm that the girls had set; their bell-like tone was true, even though they looked very old and battered.

In an instant she was dancing with them, her own feet stamping in time with theirs. She copied each movement that they made, instinctively knowing which way they would turn next. Myrina laughed with pleasure and began a steady clap to accompany them. She thought she saw a movement in the dark recesses of the cave and felt sure that the old woman was watching them. How could she not be?

CHAPTER TWENTY-TWO

Katya

M YRINA WATCHED THE three girls dance together with enjoyment. Perhaps this place was not as sinister as she had feared. When at last they all flopped down onto the rocks, laughing and exhausted, she touched the girl by the arm. "You are a fine dancer," she said. "What is your name?"

"I am . . . Katya," she told them, still gasping a little after the exertion. "Once . . . I danced in the temple for the great Moon Goddess Artemis, but nobody wants my dancing now—no coins and no food."

"The temple of Artemis," Myrina murmured thoughtfully. She felt sure that it must be the strange ornate building they had seen perched up on the cliff tops.

But the girl suddenly frowned and her mouth twisted up in anger. "My grandmother and I sit here and starve . . . and it is all the fault of Hepsuash, the girl from the sea."

Myrina was at once alert. This was surely the name

that Kuspada had used when he spoke of the new priestess at Tauris, the one he thought might be Iphigenia.

She put out a gentle hand to hush Tamsin and warn her to be careful. "Who is this . . . girl from the sea?" she asked Katya gently. "And how has she injured you?"

Katya's lip curled with fury, and Myrina feared that she had asked too much.

"Hepsuash!" Katya spat the strange name out with such forceful contempt that Myrina's sense of unease came back a hundredfold. "She was washed ashore," the girl went on, her resentment clear in every word, "clinging to a statue of Artemis. A bedraggled fish she was, a skinny, slimy eel!"

Phoebe sat still and tense, worried by the hostility that had suddenly surfaced. Tamsin looked as though she'd like to speak but heeded her mother's warning.

Myrina bit her lip as she listened, troubled by the girl's vehemence, but at least she was getting the information she needed. "But . . . how has this Hepsuash injured you so sorely?"

The girl looked surprised. "You must be strangers here," she said, scowling at them, full of suspicion now.

Myrina hesitated, unsure whether to admit that they were strangers or not. But the girl's expression quickly changed again as she looked down and saw the neat parcel of food that they had set on the rock for the old woman. It served to remind her that, strangers or not, they had fed her and left more food for her grandmother.

Even Tamsin sat very still and quiet now.

"Well, I suppose you cannot help being strangers," Katya murmured, softening a little. "I will tell you what Hepsuash has done," she continued in a more friendly tone. "My grandmother is Nonya. She was the great priestess of Artemis." She inclined her head slightly toward the cave mouth, and Myrina again had the uncomfortable sensation of movement in the darkness behind them. The old woman must be listening to what was being said.

"My mother, Solya, was to take her place when Grandmother went to join the goddess in the sky. I was to follow in my turn. All three of us lived in the temple and we were the three most respected women in the whole of Tauris."

"Aah." Myrina nodded with some sympathy. She began to understand the ragged gown that had once been so fine and the dainty, confident way of speaking.

"What happened?" Tamsin could not hold back her curiosity.

"The Taurians are so stupid!" Katya's anger came flooding back. "They found that slimy fish on the beach and instead of sacrificing her as they should have done, they all fell in love with her little flower face!"

Myrina glared at Tamsin again, warning her to stay silent.

"Well," Katya said, "they insisted that her arrival with the statue must be a message from the goddess herself. And when Thoas set eyes on her, he became just as besotted with her as those who had found her on the beach. They set up the statue on a great plinth, and Thoas insisted that Hepsuash be made high priestess. They carried her up to the temple and set her there in Grandmother's place, while we were cast out!"

"That was unjust!" Phoebe spoke low, trying hard to be fair and finding a little sympathy in her heart.

"Yes, it was," Tamsin agreed heartily.

"Why do you care?" Katya asked, puzzled by their sympathy. "Nobody else cares! When Grandmother refused to leave the temple, the king sent his guards to remove us. Once outside the temple gates the people turned on us. They stoned us in the streets! Mother died."

Both Tamsin and Phoebe gasped at that, and Myrina sighed heavily, understanding the anger at last.

Katya ignored their concern. "Grandmother and I fled to this cave," she said. "Now we live here and we have nothing. Grandmother sends me into the city to dance for coins. To dance for our food. But I am lucky if they do not pelt me."

Phoebe's eyes were bright with tears. "I am truly sorry for you," she said. "I lost my mother when I was young— too young to even remember it—and we all know what it is to be treated badly, for we were once taken as slaves."

Katya looked at her with new interest, touched by her words.

"How do you manage to survive?" Myrina asked. She could see many difficulties in this situation.

"Sometimes people forget who I am— who I was," Katya corrected herself. "And they may throw me a coin or two, but others throw stones and curse me so that I have to run."

"Poor girl," Myrina murmured. "What a way to live."

"Huh! I will not be a poor girl for long!" Katya gave a sudden sneer. "Grandmother knows things that nobody else knows . . . she has her secrets and she will see Hepsuash back in the sea, even though the king now swears that he will marry her."

"He wishes to marry her?" This was a shock to Myrina, but almost at once she remembered the richly dressed young man speaking to Iphigenia in her mirror vision. Yes, this began to make sense. Was that why she had seen Iphigenia shaking her head at him?

Tamsin and Phoebe were looking anxiously at Myrina, aware that this was not quite what the Snake Lady had expected.

Katya smiled nastily. "The foolish milk face refuses him, but whether she marries him or not is naught to us. By the time my grandmother has finished with Hepsuash she will be nothing but fish food!"

Myrina's stomach turned over with apprehension. Katya's revelations told her for certain that Iphigenia stood in great danger—and not only from King Thoas or the Taurians. While she must feel sorry for the plight of the deposed priestesses, she also feared the vicious poison of their anger. She must find out if this Hepsuash really was Iphigenia.

"We have journeyed all day and we are weary," she said, rising to her feet and taking the two girls by the arms. "We must rest now, but tomorrow we will try to bring you more food and some for your grandmother, too. We go into Tauris city to sell our horses."

Katya rose politely, looking a little disappointed that they should go so soon. "There will be no buying or selling of horses tomorrow," she told them. "It is a sacred day, and the city will be crowded. They carry the two boys through the streets in procession."

"Two boys?" Myrina murmured uncertainly.

"The two boys who are to be sacrificed at the full of the moon!" Katya seemed slightly irritated that she should be so ignorant.

Myrina was shocked again, but she tried to think fast

and not look surprised. "The sacrifice of strangers who are shipwrecked?"

"Of course!" Katya's lip had a curl of disdain. "Milk-faced Hepsuash stopped it for a while and refused to officiate, swearing that the goddess reviled such acts. At first Thoas bowed to her will; he would do anything to please her. But now that she has refused to marry him, he's losing patience with her. He says that she cannot have it both ways—either she is priestess and must officiate at the sacrifice, or she gives up that role to be his wife."

"So"—Myrina tried to get a clear picture in her mind—"she has no choice but to see these boys sacrificed or marry Thoas?"

Katya nodded. "She's a fool! I would not refuse Thoas! And if she knew him better, she'd understand that he doesn't mean what he says. She could be priestess *and* his wife, if she wanted it."

Myrina thought hard. "What will Hepsuash do tomorrow?"

"She will be brought out of the temple when the procession arrives, receive the boys, and prepare them for sacrifice. It should be Grandmother instead of her."

Phoebe's cheeks were pale. Sympathetic though she was, the way in which Katya spoke of sacrifice made her feel sick. Tamsin looked at Katya with horror in her wide eyes, though she did not speak a word.

Myrina had to grit her teeth. This grim information was very important, hard though it was to stand there calmly and listen to it. As they turned to go, the burning resentment seemed to fade from Katya's voice. "You are the first people to speak kindly to me since we were cast out," she said, suddenly sounding like a lost and lonely child.

Myrina stared for a moment, trying to adjust her thoughts quickly. "Then we will look forward to speaking to you again." She tried to sound reassuring, and the sudden change in the girl made her think that perhaps Katya was not so damaged by tragedy that there'd be no chance of winning her back. In among the outpouring of hatred were strange, touching traces of dignity and even decency.

Quietly they walked back to their tent, deep in thought. Myrina's head was buzzing with all that she'd learned; Tamsin and Phoebe were both subdued.

"Now what do you think of your new friend?" Phoebe asked.

Tamsin said nothing.

"And those guards at the temple! They were guarding . . . ?"

"Yes, Young Tiger." Myrina nodded. "I think you are right; they are guarding Hepsuash. We must find out if she can possibly be our Iphigenia."

CHAPTER TWENTY-THREE

The Chosen Ones

T HE NEXT MORNING they dressed themselves carefully and prepared to go into the city. If the streets were to be as crowded as Katya had warned, Myrina thought it better to leave the horses and go on foot. They'd certainly be able to mingle with the crowd and discover more that way. Though the city seemed a dangerous place to be taking the girls, she knew that she'd feel better if they were by her side and it would have to be a bold horse thief to get the better of Big Chief.

She was hesitating when Katya slipped out of the cave and sidled almost shyly over toward their tent. "My grandmother will watch your camp and horses for you if you want to go into the city," she said.

Myrina turned to the cave mouth to see the old woman hobble out into the sunlight and settle once again in the place she'd occupied the evening before. Nonya gave a grim nod in their direction and Myrina acknowledged it, smiling to herself. This was a strange guardian indeed, but it seemed that she had little choice in the matter and must make the best of things. After all, she was really leaving Big Chief in charge and she could be sure that he would not let a stranger near their tent or the mares.

"Tell your grandmother, Thank you," she said.

"If you wait for me, I will go with you to the city," Katya suggested. "I can show you the way."

They looked at her uncertainly for a moment. It seemed that now the girl had decided they were friends, she was unwilling to let them out of her sight.

"Very well," Myrina agreed at last, unsure that an outcast was the best kind of guide.

They waited while she washed in the stream, smoothed down her ragged skirt, and began to rake at her hair with a twig. She'd told them that she and her grandmother had been left with nothing when they were cast out of the temple; it was proving to be true. Phoebe watched Katya's struggle to smooth her hair, then went to her baggage and brought out a bone comb that Kuspada had carved from the shin of a wild boar. It was a practical and cheerful thing with a fat hog carved into the handle.

"For you." She handed it to Katya.

The girl took it uncertainly.

"For you to keep."

The girl gravely whispered her thanks and set about combing her hair very thoroughly. As Myrina watched, she glimpsed a touch of beauty in the young face. Swiftly she recognized that if Katya were dressed in a fine gown and jewels, she would make heads turn.

"Just a moment," she said and went to one of the leather-bound bundles she'd hidden away in the tent. She pulled out a long tunic of the softest light-green linen which Tabi had given her at the winter feast. It wasn't the rich floating gown she envisioned for Katya, but it was a good, practical garment that would allow for movement.

Myrina emerged from the tent and held it up in front of the girl. "It's short for me," she said. "It will suit you much better."

The girl's face fell and for a moment she almost looked angry again. Myrina's stomach gave a small twist of regret; it seemed so easy to give offense. Did the gift signify humiliation to the proud priestess's child?

"This is payment," Myrina added hurriedly.

"Payment?" Katya looked up with interest.

"Yes—payment. Today you will act as our guide. You know the city and we do not; we will be lost without you. This is payment for a day's work."

Katya took the tunic and slipped it over her head. She smoothed the sleeves down over her shoulders and arms, sighing with pleasure at the comfort that the fine woven fabric brought. She bent to rip away her old rags from underneath it.

Tamsin grinned at her. "You look like a Moon Rider now," she said.

Katya shook her head, puzzled. "Moon Rider . . . what is that?"

There was a moment of tense silence as Tamsin realized that she should not have betrayed their true identity.

But Phoebe jumped in quickly to put things right. "Dancing priestesses," she said. "Tamsin and I once saw them long ago and we have copied them ever since."

"This is not what a priestess of Tauris would wear." Katya hesitated, frowning; then her face softened again. "But it is very comfortable," she assured them.

The moment of tension had passed and Myrina was relieved. Though there were now few coins left in Kuspada's purse, she promised herself that as soon as she sold one of the mares she would make Katya a present of a new gown—and it would be a gown worthy of a Taurian priestess.

They set off for the city, Katya taking her work as a guide seriously, keeping up an informative flow of conversation. Now that she had found listeners, it seemed that the young outcast could not stop talking. Myrina was soon grateful for the skill with which the girl directed them through the outskirts and into the maze of busy streets. Some people looked at Katya with a touch of suspicion, as though unsure whether they recognized her or not.

The palace of King Thoas was very grand, situated halfway down the sloping hillside and facing the sea. Many smaller palaces surrounded it, and Katya could relate the names of all the occupants, many of whom were wives to the king.

"So if Hepsuash were to agree to marry him, she would not be his only wife?" Myrina mused.

Katya's frown returned. "Of course not." She seemed surprised at the very idea. "But the fool wishes to make Hepsuash his chief wife—she would be his queen and still she refuses."

From the palace gates they could look up along the winding streets to see the strange building they had passed the day before, perched on the highest rock, far above the city. None of them dared to ask the question, but Katya saw that their eyes were drawn to it.

"That is the temple of Artemis," she told them, her voice suddenly soft and wistful. "It is— it was where we lived—the only home I have known."

They shaded their eyes, gazing up at the lofty temple.

Phoebe touched Katya's arm. "It's a beautiful home," she said kindly.

"If I lived up there," Tamsin said, "I'd dream I was an

eagle, swooping down from my nest to fly across the sea."

Katya looked at her with sharp approval. "You understand well," she said. "That is what happens to sacrificial victims. The priestess takes them up to the very top of the tower, and if they are brave and worthy they fling themselves from it, then—just for a moment—they swoop like an eagle."

Tamsin's smile fled. "You mean . . . they swoop down and then . . . ?"

"Oh yes," Katya answered, as though it were only to be expected. "They swoop down and then they plop into the sea."

Myrina put a reassuring hand on Tamsin's shoulder.

"They . . . drown?" Tamsin's face had turned white.

"Of course—they are a sacrifice! If they have died bravely, their spirits fly at once to Artemis's hunting ground up in the sky and live there happily with the goddess forever, while their bodies feed the fish."

"But . . . what if they do not wish to throw themselves over the edge?" Tamsin was aware of her mother's warning, but was so troubled by Katya's words that she had to know the answer.

"Then the priestess must push them—that is her job! Though it seems that flower-faced Hepsuash has little stomach for it!"

"So . . . your . . . grandmother . . . ?"

Myrina slid her hand down Tamsin's arm and squeezed her hand tightly. Tamsin heeded the warning and swallowed her question, falling quiet.

People had begun to emerge from their houses dressed in their best clothes; they crowded the streets, baskets full of rose petals in their hands. "Tell us"—Myrina wanted to find out as much as she could—"where will the procession start from and where will it go to?"

"It starts from the palace, then they move slowly up the hill, winding in and out of the pathways until they reach the temple."

"Then what . . . ?" Tamsin's eyes were wide with fear. "Will they leap . . . ?"

Katya shrugged, an impatient glint in her eyes. "No, no, not today. For a sacrifice to be judged worthy by the goddess, those who are offered must undergo preparation. Today Hepsuash will come out of the temple to meet them and take them inside to begin the preparation."

Tamsin could no longer hold back and her voice trembled with accusation as she asked the question that troubled her so much. "Has your grandmother pushed people off that tower?"

Myrina held her breath, fearful that this would make the girl angry again. But Katya only looked puzzled for a moment, then answered with fierce certainty. "Of course.

It was Nonya's job. She should be here to do it now!"

"How long does it take—this preparation of the sacrifices?" Myrina asked quickly.

Katya answered with an irritated sigh. "Until the full moon," she replied. "Don't all sacrifices take place on the night of the full moon?"

Myrina saw that they must ask no more, but the very words "full moon" brought back to her the frightening days and nights in Aulis, before the intended sacrifice of the young Iphigenia. Katya was right about that—it was always the full moon, and the memory of it made her tremble, fierce Snake Lady though she was. How then must Iphigenia be feeling? And to be expected to actually push unwilling victims from a tower! Iphigenia would not willingly crush a beetle beneath her foot.

"They're coming! They're coming!"

There was a flurry of anticipation all around them; horns sounded and the palace gates were opened.

Myrina thrust away the dark feelings of despair that suddenly threatened to engulf her, forcing herself to be practical. Iphigenia had been rescued before—well, now it must be done again. She was the Snake Lady; she must think hard and draw on the craftiness that had always been her strength. At least this time it didn't seem to be Iphigenia's life that hung in the balance; only her freedom—but then to a Moon Rider, freedom was life!

Maybe she would see her friend today and then at least she could be absolutely sure that it was the daughter of Agamemnon and Clytemnestra whom the Taurians had imprisoned in the lofty temple on the rock.

All at once there was a small rush of expectation in the crowd.

"The king, the king!"

Loud horns sounded again as King Thoas rode out of the palace gates on a fine black stallion, surrounded by heavily armed guards. He was still young, with a thick dark beard and a thin, rather somber face. Myrina recognized him as the man she'd seen in her vision. His clothes were rich with cloth of gold, and a heavy diadem crowned his brow. His horse's bridle was decorated with heavy golden bulls, and his hands and arms dripped with jewelry.

The people cheered, but Myrina sensed a dutiful reticence in the applause. The king did not lift his hand to wave or respond with even a nod; he seemed unaware of the crowd that surrounded him.

"Fool!" Katya murmured under her breath as he came toward them.

Myrina thought that for a brief moment the king's eyes rested on the deposed priestess's granddaughter, as though he recognized her, but then he looked away uninterested and rode on.

Many finely dressed courtiers followed in the king's

wake and again they were cheered politely. It was only when a small but elaborate cart rattled out through the gates that warm smiles and real excitement seemed to ripple through the crowd. The cart was pulled by two milk-white ponies, and as it passed, many hands reached out to touch its gilded sides. Two young men sat in it side by side, richly dressed in white robes and cloaks, gold fillets bound about their brows. The crowd surged forward to surround the cart, throwing rose petals over its occupants.

"Sweet boys, sweet boys!" they cried.

"Hail to the Chosen Ones!"

"Bring us our harvest from the sea!"

Myrina closed her eyes for a moment, suppressing horror, as understanding flooded through her mind: the gilded curves that adorned the cart represented the rolling waves of the sea, into which the two young victims would be flung.

"If I were them, I'd jump out now and run!" Tamsin whispered.

As the cart passed close to them, Myrina could see only too well why they didn't attempt to escape. The boys sat side by side on a gilded bench, but they were tied by the ankles to the base of the cart, their hands fastened behind them with golden ropes.

"Bonds of gold," Myrina murmured. "Boys—just boys!"

CHAPTER TWENTY-FOUR

Hepsuash

B OTH THE INTENDED victims were young, but strangely neither of them looked scared. Myrina wondered if they understood what their fate would be, but then she saw that the tall, fair-haired boy burned with quiet fury. He knew well enough and he was too angry to be frightened. The other boy was dark haired and his skin was sunburned; he gazed about him with a vacant smile.

"Who is he?" Myrina murmured. She racked her brain, sure that she had seen him before.

But what happened next wiped all such thoughts from her mind, for the dark-haired one began to shake his head slowly from side to side. The vacant look fled and was replaced by one of horror as the shaking grew faster and faster. He began to mutter incoherent words.

Myrina pressed herself up close to the cart, trying to hear what he said. "No—I did not, Mother. No,

Mother—I did not!" Then as Myrina still listened, distressed, she seemed to hear him answer himself. "Yes, you did! Yes, you did! No, Mother—it was not my fault. It was the oracle; the oracle told me to do it!"

His words made no sense. The citizens of Tauris seemed undisturbed by his strange reaction, some laughing, others pleased and excited, almost as though they thought he gibbered to entertain them. Rose petals floated around his head, some settling on his hair and shoulders. Myrina felt that she had never seen anything so horrible, but she realized with some relief that he was unaware of either the rose petals or the chanting crowd. He probably had no idea of his intended fate.

"Hail to the Chosen Ones!"

"Young sweethearts! Bring us a good harvest!"

The boy shook his head, his eyes staring wildly at something far away. "No—I didn't know! Revenge was my duty! Nobody told me what he had done!"

His voice sank low, and Myrina could no longer hear, but she saw how he muttered the words faster and faster. The boy's mind was completely taken over by some other concern. She guessed that they'd have little trouble getting him to jump. It might be more of a problem if they tried to hold him back!

"Madness," she murmured. "Poor boy; he is quite mad!"

* * *

The procession wound its way up the sloping hillside, through wide streets and narrow, through open squares and alleyways, the great crowd surging after the cart, pushed and hauled more by helping hands than by the little white ponies.

"Stay close," Myrina hissed. She grabbed Tamsin by one hand and on the other side she clung to Phoebe's arm. They struggled to keep close to the poor victims in their cart, but somehow they seemed to have lost Katya among the great press of people. Myrina pushed ahead, grim faced. She hated being stuck in the middle of this crazy crowd, but she knew that she was learning a lot. She must store every detail in her head—getting Iphigenia away might depend on what she could remember.

At last, as the sun reached its zenith, the houses and huts thinned out and the procession crossed the stretch of open land that led to the temple. It seemed that nobody wanted to live very close to the sacred spot on the craggy cliff edge. Rows of guards were lined up at the entrance, confirming Myrina's suspicion that the temple was nothing more than an exquisitely decorated prison.

A strange place for a young girl to be raised, she thought, looking around for Katya. She still couldn't see her and dared not search for her as the cries of the crowd told her that the priestess from the sea was about to appear.

"Hepsuash, Hepsuash!" The chant began low and insistent; then it grew louder and louder. "Hepsuash! Hepsuash! Come to us!"

At last a movement could be seen, deep inside the dark entrance to the temple. A great fanfare of horns heralded the coming of the priestess. The chanting faded, and everyone waited in silence. Myrina clung to Tamsin's hand so tightly that she made her daughter wince. Would the priestess be Iphigenia?

Horns blared again, and a small, slender woman emerged from the shadows of the inner temple, smothered in jeweled robes, a golden circlet on her head. Two soldiers escorted the priestess on either side. Despite the heavy robes and the strange surroundings, Myrina recognized at once the pale oval face and dark hair of Iphigenia.

"It is her—our own Iphigenia," Tamsin whispered.

Phoebe, who had always loved her, whispered fearfully, "If they should hurt her . . ."

"We will not let them, Tiger Girl!" Myrina whispered. "But look around you. I do not think there are many here who wish her harm."

Phoebe saw that this was true. The crowd pressed forward quietly, eager to get a good view of the priestess, their faces bright with curiosity. Myrina did not know whether she wanted to smile or cry at the sight of her dear friend, but at least she could now be sure that her visions had not been deceiving her.

Iphigenia stood stiffly between her guards, as King Thoas dismounted and climbed the steps to stand at her side. She looked very small beside him, and Myrina saw that she averted her gaze from his. The silence continued as the cart arrived and the two prisoners were released from their ankle bonds, then led up to meet Hepsuash, their hands still tied.

"We've got to get closer," Myrina hissed in Tamsin's ear. "Can you think, Lizard, and lead us to the front?"

Tamsin's eyes shone at the request. She took tight hold of Myrina's hand and dived into the crowd, pulling her mother after her as she wriggled and slid her way through the sea of bodies, smiling with innocence at those she nudged and shoved.

Myrina grabbed Phoebe and dragged her along behind them; then at last she tugged Tamsin back. "Well done—this is close enough," she whispered. They could see clearly, but were not so close to the front that they themselves might be noticed.

The view they had of Iphigenia was so good that Myrina almost wished they'd stayed at the back of the crowd. The priestess stood on the temple steps, as poised and dignified as ever, but Myrina, who knew her so well, was shocked by the beaten look in her eyes and the pallor of her cheeks. She wanted to rush forward and snatch her away there and then, whatever might come of it. The sight of Iphigenia brought vividly to her mind the ordeal at Aulis. Then, as now, Myrina had stood at the front of a crowd, watching the twelve-year-old Iphigenia facing death with just the same pathetic dignity.

"But this is not Aulis," Myrina muttered under her breath, forcing herself to be sensible. "And it is not Iphigenia who is threatened with sacrifice!"

Then, as the Snake Lady struggled with her memories, something happened that relieved her of the urgent impulse to leap out from the crowd. The two prisoners were led up the steps to be received by the priestess, the dark-haired boy still muttering wildly, in the throes of insanity. As Iphigenia turned to look at the pair, her whole demeanor changed. Her gaze swept calmly over the angry fair-haired boy, but as she looked past him to the younger one, an expression of intense sympathy touched her face, almost of recognition. Myrina had seen this look before and knew well what it meant. Agamemnon's daughter had seen that somebody close by was in dire need of care and at once she would forget her own troubles in her concern for another.

Iphigenia turned at once to King Thoas, with outraged authority. "Why are his hands bound?" she demanded, her voice clear and strong. "This suffering is unnecessary! Sacrifice is bad enough, but a victim should at least be shown some respect!"

The king was puzzled and looked around at his guards.

"He is not going to escape from here!" Iphigenia spoke with certainty. "Untie his hands!"

The king hesitated, but a low chant rose from the crowd, a chant of support for the priestess.

"Hepsuash, Hepsuash!"

"Hepsuash has spoken!"

"Untie his hands! Untie his hands! Hepsuash has spoken!"

An expression of irritation crossed the king's face, but he nodded at the guards. "Set his hands free!"

The crowd murmured their approval and fell silent again. Myrina was cheered to see this interchange; it seemed that Iphigenia was not as helpless as she'd feared. As the young man was released from his bonds, the high priestess strode forward and took him into her arms, hugging him. Tall though he was, he accepted the embrace like a child, still trembling and muttering, his head stooping over hers. Iphigenia patted his back, just as a mother might soothe a distressed infant.

The crowd fell silent again at the sight, puzzled by Hepsuash's behavior. But the simplicity of the gesture and the calming effect the embrace had on the boy seemed to touch them and win their approval. There were a few murmurs of pity.

Myrina was strangely comforted by the sight of the two dark heads pressed so close together. Iphigenia suddenly looked strong again; this boy's frightening situation was one that she must identify with as no other could. Concern for him would bring her a new sense of purpose.

Then at last the priestess released the boy and turned to acknowledge the crowd, aware of the support they'd given her. They responded with cheers as she bowed graciously and waved to them, every inch the priestess they wanted her to be. Then, just as she turned to go back inside the temple, she raised her hand and for a fleeting moment she gave the Moon Riders' salute.

Phoebe and Tamsin both caught their breath, turning to Myrina, eyes shining. They could not answer the salute for fear they'd raise suspicion, but the message was clear.

"She knows," Phoebe whispered. "She knows that we are here!"

"Yes," Myrina agreed, smiling at them with satisfaction. "She knows!"

They watched as Iphigenia took the trembling boy by the hand and led him back inside the temple. The other victim followed, his hands still tied—nobody had suggested that he be released. The glance of grim fury that he bore was explanation enough, but Myrina's heart went out to him, too, as she watched him stumble after his companion.

The people sang out their support, chanting "Hepsuash" over and over again. King Thoas bowed awkwardly to the crowd and then followed Iphigenia into the temple. Myrina could not see clearly how it would help or hinder them, but one thing she had learned today: the people of Tauris loved Hepsuash and respected her; she was indeed their chosen priestess.

Once the king had vanished inside the temple, his guards took their place again at the top of the steps. The show was over—for today at least—and the audience began to move away.

"Now what do we do?" Tamsin looked lost. "How are we going to get Iphigenia back?"

"Our Snake Lady will think of a way." Phoebe spoke with confidence.

But the Snake Lady had no immediate answer to give and shook her head uncertainly. "We've learned a lot," she said. "Now there's a lot of thinking to be done."

They followed the crowd back down through the steep streets of Tauris.

"Where is Katya?" Tamsin wondered.

Myrina frowned at the question, unsure whether they

should search for Katya, when the rhythmic clatter of finger cymbals made them look sharply up at each other.

"Could that be . . . ?" Phoebe asked.

They turned a corner into a small square and saw that it was indeed Katya. She'd made the raised portico of a stately town house her stage and clattered her cymbals while she danced in front of it. A small crowd watched her tolerantly, still cheerful from the procession and the holiday atmosphere.

Myrina smiled; it seemed that they would not need to struggle back to their camp alone after all.

CHAPTER TWENTY-FIVE

A Little of the Truth

M YRINA LEANED AGAINST a wall to watch Katya's performance for a while, content to let Tamsin and Phoebe make their way to the front of the crowd.

As people still flooded past them, away from the temple, some stopped to watch the young dancer; others pushed past, eager to get home. Then one old woman stopped and pointed at Katya, frowning and straining to see her clearly. "Is that the outcast's granddaughter? The little witch?" she cried.

Those who'd been watching shrugged, ignoring the question.

"No," her son answered. "The outcast's granddaughter is a filthy ragged thing! This is a Sinta girl!"

"It is the outcast's girl." The woman was adamant, her voice ripe with resentment. "I'd know her anywhere." She stooped to pick up a stone.

Myrina sensed danger and took a step toward the woman. Tamsin and Phoebe turned around at the disturbance. They saw trouble brewing and both bravely leaped to their feet to join Katya in her dance, ready to protect her.

There was a gasp of pleasure and a ripple of applause from the audience when they saw that two more Sinta girls had joined the dance. The old woman's son caught hold of her arm to prevent her throwing the stone. "No—see, there are three of them, Mother; Sinta girls! Put down your stone!"

Myrina's watchfulness was noted by another bystander. "They're Sinta girls—there's their mother keeping her eye on them! How well they dance!"

The audience began to clap their encouragement in time to the rhythm of the cymbals, while the old woman was pulled away and led home.

Myrina had been a little shaken by the girls' quick action, but it seemed to have soothed the crowd's suspicions, and now the three of them filled their audience with delight. She settled back to watch again. There was no melody to accompany the dance, only the steady rhythm of the clattering cymbals, but the girls danced with the bubbling energy of youth, huge smiles of enjoyment on their faces. Now Phoebe took the lead, imitating the delicate grace of a young foal. Katya and Tamsin watched and followed, their own movements harmonizing with hers as though they'd been dancing together all their lives.

"They prance like Sinta foals!" the audience murmured.

"Half girls, half horses!"

The watchers were entranced, and soon coins rained down at the dancers' feet.

Myrina smiled with a touch of regret. What a fine Moon Rider Katya might have been.

At last people started to wander away and the girls stopped dancing, scrambling to pick up the coins.

"I've never been paid as much as this." Katya spoke with breathless delight. She searched the pavement eagle-eyed, to make sure that every last coin was found.

Tamsin and Phoebe handed the money they'd collected over to Katya, who took it eagerly at first; but then she paused, her brow wrinkled with uncertainty. "No—you should have some!"

Myrina watched with a quiet smile as Katya snatched up a handful of coins and held them out to Tamsin and Phoebe.

Tamsin's hand went out eagerly, but then she looked at her mother, doubtful for a moment.

"Yes," Myrina said. "You should all take your share of the earnings—that is very fair of Katya!"

On the way back they stopped to buy fresh white

barley bread, goat's cheese, and dates. "Wait till Grandmother sees this feast," Katya crowed.

Myrina smiled again. Disguised as a Sinta girl, Katya looked as though she might well be able to earn her own way again.

When they returned to their camp, they were greeted by cheerful whickers of welcome from Big Chief and the mares. Katya's grandmother was still sitting there on her rock, grim faced as ever, but it seemed that she'd kept a good watch on their tents and belongings. Myrina bowed her thanks from a distance and was answered with a curt nod. Katya ran up to the cave to display her earnings and the food she'd bought.

Myrina was not surprised when the girl came striding back to them through the grass. "Grandmother says will you come and eat with us?"

"Of course we will," Myrina replied.

Somehow, without ever meaning to, they seemed to have thrown in their lot with these two strange women.

They washed in the stream and then wandered over to the cave. Nonya solemnly directed them to sit on comfortable rocks while they ate; then she brought out from the cave an astonishing, beautifully decorated golden cup, which she filled with stream water and offered to her guests.

Myrina was so surprised at the sight of such a precious

object appearing from the rugged interior of the cave that she struggled for words, uncertain whether to admire its beauty or just drink from it as though it were a plain Sinta beaker.

Nonya watched her for a moment, then opened her mouth and gave a sudden burst of wild throaty laughter. Myrina smiled, still unsure how best to react.

Nonya's laughter fled as quickly as it had come. "Eat!" she directed them in the Scythian language.

They ate the bread and cheese in silence, but as they progressed to the dates the girls began to grin at each other and exchange words of appreciation at the sweetness and succulence of the fruit. When they'd finished, Katya got up with a touch of delicacy and went to the stream to wash her hands.

Tamsin followed her. "Teach us to clatter the cymbals as you did today," she begged.

"If Phoebe will show me the horse dance." Katya glanced hopefully back at Phoebe, who rose willingly to her feet and went to join them.

As the girls wandered away there was a moment of silence, then Nonya turned to Myrina with curiosity. "Why . . . you come here?" she asked.

Myrina smiled; she was ready for this one. "I come to sell horses," she told her. "I am a widow and must earn my bread, so I deal in horses."

"Sinta horses."

"Yes," Myrina agreed.

Nonya gave her a crafty look. "But . . . you are not a Sinta woman!"

Myrina looked up sharply and again Nonya gave her throaty laugh. This old woman was no fool, and she must be careful.

The laugh stopped as suddenly as before. "Where . . . you come from?" Nonya asked.

Myrina frowned; she sensed that Nonya would know if she lied. Perhaps it would be best to give away a little of the truth and try to gauge the old woman's attitude.

"I hear that strangers are not welcome here," she said, hoping that she sounded like a woman who would frankly speak her mind. "So, knowing that, I fear to tell you where I come from."

"Huh!" Nonya gave a short and bitter laugh. "You are wise to be careful, but these people are stupid—they do not understand their own traditions. It's only the ones that are washed into the harbor by the goddess that must be returned to her."

"Well . . ." Myrina took her courage in both hands. "I will tell you then that we crossed the Inhospitable Sea and we were shipwrecked and washed ashore, far away to the east, in the Sinta lands."

Nonya's eyes were wide. "You crossed the Inhospitable

Sea? Foolish ones! Don't you know what lies at the bottom of that sea?"

Myrina shook her head, wondering if she'd said too much.

"Every Taurian knows the story from childhood," Nonya explained. "That's why we do not often venture out onto the sea ourselves. The Bogatyr was the first man who ever lived and he possessed a magical arrow, a most fearsome weapon that would destroy the whole world if it was ever used. Have you never heard of this?"

"No," Myrina admitted, but she could not hide her curiosity. Nonya's words had brought to mind the Old Woman Atisha and the fascinating stories she used to tell.

"Well . . ." Nonya continued, pleased with the respectful attention she was now being given, "the Bogatyr was both wise and strong and while he lived he could trust himself never to use this terrible weapon, but as he grew older he was troubled by the sight of his three sons fighting and quarreling among themselves. He realized that he couldn't trust any of them to shoulder the responsibility of possessing the magical arrow . . . so . . . one day he took up his bow and he shot his magical arrow right out into the middle of the dark Inhospitable Sea."

"Aah." Myrina sighed, recognizing the deep wisdom that was hidden in the story. "It would be safe there and nobody could find it."

Nonya nodded. "But now . . . do you understand why we do not venture across the water?"

"I think I do." Myrina paused for thought. "The sea . . . has its own dark secret."

Nonya smiled fiercely. "It has! The arrow lies there on the seabed in the deepest depths, but sometimes the sea rises up and boils and thrashes, for that fearful weapon still burns with anger and tries to surface and kill us all. The fishermen who dabble at the edges of the sea live with this danger every day; they accept that the goddess takes one or two of them as they struggle to feed their families. But ignorant strangers come sailing far across the sea, with no respect at all for what lies hidden beneath it. If the goddess sees them she washes them into Tauris harbor and there they must answer for their ignorance— they are the Chosen Ones."

Myrina sat very still, wondering if she had admitted to transgressing the strange rules of this place or not. "And we . . . ?"

"The goddess would have no claim on you," Nonya told her gruffly.

"I am glad to hear it," she said with relief.

She relaxed a little, feeling that she was slowly winning some approval from the old priestess, but what came next shocked her again and made both her mind and her body quail.

"It is Hepsuash," Nonya snarled, and the bitter resentment that she felt was evident in her voice. "It is Hepsuash whom the goddess demands! She was washed ashore and she should have been sacrificed, with her sweet face and her gentle voice."

Myrina pressed her lips tightly together, not trusting herself to speak.

The sneer in Nonya's voice turned to anger. "But what do the stupid Taurians do? They claim her as their chosen priestess, just because they found her clinging to the goddess's image. I know the real reason behind it—that fool Thoas drools over her wan white face. As soon as he set eyes on her I saw it and I had been hoping . . . bah!" Her mouth twisted with bitter disappointment and she turned her head for a moment to gaze out of the cave toward her granddaughter, dancing outside on the grass with Phoebe and Tamsin.

Myrina's mind buzzed with questions she dared not ask.

But Nonya was speaking angrily again. "The people would follow me if I just had the chance to speak to them and be listened to as I once was. Thoas is so bewitched with Hepsuash that he would make her his queen, so now the people dare not insist upon her sacrifice for fear of upsetting their king."

Myrina had seen for herself that this was far from the truth, but silence seemed the least dangerous route to take. Her stomach churned as she listened to the poison in Nonya's words. She must somehow manage to squeeze out a little judicious sympathy for the woman.

"Katya told me what happened and I understand your anger. I know a little of what you feel, for I, too, was once a respected priestess, a Moon Rider, a follower of Earth Mother Maa. I traveled with my sister priestesses about the southern shore of the Inhospitable Sea, bringing the Earth Mother's blessings with our dances and songs. We fought to defend Troy, and after the city fell we made our homeland beside the River Thermodon, until we were captured by slavers. To lose respect and power when it is not your fault is a hard and bitter thing indeed!"

A flicker of interest crossed the old woman's face, but then the wicked laugh bubbled up from her throat again and her words left Myrina cold with fear. "Don't you worry; I have the means to see off Miss Milk face!"

Myrina looked up at her sharply and could not stop herself from demanding, "How?"

But Nonya only smiled nastily in answer and shook her head. "The goddess will get her sacrifice; Hepsuash will fly into the sea, and I shall be Priestess of Artemis once again."

The girls twirled and leaped together in the distance, happy and laughing, their faces and arms colored pink and gold with the warmth of the sinking sun, but in the shade of the cave Myrina shivered. She forced herself to sit quietly for a while, giving a nod of acknowledgment to show that she'd heard Nonya's words and understood them.

How could she hope to shift the old woman's bitter hatred of Iphigenia? How could she bridge the huge gap in their understanding? She must get away from this terrifying old woman and think.

She yawned. "I am weary," she murmured, rising to her feet. "Tomorrow I take one of my mares into the city to sell. I must rise early to brush her coat and make her look her best. I thank you for your company."

Nonya nodded, accepting the excuse. "You come and eat here tomorrow night?"

It was the last thing that Myrina felt like doing, but she reminded herself that staying close to the enemy meant knowing when they'd make their move. "Thank you," she agreed.

CHAPTER TWENTY-SIX

Nonya's Secret

MYRINA LEFT TAMSIN and Phoebe dancing with Katya, for she needed to be alone. She went into her tent and searched out her mirror. She knew that it would take time to bring her visions; her head buzzed and her heart was full of dread.

At first she tried to mirror gaze in the safety and privacy of the tent, but nothing came to her, not even a glimpse. So she went outside and wandered away from the laughing girls and the cropping horses, heading toward the stream. She found a spot where blue iris flowers bloomed in the marshy ground. She flung herself down on a rock, grateful that there was nobody about. The water rushed past her feet, soothing her spirits a little.

"Iphigenia first," she murmured; she must see that her friend was still safe.

It took a while, but at last the sound of the stream made

her eyes droop, so that the sight of her own face faded and she focused on the gentle sway of the flowers in the fading sun. The blue of the irises darkened to purple and then black, and at last they merged with the heavy, curling tresses of Iphigenia's hair. The priestess sat by an open window overlooking the sea, high above the terrifying drop, but Iphigenia seemed unaware of the view; she was intent on pounding herbs in a small bowl and mixing in a little wine.

"She prepares a soothing potion for the mad boy," Myrina whispered.

That was enough; it was all she needed to know. Iphigenia was safe and her own fears had fled with her concern for another.

She let the vision fade and caught a glimpse of Cassandra, who was sitting beside a bed, stroking the curly hair of the Mouse Boy. It seemed the princess's unexpected role as a mother suited her well.

Then with a lurch of apprehension Myrina let her thoughts wander to the camp of the Moon Riders and Kuspada. What would she see there? Would the blacksmith have a young woman at his side? Might Kora have won him with her warmth and good humor? The camp seemed still and peaceful, but one man still sat huddled by the embers of the fire; he was wrapped in his cloak, a spear in his hand, keeping watch. It was Kuspada, his face tranquil but unsmiling; he was alone. She longed to call to him, to tell him how much she missed him and how lonely she felt. If only she'd allowed him to come along, she'd not be feeling so helpless and desolate now.

But then she forced herself to recognize that it was her very vulnerability that had helped her to gather so much information so quickly. It was almost as though a woman traveling with two children were invisible. Had Kuspada ridden here with her, she never would have spent the evening sitting in Nonya's cave, learning so much as she listened to her terrible plans.

At last, reluctantly, she let the image of Kuspada fade, assuring herself that she'd really made a very good start. Subtlety was the answer; hope must lie in that. Nonya had confided in her and she might tell her more, even though it was hard to sit there quietly listening to the hateful things she said.

Myrina remembered how Hati used to tell her that to hunt a creature you must think as that creature. "You must understand what the creature needs, what it feels. Only then can you destroy it. You will be left with a great sense of sadness and respect for the vanquished one and that is only right."

"Yes," Myrina answered, as though her grandmother had whispered in her ear.

She knew that she must struggle to understand Nonya;

only then could she hope to change her foul plans. Nonya and her grandchild had suffered great injustice—she must acknowledge that.

She sighed again, then rose to her feet and walked back to the camp, swinging her mirror in her hand. All was not lost. She must keep her nerve and let her snakelike sense tell her when to seize the moment.

The girls had settled in their tent and the camp was silent now, though Myrina thought she saw the glimmer of Nonya's white face still watching at the mouth of the cave. Did the woman never sleep? She crawled inside and snuggled close to Tamsin, wrapping her arm around the sleeping child. She shut her eyes, her spirits light enough now to allow her to sleep.

In the morning Myrina set off into Tauris again, this time taking Moonbeam, the silver-white mare, whose coat gleamed from the comb. Katya and the girls followed on foot, dressed alike and full of energy, ready to dance again. That day they earned more coins; but even better, they attracted a fine crowd who examined the silver mare with admiration. Myrina was just about to sell her to a fellow who offered her a good price and wanted a mount for his daughter, when a young man arrived on horseback, dressed in the royal livery.

"Ledus," Katya whispered. "The king's ostler."

The first buyer looked disappointed at Ledus's approach, and without even waiting to hear whether Myrina would accept his offered price, he backed away, allowing the ostler to come forward.

"Bring the mare to the palace!" Ledus told Myrina after only the most cursory inspection.

The certainty of obedience and the condescension in his voice grated on Myrina, but she knew that she could not afford to give offense, so with a warning glance at the girls she took hold of Moonbeam's halter and started to lead the mare toward the palace gates.

The girls followed for a little way, but then Katya stopped, her brow drawn tight with worry.

Myrina saw that there was something wrong when she looked back to check on them. She stopped and waited for them to catch up. "What is it?"

Katya spoke low, under her breath. "No one has recognized me while I've been with you. Nobody has called me witch. But they know me better in the palace, and Thoas—he will recognize me."

Myrina quickly understood. She'd been puzzled at the familiar way in which Katya and her grandmother sometimes spoke of the king. It was one of the things she wanted to ask about, but she had been afraid of seeming to pry.

"Go back to our camp and wait for me there," she told them, thinking that maybe it was best for the girls to be safe by the tents and horses.

They turned willingly enough, aware that the situation might be delicate, and marched away together, Phoebe leading Tamsin protectively by the hand, leaving Myrina to follow the guards through the palace gates.

She and Moonbeam were led into a paved courtyard, where she was asked to put the mare through her paces. As she trotted around the enclosed space she glanced upward and saw that King Thoas watched from a balcony. She urged Moonbeam to canter, then demonstrated the reliability of the horse by swinging her legs down to touch the ground briefly on one side, immediately springing back over Moonbeam's haunches to repeat the trick on the other side. All the while the beautiful silver mare pranced steadily on and Myrina resisted the temptation to show what she could really do, fearful that King Thoas might see through her claim to be an ordinary Sinta widow woman.

When at last Moonbeam slowed to a walking pace, the king came down from the balcony, solemn as ever, but nodding his head. "Yes," he said. "This mare is just what I need for a special gift. No woman could resist her grace and beauty."

Myrina slipped to the ground and bowed at his approach. "Any of your wives must delight in such a steed," she agreed.

The king shook his head. "This is for one who is not my wife, but I hope she may still be persuaded . . . This mare is for the priestess Hepsuash!"

Myrina's heart thundered. Maybe Maa had taken a hand in this! If she snatched at this bit of luck, it might bring her the chance to be admitted to the temple. "I could deliver the mare for your majesty." She spoke quickly, hardly daring to breathe in case she gave her eagerness away.

The king nodded, looking thoughtful for a moment, and Myrina believed that her craftiness had worked; but then he shook his head, thinking better of it. "No. This is one gift that must be delivered in person." He beckoned Ledus over to him. "We shall go at once!"

Myrina bowed meekly, but her heart sank at the missed opportunity.

Ledus gave her a purse of gold coins, and the very weight of it told her that she had been more than well paid. She left the palace on foot with her heart in her boots, while King Thoas set out on his stallion for the temple, leading Moonbeam by a silver halter. Myrina wandered back through the streets, blundering up a blind alleyway, miserable and frustrated. She had come so close to being allowed into the temple. Despite a few more wrong turnings, her Moon Rider's instincts at last led her back to Big Chief's corral.

The girls were impressed by the payment, but they quickly sensed that Myrina was disappointed and tired. Katya tried to offer comfort the best way she knew: "Grandmother says eat with us—she has set up a spit and is roasting shoulders of goat that we bought from our dancing today!"

Myrina forced herself to bow with courtesy and thank the girl.

That night, as the girls danced in the rosy light of the setting sun, Myrina sat by the stern old woman and listened well. She came to understand that Nonya had been a friend to Thoas's mother, who'd died when he was very young. Katya had played as a child with the young Thoas, and it had long been the old priestess's plan that her granddaughter might become not only priestess of Artemis, but also one of the king's wives, and maybe even queen.

"Is it the custom in Tauris for a woman to be priestess and wife?"

"Oh yes," Nonya answered indignantly. "Any woman is honored to be a wife of the king! Don't you moon priestesses marry?"

Now it was Myrina's turn to look sad as Tomi's face swam in front of her eyes. "We Moon Riders would give up our role as priestess after seven years and then we would choose ourselves a husband."

"You would choose a husband?" Nonya's eyebrows shot up in surprise.

They sat in silence for a while as Nonya contemplated this surprising possibility.

"Did Katya wish to marry Thoas?" Myrina asked.

"Huh! They were the closest of friends as little children, and fought and exchanged insults. Now he has deserted us, she cannot find a good word for him, but . . . I think without Hepsuash . . ."

Myrina sighed; there was so much to weigh up and think about, but she did not want the conversation to dwell yet again on the deep resentment Nonya felt toward Hepsuash. "I have been thinking about your troubles," she said, "and I would like to see a way to help. What would you say if Hepsuash were to disappear?"

"She will disappear beneath the waves and I will see to it!" Nonya spat back.

Myrina suppressed a sigh; she'd been too forthright. She sat quietly for a moment then tried again. "But what if Hepsuash were to leave quietly and willingly of her own accord?"

Nonya thought for a moment, then shook her head. "He wouldn't let her go; there is only one way—she must die!"

Myrina tried a slightly different approach. "But how could you reach her? She is guarded day and night!"

Nonya's answer took her breath away. The old woman

gave a sly smile and bent to snatch up the beautiful golden cup. "How do you think I came by this?" she said, twirling it around in her fingers so that it gleamed with rich colors in the fading light. "It came from the temple of Artemis. They have cast me out, so they think, but the priestesses kept their own secrets and passed them on, mother to daughter. I can go in and out of that temple at will. It will only take me a moment to overcome that little weakling Hepsuash!"

Myrina found it hard not to smile at the thought; weak though she might appear to be, Iphigenia was warrior trained and no coward. But she must ignore the question of that threat in order to find out more about this startling revelation. "A secret way?" she murmured.

"Ha! A very secret way!"

Myrina's head was spinning again. If she could use this secret way to get into the temple and speak to Iphigenia, it would solve all her problems. If she had the horses ready, they could simply leave and ride away together. Awareness slipped into her sharp, snakelike mind. She should have asked herself why the old woman sat in the mouth of the cave day and night. Why she sent her granddaughter to beg, while she stayed here like an ancient stone guardian. Was the cave itself the secret entrance to the temple?

CHAPTER TWENTY-SEVEN

Trust

T HE REVELATION OF the old woman's secret sent Myrina's thoughts spinning wildly; she must find patience. She deliberated for a moment, then went back to her first line of attack.

"Supposing Hepsuash were unhappy in the temple," she persisted. "After all, she has not chosen to be priestess. Maybe she longs to get away and would willingly go."

Nonya frowned and said nothing.

Myrina tried again. "It seems Hepsuash does not wish to marry the king."

Nonya's answer came back at once. "She is a fool!"

Myrina's forbearance was wearing thin. "If Hepsuash holds such a sway with King Thoas, she could appoint a new priestess in her place! Such a one could be you!"

Nonya stared at her with disbelief. "Now *you* are the fool! You think Hepsuash would help me? Give me my rightful place again?"

"Yes—why not?"

Nonya scowled and scratched her head in puzzlement. Myrina saw the old woman's terrible confusion. It was as though she briefly glimpsed a time long gone, a time when generosity had not been so difficult a thing to imagine.

"Hepsuash help me?" she muttered, as though asking herself if such a thing could be possible.

Myrina sensed that she had made a tiny movement in the right direction, but feared that if she pushed it further she might lose everything. "Think about it," she said.

She got up to leave, thanking her hostess courteously.

Nonya acknowledged her with an absentminded nod. "Hepsuash . . . ?" She repeated the question, but this time she seemed to find the answer. "Yes. Thoas might listen to Hepsuash!"

A smile touched the corner of Myrina's mouth as she walked through the meadow; she felt sure that she had managed to shift the ground—just a tiny bit.

That night she sat out by the stream, mirror gazing with the aid of a bright, waxing moon. She was cheered by the sight of Iphigenia wandering down to the temple stables to stand in the straw and stroke the silky silver mane of Moonbeam. She felt sure that Iphigenia had recognized Moonbeam as a Mazagardi-trained steed. Agamemnon's daughter had lived as a Moon Rider for many years and knew well the secret Mazagardi calls that would make a horse obey her every command. Such a skill might prove useful.

The following day Myrina led her remaining five mares into Tauris and succeeded in selling one to the patient man who had wanted to buy Moonbeam the day before. She didn't feel that she needed the money—Thoas had already paid her so well; it was more that she needed something to distract herself with so that she wouldn't dwell on the dangers of what she meant to do that evening. What she planned might go very wrong, but there were only two days now before the night of the full moon and she felt that she must act. What would Iphigenia do, faced with the dreadful choice between marrying Thoas and killing the two young men? The Snake Lady must persuade Nonya to trust her.

By the time the sun started to sink she had sold the other mares and set off back to the camp. They shared their meal with Katya and her grandmother, just as they had the night before, and when the girls stood up to dance, Myrina took a deep breath and prayed to Mother Maa that the goddess would guide her tongue.

Nonya leaned back against the cave wall, warmed by her fire and sated with food, looking as content as it was possible for her to look.

This was the moment to speak, Myrina told herself. "You have made us most welcome here," she said. "I cannot thank you enough. Though we were strangers you made us welcome. Tell me why?"

Nonya looked across at her, surprised but still good-humored. She shrugged and mumbled one word: "Kindness," she said. "You gave us kindness when those who were not strangers showed us only cruelty."

Myrina was pleased with the answer, but she still had a long way to go and dared not allow her determination to slip away. "You let your granddaughter go into Tauris with me; you trusted that she would be safe."

"Yes?" Nonya frowned, uncertain what this might mean.

"Do you trust me?" Myrina asked, fixing the old woman with a straight and steady gaze.

There was a pause, but then Nonya answered her with a touch of irritation. "Yes."

"Then I shall put my trust in you, though it may be a very dangerous thing for me to do."

"What do you mean?" The old woman was alert now. She was no fool.

"When you asked who I was and where I had come from, I told you only part of the truth."

There was no surprise. "I knew that!"

"Now I tell you the whole truth."

"Well?" Nonya leaned forward to listen, her eyes bright with interest.

Myrina made the sign of Maa behind her back. "Hepsuash . . . is a Moon Rider," she admitted. "A lost priestess of Maa, just like me. She is my friend and I have come to take her far away from here."

Nonya raised her eyebrows, but not a muscle of her mouth moved.

"If you take me into the temple by your secret way, I swear that I will bring her back at once and she and I will ride away. But more than that . . . if you wish it, I will make sure that she instructs the king to reinstate you in her place."

Nonya still did not speak, but her eyes narrowed in thought.

"Will you help?"

There was silence between them, and Myrina found it hard to breathe as she waited for a reply.

At last the old woman spoke. "If you play me false in this, you will be my sworn enemy for life." The threat in Nonya's voice left no doubt that she meant what she said.

"I will not play you false," Myrina told her with unflinching certainty.

The old woman stood up and frowned at the girls, who were swaying happily out on the grass, chinking Katya's finger cymbals in a steady rhythm. "I would not take my granddaughter along—there may be danger in this."

Myrina nodded in complete agreement. "Nor will I take my girls! The three of them may stay here."

"Hostages against treachery," Nonya suggested, her eyes dark with sinister meaning.

"Yes," Myrina said. "We go when night falls? I will come back to you."

Myrina walked back to her tent and at once began to pack her bundles so that their camp would stand in readiness to be moved should she manage to return with Iphigenia. As the sun began to vanish below the horizon, she called Tamsin and Phoebe over to her and explained what she was about to do.

"We come with you, Snake Mother," Tamsin insisted.

"No." Myrina was ready for this. "You and Phoebe must stay here and watch the horses and the camp. We may need to leave at once when I return. Call Katya over—she may sleep here with you."

But Katya's eyes were bright with a sense of responsibility as she ran through the grass to speak to them. "Grandmother says that I must guard the entrance to the sacred cave."

"We will all guard it," Phoebe told her.

Myrina nodded. "Then we shall pack up the tent."

Big Chief gave a low whicker of concern as she issued the Mazagardi order to stand guard over their neatly rolled goods, then they all walked back through the darkness to the cave. Nonya lit two tapers from the glowing embers of her fire and the girls settled down together in the cave mouth, wrapped in warm Sinta sleeping bags.

"Ha! Now we will see what trust will mean." The old woman's eyes glinted in the light of her taper, and Myrina bit her lip, praying that she did right to take this action.

Nonya led the way deep into the recesses of the cave until they came to a place where the rocky sides narrowed and it was impossible to see a way ahead. The light from the tapers cast dark shadows that shook and shimmered as they moved. It seemed they were making their way toward a blank rock face, but Myrina followed the old woman, confident that she knew what she was doing. They continued toward a dark cleft that looked far too narrow for a person to pass through, and Nonya chuckled at the expression of consternation on her companion's face. "Once through this narrow gateway, you will see the sacred way."

Myrina could not believe her eyes as Nonya attempted to slide into the narrow space, but suddenly the old woman vanished and it was only when she put her own face up close to the gap that she saw how cleverly it worked. The narrow split in the rock was just wide enough for one fairly slender person to squeeze through to the left; then she must turn sharply to the right, where the rock sides opened up again like the shell of a whelk.

Once through this narrow twist and turn, Myrina saw in the flickering light of the tapers that they stood in a good-sized natural cave with plenty of headroom; beyond it was a passageway where neat, even steps had been cut.

"Ha! Now you see my secret way!"

"How long has it been here?" she asked.

"It is older than the ancient priestesses . . . older than time."

Myrina could believe it, for as they began to ascend the steps she saw that they were worn with the passage of many feet but still quite easy to climb, each step well spaced. Nonya led the way and Myrina followed, her heart beating fast.

"Prepare yourself for an uphill journey!" the old woman warned. "The sacred way is long and the temple is high!"

Myrina knew that must be true. They plodded onward, around many sharp bends. In some places the roof came down so low that they could stretch up a hand to touch it. It was as though a natural passageway had been worked on and widened wherever it was needed.

Nonya's breathing grew harsh as the steps rose higher and higher.

"Stop for a rest," Myrina advised.

"We . . . are almost there," the old woman gasped.

"I . . . know every twist and turn of it."

"I see that you do!"

At last the sacred way leveled out and the sound of muffled voices could be heard, as the temple guards grumbled at each other through the night to keep themselves awake.

"The slaves will be sleeping," Nonya whispered.

"Where will we come out?" Myrina asked, fearful that Nonya would emerge first and attack Iphigenia.

"In the priestess's chamber; she, too, will be asleep by now."

"But . . . my friend must have discovered this secret."

Nonya laughed. "That I do not think!"

"Why?"

"You will see. Here is where the passage ends."

They had come up against a solid stone wall, but Nonya put out her hand and felt carefully. She counted to six under her breath and then moved two along. "This is it!"

She threw her weight forward, and with a slight grating sound the stone that she pressed against gave a little. Myrina quickly understood and reached forward to help as the stone pivoted smoothly, leaving a gap just wide enough for one person to climb through.

"Let me go first?" she begged.

"Huh! So much for trust!" Nonya grunted. She blew

out her tapers and bent her head to climb through the space with surprising alacrity. Myrina hurriedly struggled through after her, hampered by the sudden darkness. The hole was hidden behind a heavy wall hanging that swung in her face, restricting her movement, but she quickly fought her way past it and stepped out into a fine bed-chamber lit by an oil lamp.

Her worst fears had not been realized, for the old woman stood blinking in the dimly lit chamber and coughing at the smoke from her tapers. Iphigenia was awake and sitting on the balcony that overlooked the steep drop down to the sea. Now she rose shakily to her feet, alarmed at the sight of Nonya in her room.

Myrina quickly strode forward to greet her, arms wide open.

"Snake Lady!" Iphigenia cried. "It is you! I knew you were close by!" They hugged each other tightly. "But what and how . . . ?"

"There is no time to lose," Myrina told her. "We can leave at once! You must remember Nonya, who was priestess here before you. She has a secret way in and out of the temple, and I have promised her that we will see her reinstated. You must leave a message for the king ordering him to return her to her position as priestess in your place."

"I would willingly do so," Iphigenia said. "But . . . there is something . . ."

"What?" Myrina asked. She did not like the way Iphigenia's face had clouded over at the mention of leaving. "You cannot wish to stay!"

CHAPTER TWENTY-EIGHT

Agamemnon's Curse

ONYA SHUFFLED UNEASILY and frowned as though she was beginning to doubt the Snake Lady's promise. Iphigenia saw that she was angry and turned to appeal to her directly.

"Old One"—she addressed her with courtesy—"I wish nothing more than to leave this place and see you high priestess once again, but something has happened that I could never have believed possible and it changes everything!"

Nonya sprang forward and caught her by the arm. "I knew it," she snarled. "I knew it. I should never have trusted you moon priestesses!"

"By Maa!" Myrina cursed beneath her breath. Her carefully laid plan seemed to be going very wrong.

"No!" Iphigenia tried to soothe the old woman by stroking the hand that clutched at her. "I do honor you, Priestess. Believe me, this role has been forced upon me.

I would willingly see you in my place, but . . . I cannot leave yet. I cannot leave alone!"

"Two-faced one!" Nonya bellowed.

Myrina tried to push herself in between them, her heart thundering, panic rising at the noise that the old woman was making. "You must listen to Hepsuash—let her explain!"

"You swore to me! You swore me false!" Nonya wouldn't listen and she turned so fast that neither of them could stop her snatching the hunting knife that swung from Myrina's belt. She lunged at Iphigenia, but Myrina's arm shot up between them, catching the intended blow, her arm ripped open from elbow to wrist, just as two temple guards burst into the chamber. They grabbed the old priestess, one on either side.

"The old witch! Curse her!"

"How did she get in here?"

"Trying to murder Hepsuash!"

"And another one!"

"No!" Iphigenia intervened at once, concerned at the blood that flowed from Myrina's arm. "She was defending me . . ."

"Yes!" One of the guards confirmed her words. "I saw her step between them and prevent the witch from harming Hepsuash!"

"This is Myrina, a novice priestess." Iphigenia spoke

quickly but she kept her voice steady. "I have chosen her to train for temple duties!"

The two men kept tight hold of Nonya, who screeched ferociously and hurled a mouthful of spit in Iphigenia's direction. The captain of the guard appeared in the doorway and ordered Nonya to be taken away and locked up. "How could this happen?" he demanded. "There will be trouble when Thoas hears of it!"

"Take her away and keep her safe!" Iphigenia ordered. "But do not harm her or treat her ill! The goddess will punish you if you disobey me."

Nonya was dragged away, but they could hear her cursing them both roundly until the sound of her anger faded into the distance.

"Priestess . . . are you hurt?" The captain spoke with respect.

Iphigenia shook her head.

"Shall I send some of the slaves?"

Iphigenia nodded quickly. "Tell them to bring water and clean cloths. Myrina has protected me; now I will see to her needs. I wish a little peace to compose myself and allow this injured one to rest."

The man bowed and quietly left the room.

"I promised the old woman . . ." Myrina murmured, her voice suddenly weak. "She has a right . . . to curse us both, for I promised that you and I . . ." But the color fled from her face and her words petered out as she slumped back onto the couch, faint with loss of blood.

Iphigenia made Myrina lie down. "Be still . . ." She quietly took charge. She ripped a strip of cloth from her own gown to stanch the flow of blood, tying it tightly about her friend's arm.

Three temple slaves came into the chamber, carrying the things that Iphigenia had requested.

"Do not even try to speak!" Iphigenia warned. "Lie back and let me tend this wound or you will be good for naught but worms!"

The weakness of blood loss overcame Myrina as she watched Iphigenia with the ghost of a smile. Then everything went black.

When she opened her eyes she found that she was in Iphigenia's bed and bright sunlight filled the room. She was dressed in a beautiful silken priestess's gown, similar to the one that Iphigenia wore, and though her arm throbbed, it had been skillfully bandaged. She lay there puzzled for a moment, but as she looked at Iphigenia's face bent over her with concern, the memory of all that had happened last night came back.

"I cannot lie here," she complained, struggling to sit upright. "The girls are left alone and I must not leave Nonya imprisoned in her own temple."

"No." Iphigenia bent to speak low to her. "But we must be careful and not raise suspicion. There is something I must tell you and somebody I wish you to meet. We have to talk together and it cannot be explained in a moment."

Iphigenia's serious tone of voice made Myrina lie back again. She acknowledged that she was still too weak to drag her friend away at once, so she must just trust to the good sense of the young girls who guarded the cave and the devotion of Big Chief.

Iphigenia sat down on the bed and took her hand. "You must listen with patience," she insisted. "There is much to tell."

"Patience is not my greatest quality, as you know," Myrina said. "And I have much to tell *you*, but it must wait a while."

"How to start?" Iphigenia struggled to find the right words. "When I mirror gaze, I have sometimes seen a face." Myrina huffed with impatience.

"This is important!" Iphigenia reproved, speaking sharply. "This face—I have glimpsed it in my mirror all through my years with the Moon Riders."

"Whose face?"

Iphigenia shook her head. "I didn't know then, but I do now!"

"Those we see are those we love!" Myrina protested. "How can it be possible to love and not know?"

Iphigenia looked at her steadily. "Oh, you can love and not know, if you are from Agamemnon's family."

Myrina fell quiet, knowing only too well the strange and terrible childhood that Iphigenia had suffered. "And now you do know who it was?"

Iphigenia nodded. "It is the young man who is to be offered for sacrifice, the dark-haired one. As soon as Thoas presented him at the temple, I recognized him as the face in my mirror visions."

Myrina remembered the moment when she had stood with the girls at the front of the crowd. She herself had seen that something important passed between the young sacrificial victim and the quiet priestess.

"The troubled one!"

Iphigenia nodded sadly.

Myrina sighed. Had Iphigenia fallen in love at last? Surely she could not look with love on a man so young and half out of his mind. "Do not tell me that you want to stay here with him. He is due to be sacrificed in two days' time! I was there in the crowd and I felt desperately sorry for him, too, but I thought that you looked on him with motherly concern, not love!"

All at once Iphigenia laughed, and the sound of it amazed Myrina.

"I do love him," she said. "But not in the way you think. It is not motherly love either—the love I feel for him is . . . a sister's love!"

"A sister's love?" Myrina struggled to understand and then she began to remember that terrible time when Agamemnon had offered the young Iphigenia as a sacrifice.

"A brother . . ." She frowned. "Yes, you did have a brother."

Iphigenia nodded, smiling.

Myrina saw it more clearly now. Clytemnestra, the queen of Mycenae, had traveled to the town of Aulis with her daughter, both of them dressed in rich wedding clothes, believing that Iphigenia was to be the bride of the great warrior Achilles. They'd traveled in a litter and in Clytemnestra's arms there had been a baby boy, new born.

"Orestes!" she murmured. "You had a brother Orestes. Somehow . . . I have never thought of him!"

"But I have," Iphigenia said. "It was his face that I saw in my visions, even though I did not know him as my brother. But when he started to tell me who he was and where he came from I suddenly understood why I had seen him in my mirror!"

"Does he know who you are?"

"Yes—he does now, and that knowledge has soothed his troubled mind. His ship is anchored just a little way up the coast, but he and his friend Pylades came here searching for the ancient image of Artemis. They heard of a statue washed up by the sea and thought it might be what they were looking for."

"You and I know that to be the figurehead from Neoptolemus's slave ship."

But Iphigenia would not be distracted. "I believe the Moon Lady saved me for a purpose," she insisted. "She washed me into Tauris harbor to meet my brother."

Myrina frowned and rubbed her arm. This certainly altered things; her plan was completely thrown. "You say he has a ship?"

"Yes . . . but it is anchored in a hidden bay to the east. He and Pylades set out in a smaller boat to seek the statue and were blown into Tauris harbor. It is hard for a boat to escape once it has slipped through the narrow channel."

"I have seen it." Myrina nodded. "And the crazy Taurians snatched them from the sea and named them as the Chosen Ones."

Iphigenia's face fell. "I cannot see how we can leave at all, but I know this—I cannot leave without my brother."

Myrina sighed. What should they do now? She remembered the battered ship they had passed, anchored at Yalushta, where the coastline split into two levels. "I saw his ship. An ancient galley with Agamemnon's symbol blazoned on its sails, the *Castor and Pollux*."

"That is it," Iphigenia said.

"Then it is simple," Myrina insisted. "We must all escape together down Nonya's secret way."

But a cloud of sorrow shadowed Iphigenia's face. "It is not so simple," she said. "The Chosen Ones are guarded day and night and, though I may go to speak with them, the guards never leave their side."

Myrina frowned again.

"And there is more to tell! More horror—perhaps the worst of all!" Iphigenia's mouth twisted with a painful bitterness that Myrina had never seen in her before. "My mother is dead . . . murdered by my brother."

"What!"

"Orestes visited the oracle at Delphi, and the powerful, priestess whom they call the Pythoness told him to avenge his father's death; he must go to Mycenae to kill Agamemnon's murderers."

"Those Achaean priests and priestesses have much to answer for!" Myrina spoke angrily. "Why do they always want blood? The Pythoness must come from the same mould as Chalcas! They call the Moon Riders barbarians, but we cannot compete with their pointless blood lust!"

Iphigenia's face was white with pain.

"Did he do it?" Myrina asked her gently.

"Yes, he did." Iphigenia spoke low. "My brother has killed his own mother and mine."

Myrina shuddered. Even to a tough warrior woman

like her this was a terrible thing. "To kill in battle is one thing," she murmured, shaking her head, "but to kill the one who bore you! Can you still love him?"

Iphigenia's face was racked with grief, but she nodded. "He is . . . little more than a child, and he is broken up with sorrow and guilt. My mother died in his arms and whispered to him that his sister still lived. She told him that he could redeem the sin he'd committed if he found his sister and made his peace with her! So he has been searching for me ever since."

"And his search for a statue?"

"He was sent before a great council at Athens in judgment for his matricide. They banished him, saying that he could return to his home only if he found the ancient image of Artemis."

Myrina's eyes were full of tears, and her voice broke a little. "Such a quest is impossible to fulfill. What does it mean—the ancient image of Artemis? I knew when I saw him in the procession that his sanity had fled. Now I understand his madness," she whispered. "But . . . he has found his sister and I think he has made his peace with her! That is the most important thing."

Iphigenia nodded as tears spilled down her cheeks. "We do not need an old priestess to curse us! In my family we are cursed from birth to death at every turn."

Myrina held out her arms, and Iphigenia laid her head

on her friend's shoulder and wept bitterly, with huge racking sobs that made her slim frame shudder. They hugged each other tightly, and Myrina cried, too, rocking her friend gently. Through all the years of bitter struggle and despite all her harsh memories, Iphigenia had never, ever wept like this. She'd never truly allowed herself to weep for her father's treachery nor for the tragic chain of death and revenge that had been set in motion when Agamemnon commanded his young daughter to go to Aulis as a bride.

CHAPTER TWENTY-NINE

A New Plan

A T LAST THEIR sobbing quieted a little and they began to dry their eyes.

"How is your arm?" Iphigenia asked, pushing her own misery aside.

Myrina stretched it out and flexed her fingers. "It is very well bandaged." She smiled and then hiccuped. "It will mend. But now, my dear friend, we must think carefully what to do. If you can find it in your heart to forgive your brother, then none of us have the right to wish him ill. Your forgiveness means everything; your forgiveness must have the power to banish this curse forever!"

"Thank you." Iphigenia clasped her hand. "You see why I cannot leave without finding a way to free both Orestes and his faithful friend Pylades."

"Yes," Myrina said. "And it seems we have little time. But there is something that I must honor. I made my promise to Nonya, and though the woman will never listen and casts blame as fast as lightning, still I would not leave without reinstating her as high priestess in your place."

Iphigenia was of the same mind. "I will do all I can to achieve such a thing. I'd give anything to exchange places with her, though I wish she'd repudiate this terrible belief in sacrifice."

Myrina's brow was furrowed. "Is there any way we can get Orestes and his friend up here to your room so that we can take them down the secret way?"

"No." Iphigenia was quite definite. "I have power of a kind, but it is very limited. The guards will not let them out of their sight, but I may go to their prison and speak to them."

"One thing may help." Myrina took her friend's arm. "I saw you receive the sacrificial victims—I was there in the crowd—and I do know that you are loved and honored as Hepsuash. Now tell me—what kind of a man is Thoas?"

Iphigenia sighed. "He is a spoiled and stubborn young man, but . . . not wicked, I think. He begs me to marry him and of late I have given him a little hope, just to fend him off and keep him as my friend. I do not like to be deceitful, but . . ."

Myrina clasped her hand. "You have learned from the Snake Lady! And I think you have learned well. What other choice do we have? Thoas has a huge army to back him! We could go down fighting, you and I. We could stand back to back and send many of these Taurians to their goddess's hunting ground. But a little trickery might save our lives and theirs. King Thoas is besotted with you."

"No." Iphigenia smiled, shrugging her shoulders. "He loves women. He has more wives than any other king I've heard of. He's intrigued with me and swears that I am different. I make him feel at peace, he says, but he will soon tire of peace! This month it is me; next month it will be another."

"If this is true . . ." An idea began to come to Myrina that might help them get away and please Nonya at the same time.

"I am the first woman to be unwilling to marry Thoas, which seems to make him all the more keen," Iphigenia said.

"But he listens to you and respects what you say?"

"Yes," she agreed with a wry smile. "Yes, he does, but he will not listen to my pleading for the lives of the Chosen Ones. Sacrifice has been a long and ancient tradition here: the people are so stupid, they fear that the goddess will be angry and make the sea dry up if they do not feed these poor bewildered strangers back into it."

Myrina smiled at the irony of Iphigenia calling the Taurians stupid just as Nonya and Katya had done.

Perhaps they had more in common than they realized. "I think I see a way . . ." Her spirits rose a little as a new plan slowly began to form in her mind. "If you told Thoas that you had discovered that these young strangers were guilty of murder—which is quite true—and swore that they must be purified by washing them in the sea . . . would he agree to that?"

"Yes, that might be possible. I think we'd be well guarded, but . . ." Iphigenia's face lit up with understanding. "I begin to see!"

"And you must bring the old figurehead, too!"

"That figurehead saved my life," Iphigenia told her seriously.

Iphigenia insisted that Myrina rest while her wound began to knit and she regained her strength. When they were alone they spoke together of their plans, but while the temple servants hovered around to wait on them, they tried to make the most of good food and drink, though Myrina thought often of the three girls left guarding the cave and the horses.

As darkness fell that evening they went down to the sacred inner temple, where the two young sacrifices were kept in surroundings more luxurious even than the priestess's chambers.

They found them both thin and pale, beside platters piled high with honeyed dates and sweetmeats that they couldn't bring themselves to touch. "A gilded cage!" Myrina hissed.

But at Iphigenia's warning glance, she fell silent.

Orestes went at once to his sister, the deep, instinctive affection between them clear to see. Iphigenia spoke quietly to the boys, explaining the plan, and Pylades turned his head to listen, alert and suddenly hopeful. Myrina warmed to him, understanding his anger. She remembered the time long ago when she'd been companion to the young Princess Cassandra, also thought by many to be mad. It had not been an easy friendship at first, but Cassandra had turned out to be the most extraordinary person Myrina had ever known. Now she looked at Orestes and thought that even he might be hauled back to sanity and redeemed by his sister's love and care. Perhaps Pylades would be rewarded for his devotion in the end.

"Do you understand?" Iphigenia took her brother's hand.

"Of course I do," Orestes said, but when she asked him to repeat her words, he shook his head and couldn't. His sister soothed him and told him it didn't matter, while Myrina spoke fast and low to Pylades, making sure that he at least would know what to do. "You are a true friend," she told him. "Believe me, I know what such friendship costs!"

"We were raised as brothers," Pylades said simply.

"And brothers you are!" Myrina agreed.

She explained their plan to him and felt confident that she could rely on his nerve and good judgment to steer his friend through the ordeal that lay ahead. They returned to the priestess's chamber and ate a good meal. Iphigenia sent one of the temple guards off to Thoas's palace with a message that she must see him early in the morning, for an impediment to the sacrifice had arisen. While she was giving these orders, Myrina secretly packed away some of the fruit and soft white bread from the table. Then Iphigenia dismissed the servants, giving them the impression that she and Myrina were settling down for the night.

As soon as they were alone, Myrina drew back the hanging that covered the secret entrance to the passageway, taking up the bundle of food that she'd prepared. They both paused, looking fearfully at each other for a moment. "Do we do right?" Iphigenia murmured.

"What choice is there?" Myrina asked. "Until the full moon," she whispered, kissing her friend. "I pray you will not forget Nonya."

"I will not!" Iphigenia whispered. "Blessings of Mother Maa! Until the full moon!"

Myrina hurried down the steep rocky steps, her wounded arm bound tightly in protective leather, still wearing the beautiful priestess's robe. Her heart thundered with excitement. She needed every drop of courage she could muster and every bit of snaky craftiness, too.

The three girls were sitting together in the cave mouth just as she'd left them, but they rose to their feet with wild relief when they saw her.

"Where is Iphigenia?" Tamsin demanded anxiously.

"What a beautiful dress!" Phoebe frowned. "Aah! You are wounded!"

"I am strong enough and there is no time to explain," Myrina told them. "Iphigenia is safe for now and I need you all to ride fast with me to find the Achaean ship, the *Castor and Pollux*, that we passed on our way to Tauris. Fetch me the horses and some proper riding clothes!"

Tamsin and Phoebe ran at once to obey her, but Katya looked at Myrina with suspicion.

"Where is my grandmother?" she asked.

"She, too, is safe enough." Myrina grabbed the girl by the shoulders and spoke firmly. "You must trust me, Katya, and come with us. I know it is hard, but you must believe me."

"I haven't the skill to ride," she protested. "I will stay here and wait for Grandmother!"

"No!" Myrina insisted. "You ride with me. You are all important to our plans and if you wish to see your grandmother safe and happy again, you will do as I say!"

Phoebe stumbled into the cave mouth with a bundle of Sinta trousers and a smock. Katya watched uneasily as Myrina stripped the silken gown over her head and struggled into comfortable riding gear.

Phoebe picked up the gown and made to lay it inside the cave, but Myrina told her to roll it up carefully and put it into one of the bags.

Big Chief neighed a warm, impatient welcome as Myrina strode across the grass to him and leaped onto his back. Tamsin and Phoebe mounted their horses and they all turned back to Katya, who hesitated in the cave mouth.

Myrina wheeled Big Chief around. "Trust me!" she begged.

Katya sighed and came across to them, holding out her arms so that Myrina could lean down from Big Chief's back and haul her up behind her.

"Hang on tight!" she hissed.

Katya wrapped her arms around Myrina's waist and gritted her teeth, ready for the ride of her life.

All three horses set off, their ears pricked, manes flying as they lengthened their stride, heading toward the sea and the high cliff tops in the bright moonlight.

They galloped on, skirting the temple of Artemis. The building stood almost in darkness, still and quiet.

"What is happening in there?" Phoebe shouted.

"Tomorrow you will find out. Iphigenia will not let us down."

They rode through the night, never stopping until Myrina saw the furled brail sail of the *Castor and Pollux* down below them in the harbor at Yalushta, just as the darkness began to lift and a rosy glow crept up from the east.

Halfway down the steep grassy slope they dismounted to drink from a clear stream. They rested while they ate the bread and fruit that Myrina had brought from the temple and the horses grazed.

"Now," said Myrina, her voice tense with the importance of what she had to say, "I will tell you what Iphigenia and I have planned. You must listen carefully, for we may need your help. It is a dangerous undertaking, but in order to free Iphigenia and deal fairly with Nonya we must take this course of action. Now, first there is something that I must explain—do you remember me telling you long ago that Iphigenia had a baby brother?"

The three girls listened, openmouthed, fascinated and concerned.

"Do you all understand?" she asked when she'd finished.

"Yes." All three nodded gravely.

CHAPTER THIRTY

The Castor and Pollux

THERE WAS NO time for them to ask more questions, for Myrina had seen the first signs of movement aboard the *Castor and Pollux*. She stood up and firmly spoke the order to 'follow' into Big Chief's ear: *"Zeygut! Zeygut!"* Then she marched down the hillside, her bow strung ready on her shoulder, a full quiver of arrows strapped to her thigh. The girls and horses followed obediently at her heels.

As they got closer, Myrina was surprised at the lack of activity aboard. When they eventually stood on the quayside, looking down on the two decks, they understood that what they'd seen from the hillside was just two young oarsmen lowering a bucket over the side into the sea. Now they hauled the bucket up and began to splash water over their bleary eyes. Other oarsmen lay about the deck snoring as though they'd supped a great deal of wine the previous night. Myrina's heart sank at the sight of them.

This was not going to be easy, but there was no other way that she could think of.

"Hey there!" she shouted. "Get me your captain!"

"Who asks?" one of the young men replied, eyeing her and the girls, unimpressed.

"One who brings a message from your master!"

The two men looked at each other and laughed. "Our master? Our master has deserted us and anyway—he's a madman!"

"He's a dead madman!" The other grinned at his own wit. "We can't take orders from him."

"Who do you take orders from?" Myrina bellowed.

"Not from women!" the bigger sailor sneered, making an obscene hand gesture toward them.

He had gone too far.

"So it has to be done the hard way!" Myrina spoke with quiet anger. She slipped the bow from her shoulder and sent an arrow whizzing down to pierce right through the offending hand.

"Aagh! Curse and blast the bitch," the sailor yelled, clutching his wounded hand frantically, while the other man pulled him back behind the mast, suddenly white-faced and frightened.

"Fetch me your captain!" Myrina ordered.

The smaller sailor turned to obey, but a tousle-haired fellow had already appeared beside him, yawning and scratching his beard. "Who wants me?" he growled. "What time of day . . . ?" He stopped, surprised to see a young woman and three girls staring angrily down at him, all armed with bows; three fine Sinta horses, ears pricked, waiting behind them. "And who . . . ?" he murmured.

"I am Myrina the Moon Rider!"

"Moon Rider!" He laughed. "The ones they call Amazon? No wonder Troy fell if this was all they had to defend them!"

Fuming, Myrina fitted another arrow to her bow; there wasn't time for this. "Are you the captain of this ship?"

"I'm the captain—so what!"

"Watch her!" the smaller sailor cried. "Those arrows are double barbed. See what she has done to Phestus!"

The captain looked quickly back at her with grudging respect.

"Let me come aboard then." She still threatened him with her bow. "I have a message from your master Prince Orestes."

The man was impressed that at least she knew the name. Most of the crew were awake now and scrambling to their feet.

"Come aboard, my lady!" He bowed with mock courtesy, indicating a rope that they could climb down.

Myrina lowered her bow and replaced the arrow in her

quiver. She swung down the rope and leaped lightly aboard. "There is no time to be lost," she told him at once. "You must set your oarsmen in place and unfurl the sail while the wind blows in your favor. Your master has need of you and will join you to the west, outside the deep cut in the cliffs that is the entrance to Tauris harbor."

The girls watched tensely from the quayside as seamen gathered about Myrina, cursing and grumpy that their sleep had been so rudely disturbed.

"What do you say?" the captain asked his crew, still grinning as though this was a joke. "Do you wish to row to Tauris in search of the lunatic prince?"

There were more foul jokes and nasty laughter. Myrina gritted her teeth—this was not going well. She looked up to see that the sun had risen from the sea and had now moved above the horizon. She was too close to draw her bow and send an arrow shooting into the captain's heart, so she ducked lightly forward and snatched the short sword that dangled from his belt. Before he had realized what she was doing, she had it at his throat.

"What the . . . !" He was at last alert to danger and fully awake. One of his crew threw him a sword, but as the rest of his men ran to get their weapons, Phoebe bellowed, "Hold! First man to move gets an arrow in his throat!"

Both she and Tamsin had an arrow nocked and ready and a good vantage spot up on the quayside. Katya had taken the short meat knife from her belt and held it ready to throw. Even though the girls were so young, the sailors were wary; the man with an arrow in his hand still groaned and struggled to pull it out.

"Huh!" The captain was angry now. "Stay back, men. I don't need you to help me fight women!"

He swung his weapon up, skillfully knocking Myrina's stolen sword away from his throat.

"Ha!" He smiled again.

"That's it!" his crew shouted. "Kill the bitch!"

Myrina recovered and grasped the sword again. She and the captain circled each other, their faces grim. Shouts of encouragement came from all around; but still wary of the arrows that might fly down on them, the crew did not interfere. Rather they settled themselves to enjoy a bit of sport.

Myrina bit her lip. What was she doing? The sword had never been her weapon, and her wounded arm was throbbing painfully inside the leather strap. If only she had the warrior skills of Penthesilea, she'd soon polish him off! But with the memory of her brave friend came a cheering flow of warm courage and strength. "Penthesilea is with me," she told herself.

She took the sword in both hands and swung it fast in a neat figure-of-eight, as though it was naught but a light dancing stick. The unexpected movement sent the captain lurching to the side while Myrina swished the point at his ribs and managed to slice him.

A surprised groan came from the crew.

"Agree to my orders and the fight is over," Myrina offered, holding back for just a moment.

The captain gave no reply, but clutched at his side, staring amazed at the blood that oozed out between his fingers.

Myrina raised her sword again, but the captain moved quickly now and grabbed her arm where the leather binding covered her bandaged wound. Myrina could not help but grimace at the pain it caused.

"What is this?" the man bellowed. "Fresh blood?"

Myrina saw with dismay that blood trickled down from her own reopened wound.

"What madwoman fights with a wounded arm?" the captain demanded. Reaching forward he ripped the leather away, revealing Myrina's blood-soaked bandage.

"Leave me be," she warned.

He looked at the bloody wound, then a puzzled expression came to him. When he spoke again his words were softer and more respectful. "Let us not fight, you and I! What are we fighting for?"

But Myrina still struggled to grasp her sword. "Will you muster your crew and set sail for Tauris?"

He let go of her arm and scratched his head. "Very

well," he agreed at last. "It seems I must."

Myrina lowered her sword slowly. "Give the order then."

"All hands!" he shouted, still gasping for breath. "To the oars!"

The men looked surprised, but they obeyed, reluctantly moving to the thwarts. The captain shook his head at the mess of blood that dripped down his side.

"I'm as mad as my master," he muttered.

Myrina turned to Phoebe, pointing up at Big Chief. "Fetch my healing bundle!" she cried.

The girls had already lowered their bows, relieved that the fight was over. Now all three slipped down the rope ladder onto the deck, their arms full of baggage. The captain sat down on the lower rung of the ladder that led to the afterdeck, looking more surprised than ever as Myrina calmly searched in her bundles. Having found what she wanted, she began to pull away his clothing, pinching the wound together and applying ointment to his cut.

"What about you?" he asked.

"I will see to myself once we are under way," she snapped.

Tamsin held out bandages, but she bared her teeth at the captain. "If you had hurt my mother, I'd have killed you myself."

The man could not help but smile at such fierceness from one so young. Phoebe bent to help fashion a pad of healing herbs that Myrina strapped about his chest. Katya watched it all wide-eyed and quiet; her new friends were proving to be more ruthless and capable than she'd ever realized.

The captain sat back, rubbing his eyes in astonishment. "I have never before been stabbed, then patched up by the same one!" he murmured.

"Ha!" Myrina almost laughed. "Who better? For a Moon Rider the first lesson in fighting is how to stanch wounds. See what our young tiger can do!"

They both turned to watch Phoebe, who had gone unbidden to Phestus, the man with the arrow stuck through his hand. She neatly snapped off the flight close to the wound, then took hold of the double barb that had pierced right through the hand. With a movement that was both strong and swift, she pulled the narrow shaft right through.

The man gave a sharp cry and fainted, but he quickly came to again to find that his young helper had stopped the flow of blood and was now neatly bandaging his hand.

The captain watched it all, blinking and rubbing his eyes. "I think I am still asleep and dreaming," he murmured.

"You are not asleep!" Myrina hauled him roughly to his

feet. "And you need all your wits about you! What is your name?"

"Seris . . . madam! Captain Seris!" He bowed, courteous at last.

"Well, Seris—if you are any kind of a sea captain, get us to Tauris harbor as fast as you can!"

CHAPTER THIRTY-ONE

Swim for Your Lives

S THE SHIP moved away from the quayside,
Phoebe came to help Myrina dress her own
freshly bleeding wound, but then they both
noticed Tamsin's small chin trembling as she held back
tears.

"What is it?" Myrina asked.

"The horses!" Tamsin whispered.

Big Chief snorted loudly on the quayside, his ears set
back in distress. Snowboots stamped her hooves, and
Sandmane snaked her head in anxiety as the oars dipped
in unison and the great ship moved away. Myrina had a
moment of panic. How could she have forgotten the
horses? Though the galley was large enough to find room
for the beasts aboard, she dared not lose more time by
going back for them. She stumbled over to the gunwales
and shouted like a fisherwoman, cupping her mouth with
bloody hands, putting every last drop of strength into her

lungs. "*Zeygut! Zeygut!*" she cried. "Follow!"

Big Chief tossed his head and snorted again. How could he follow a ship setting out to sea?

"*Zeygut!*" Myrina shouted again, waving her arm toward the high cliffs.

Tamsin clapped her hand to her mouth to cover her distress, but at last, as the crew raised the brail sail to catch the wind, Big Chief turned away from the water and began to lead the two mares back up the steep cliffs that soared away toward the west.

Tamsin and Phoebe watched them anxiously from the deck as the sun rose steadily to its zenith. The *Castor and Pollux* sailed westward up the coast, while the dark silhouettes of the horses could be seen in the distance, keeping a steady pace, the ship forever in their sights.

Once under way Captain Seris began to take charge of his crew with enthusiasm. He marched up and down the length of the ship, groaning a little as his side twinged with pain and snapping at anyone who did not keep good time. Soon he had the ship skimming over the waves, and Myrina's spirits rose.

"Well . . . my fine Amazon," Seris asked her at last, "are you going to tell me what we are to do when we get to Tauris?"

Myrina was still half annoyed by his manner, but she

knew that quarreling further with him would only slow them down again so she answered him back in kind.

"Well, my fine captain"—she eyed him with a touch of humor—"you are going to anchor out here in the sea, close to Tauris harbor, and send one of your small boats in through the narrow cut with a crew of brave fellows to rescue your master and his friend!"

"Just one small boat? That will do? We believed the Taurians had sacrificed Orestes to their fierce goddess! Will they give him up to us without a struggle? Will one small boatload be enough to batter down the walls of King Thoas's jail?"

Myrina made a wry face; she knew that his questions were far from serious, but they brought to the surface her own real doubts. She wasn't sure about her plan but it was the best she could think up, so they must make it work.

"We will need two boats," she corrected herself. "Orestes will be there bathing in the shallow water and his sister—Iphigenia—will release him. Then we—"

"What!" Captain Seris cut in, giving her his full attention. "Iphigenia! You cannot mean . . . ?"

Myrina turned to him with a long, hard look. She was reluctant to put her trust in him, but without it they would have little chance of success. "Yes," she said quietly. "His very own sister."

Now the man stared at her with renewed respect, giving a low whistle, all trace of humor gone. "Tell me how."

So as the ship rose and fell, cutting along the coast of the Inhospitable Sea, Myrina explained as much as she could. Seris listened, shaking his head with amazement, and she saw that a touch of excitement gleamed in his eye. Was his appetite for adventure returning?

"Well?" At last she paused in her telling. "Can we do it, do you think?"

Seris grinned wolfishly. "We will do it or die trying!" he told her.

Now Myrina laughed. "I hope it will not come to that."

As the ship sailed on, Tamsin kept her worried gaze fixed on the distant movement of the horses, but as they arrived at the outer entrance to Tauris harbor the beasts could still be seen, looking down on them from the high cliffs close to where the temple was situated. Myrina went to speak to the girls.

"I want to know that you are both safe aboard the *Castor and Pollux*; as soon as I have Iphigenia free we will meet again in the Bay of Yalushta."

"And then will we ride back to find the Moon Riders?" Phoebe spoke with longing.

"Yes, we will."

"And will Iphigenia ride with us?" Tamsin asked.

Myrina hesitated and then sighed. "I think she may choose to go with her brother to Athens."

"And not with us?" Tamsin found it hard.

"But we will know that she is safe and free." Myrina tried to comfort them although her own heart was heavy at the thought of losing Iphigenia yet again.

"You will make sure Snowboots and Sandmane are safe?" Tamsin looked at her mother solemnly.

"I will do my best." Myrina was unwilling to make more promises that she was not sure she could keep. "Now, Katya"—she touched the older girl's arm—"you and I have much to do and to talk about. I believe we will see your grandmother safe and content, but you are going to have to be brave."

In the center of Tauris a crowd was gathering as the sun began to sink in the west. News had flown around the town that Hepsuash was angry. The people came out into the streets, dressed in their best, ready for the sacrifice, but the gossip was all about the extraordinary things that had happened last night.

"The guards are saying that the old priestess, Nonya, was discovered in the temple trying to murder Hepsuash!" one old woman whispered to her daughter.

"No! How could she get in there?"

"Dark powers . . ." Her friend gave a sharp nod. "She always did possess dark powers! That's why we call her witch!"

"Well . . . they say Thoas is furious," the old one whispered. "He has thrown his captain of the guard into jail and put Ledus in charge! He says that his warriors are as stupid as beasts, so they might as well have the ostler lead them!"

Soon a new rumor swept through the town—that Hepsuash was insisting that the two Chosen Ones be taken down to the beach and purified in the sea.

"She vows that if she must perform a sacrifice she will do it her way."

"Both the Chosen Ones and the sacred statue of Artemis must be washed in the sea."

Gradually, as the word spread, people began to head for the small beach by the harbor instead of the temple on the hill. An atmosphere of excitement grew at the news of this impromptu ceremony, and though there had been little time to prepare for it, the townsfolk came down to the water's edge, carrying wreaths of flowers.

The only ones who were not enthusiastic were Thoas and Nonya. The old priestess glared around her furiously as she was led down to the sea in chains. The crowd murmured that Hepsuash intended to drown her as punishment.

"Serve her right!"

"Drowning's too good for her!"

"Look—here they come!"

The king rode in procession down to the harbor, following Hepsuash, his face glum. Somehow he felt that he'd been tricked, though he couldn't be sure exactly how or why. How could Hepsuash, whom he'd loved for her peace and gentleness, suddenly make up her mind to waste the two lives that she'd once so stalwartly defended? This was not the outcome he'd wished for when he insisted that the sacrifice should go ahead.

Nonya's eyes never left the small figure of Hepsuash, who rode on Moonbeam, her face impassive.

When they reached the beach, Iphigenia dismounted and ordered the two young men into the sea, their hands still tied with golden ropes; two slaves who carried the figurehead statue of Artemis received the same command.

"This must be purified, too."

It was only when she followed them into the water that she allowed herself a glimpse in the direction of the narrow cut in the cliffs that formed the harbor entrance. "Will they come in time?" she murmured.

As the people watched, Iphigenia waded into the sea with the Chosen Ones carrying a small pitcher made of gold. "Deeper!" she ordered.

Farther and farther out they went, while the Taurians watched fascinated by the new ceremony that Hepsuash had invented. Her fine priestess's robes were soaked but she ignored the water until it almost reached her shoulders. Orestes and Pylades followed obediently until the water rose well above their waists. Iphigenia began to scoop up pitchers full of seawater and pour them over the heads and shoulders of the two young victims, whispering to them all the time, as though it were some religious chant. The crowd was hushed and respectful. What would Hepsuash do next?

At last Iphigenia glanced toward the narrow cut and saw what she wished to see. Before anyone could tell what was happening, she had brought the sharp sacrificial knife from the pouch at her waist and sliced through the golden bonds of the intended victims.

"Swim," she told them. "Swim for your lives!"

The Chosen Ones were ready for this command. They launched themselves in the direction of an oncoming boat, gliding fast through the water to safety.

"What is happening?"

"Where are they going!"

"Ah! Two boats are coming!"

"What is this?"

Shock and surprise at what had happened took a moment or two to sink in, but then the crowd began to stir, shouting at each other. Thoas looked up from his gloomy thoughts and quickly knew why he'd sensed deceit.

"Hepsuash!" he growled. "What have you done?"

The two young men swam on toward the boats, but Iphigenia turned her back on them to face the anger of King Thoas and his people.

CHAPTER THIRTY-TWO

A New Hepsuash

"TAKE HEPSUASH CAPTIVE!" the king ordered his guards.

But it wasn't easy for the guards to struggle through the crowds to get at the deceitful priestess. The howling of threats and promises of vengeance faded a little as the Taurians saw that their Lady from the Sea had no intention of evading their anger. She walked slowly back to face them, carefully sheathing her knife. It looked as though she would speak to them.

"Take her!" Thoas ordered again, but the crowd stubbornly stood in the way, quieter now.

It seemed they wanted to hear her speak.

In the distance Orestes and Pylades were hauled into the first boat, which turned swiftly and rowed back through the narrow crevice that led to the open sea. People watched with wild curiosity as the second boat came steadily on toward them.

At last Ledus managed to break through the crowd and march with a group of determined guards, swords drawn, toward Iphigenia. But before he could reach her, a cry rang out from the oncoming boat. "*Lakati! Lakati!*"

It was Myrina crying out the Mazagardi command "defend." No sooner had she shouted the strange words than the sound of hooves and the bellow of charging horses could be heard. Big Chief had made his way down from the cliff tops to the foreshore, just a little way from where the crowd gathered. Now at Myrina's command he galloped furiously through the shallow water to where Iphigenia stood, followed by Snowboots and Sandmane. Hepsuash's own mare, Moonbeam, splashed forward into the sea and they quickly formed a protective ring about the small figure of Iphigenia, snorting fiercely and tossing their manes. The armed men backed away.

Thoas's mouth dropped open as he watched; then at last he managed to cry out, "What kind of witchery is this, that even animals defend the woman?"

The people were frightened and staggered back. Iphigenia leaped lightly onto Moonbeam's back. Then she urged the mare forward, still flanked on three sides by the other horses.

"Thoas!" she called. At once the Taurians fell silent, every one of them straining to hear what she would say. "Thoas . . . I beg forgiveness."

Her voice dropped lower, but the silence was so great that all could hear.

"Taurians," she said, turning her head to encompass the whole of the gathering, "I beg forgiveness of you all. I have deceived you, but I had no choice. You would force me to commit murder, but no goddess of mine would wish for the blood of innocent strangers. You deserve to know the truth about me. You took me from the sea and honored me as your priestess, you called me the Lady from the Sea, but I am not your Hepsuash! I was born far away from these shores and given another name—I am Iphigenia!"

There were gasps all around and Thoas turned a little pale, but he waited for her to say more.

"Yes—I am the daughter of Agamemnon, lost to my family and cursed by my father. But now I beg your forbearance and understanding of my actions; for I have discovered that the dark-haired boy whom you would have sacrificed is none other than my brother Orestes!"

There were more gasps of shock and a few murmurings of sympathy. Thoas scowled, trying hard to take in what it all meant, but Iphigenia continued, anxious not to let her moment slip away.

"You were right to set me in the temple of Artemis, for the goddess has always favored me ever since she saw me rescued so many years ago from the sacrificial knife!"

Myrina watched from the second boat with admiration, her heart in her mouth. She of all people knew how hard it was for her quiet friend to speak these words to such a huge and dangerous audience. Gradually Iphigenia's voice gained in strength. "The goddess is angry indeed. She does not want blood sacrifices dropped into the sea; what she wants is respect."

She turned her head to where Nonya stood, still in chains, at the water's edge. "And the goddess demands respect for those who have served her in the past, handing on the role from mother to daughter, year after year."

Suddenly all eyes were on Nonya, who looked bewildered. There was a sense of unease as many of those present remembered guiltily that they had chased the old woman away and stoned her daughter. They were astonished to hear Iphigenia suggesting that they take the grim old priestess back into their hearts. But Agamemnon's daughter was not finished with them yet.

"I will not steal away from Tauris like a thief," she insisted. "I will not go like an ungrateful child and leave you without a priestess to lead your worship. I give you my sacred statue of Artemis and I bring you a new Hepsuash; a new girl from the sea."

Myrina saw Nonya's head shoot up, her face full of suspicion again, but as Iphigenia swung out her arm to indicate the approaching boat, Nonya—along with all the

Taurians—suddenly smiled with wonder and under-standing.

"Here is your new Hepsuash," Iphigenia cried.

There in the prow of Myrina's boat sat Katya. She was dressed in the beautiful blue priestess's robe that Myrina had worn as she escaped through the tunnel. Myrina had twisted her hair into a high coif, a golden diadem made by Kuspada was set in her shining locks, and a necklace of Sinta gold gleamed about her throat.

"Stand up!" Myrina whispered. "Make sure that they can all see you!"

Though the boat wobbled a little, Katya rose grace-fully to her feet. There were gasps of admiration; in the soft pink light of the setting sun, this slim young woman with her head held high gleamed like a goddess herself.

"Take her to your hearts," Iphigenia cried.

There was a small outburst of applause, then they began to chant a welcome. "Hepsuash! Hepsuash! Come to us! Hepsuash!"

The Taurians sang with wild enthusiasm, waving and throwing flowers toward the little boat that carried their new priestess. Almost every eye was on Katya, but Myrina looked in a different direction. She turned her head first to observe the king's reaction and was well pleased with what she saw. A smile touched the corner of Thoas's mouth as his eyes lighted on Katya with some surprise,

311

but also rapt admiration.

Then she searched for Nonya and was relieved to see that the old woman returned her look with a small fierce nod. Myrina was satisfied; this strange way of keeping her faith with Nonya had been accepted.

Iphigenia slipped down from Moonbeam's back, waving forward the two slaves who carried the figurehead statue. She helped Katya out of the boat and led her by the hand through the shallows and onto the beach, where she presented the statue to her while the crowd cheered wildly.

Katya held up her hand to speak and everyone fell quiet. "If you wish it, I will be your Hepsuash, but first I must beg a favor of your king."

Everyone looked at Thoas, but he could only stare at the beautiful new priestess with astonished admiration.

"Please," Katya pleaded with quiet dignity, "set my grandmother free."

Thoas tore his eyes away from her face for just a moment, and without hesitation he ordered the guards to release the old woman from her chains. Nonya stared at her granddaughter openmouthed, as though she were a stranger, but then at last she smiled and respectfully bowed her head. Katya ran to take her grandmother into her arms while they both cried tears of joy.

Myrina jumped out of the boat and splashed through

the shallows to Iphigenia. They exchanged a look of wondering relief; it seemed their plan had worked, but Myrina saw that there was still a touch of anxiety in Iphigenia's eyes.

"What is it?"

"I know these people," Iphigenia answered. "They are as changeable as the weather. Let us go before Thoas thinks better of it."

Myrina understood and whistled for Big Chief, who came at once to her side. Then she turned and nodded at Captain Seris, sitting in the prow of the second boat. In a quiet voice he gave the oarsmen the order to turn about. Myrina and Iphigenia walked slowly through the crowd toward the bottom of the steep cliff pathway that led up through the town toward the temple. Nobody stopped them or even seemed to notice the horses following in their wake. The crowds had come out to be entertained by a spectacle and, though the terrible swooping of the sacrificial victims had been denied them, something even more surprising had taken place and fulfilled their need for excitement.

Myrina found it hard to keep to the slow and steady pace but at last she felt confident enough to mount Big Chief. Iphigenia leaped up onto Moonbeam, and they trotted farther up the hill, Snowboots and Sandmane still following. At last, when they were halfway up the steep winding path, they looked back and saw that lamps had been lit down on the beach as darkness gathered all about the town. Thoas had called for his golden carriage and was handing Katya into it before he took his seat beside her.

"Is that Nonya he's inviting in now?" Myrina asked.

"Yes, I think it is," Iphigenia agreed with a smile. "Can you hear them singing?"

The crowds surged all about the carriage, chanting the name Hepsuash.

"I think the old one is happy enough," Myrina said with satisfaction. "And look out there—Captain Seris has passed through the cut into the sea."

"Have we done it, do you think?" Iphigenia asked, her voice faint and husky now.

Myrina laughed. "I think we have!" She bent and whispered low in Big Chief's ear, "*Thozeley!* Fast horse!"

Big Chief was eagerly waiting for this command. He pricked up his ears with pleasure and lengthened his stride. They cantered past the lights of the temple, giving Iphigenia's ornate prison barely a glance, and galloped away over the high cliffs, back toward Yalushta Bay, where they knew Captain Seris would be heading, his master safely back aboard the *Castor and Pollux*.

CHAPTER THIRTY-THREE

A Brave Challenge

THE RIDE WAS SHEER pleasure to Myrina, compared to the urgency and anxiety she'd felt as she'd covered the same ground the night before. Could it really be such a short time since she'd gone racing to Yalushta with the girls, a crazy plan of action in her head?

The full moon gleamed above them, and Myrina's spirits rose. She should have been more confident: the full moon had meant freedom when they'd ridden away from Aulis; now it signified freedom once again. They were galloping wildly away from danger, and Iphigenia had made the bravest speech of her life; this was what being a Moon Rider really meant! There wasn't time to take the mirror from her belt to seek the images of those she loved, but soon she would follow her friends northward across the Sinta River. Now that Iphigenia was safe, she could set Big Chief's head for the east and the Moon Riders' camp.

They had to slow up as the path began to slope steeply downhill. As the first touches of dawn came, they saw the neat dip and lift of the oars of the *Castor and Pollux* below them. Seris had his men under firm control as the ship moved steadily against the wind to the appointed place, its master safely aboard.

They were waiting there by the quayside as the ship arrived, and there was a great deal of hugging and crying when Tamsin and Phoebe were reunited with Iphigenia.

"Must you go so soon?" they begged.

Iphigenia smiled and hugged them again. "I thought I had lost all my family, but now I have found my brother again," she explained.

They swallowed their pleading, trying hard to understand. Iphigenia still had a sense of urgency and feared that any moment Thoas might send his warriors swarming after them over the cliffs.

Seris tried to reassure her that in Yalushta they would be able to see an army coming well before they could get close. He insisted that they must wait a little while to take on board enough supplies to see them back across the sea to Athens.

"We will wait until you go," Myrina insisted, grateful for this small space of time to be together. Now that she was suddenly faced with the parting, she felt as sad as the girls.

Orestes strode about the deck, calm and cheerful, Pylades at his side. Myrina could not believe that this was the same boy whose insane muttering had disturbed her so. The young men delighted in their freedom, glad to see their crew again and grateful for the part they'd played, late though it might be. There was joking and relieved laughter as they appeared once more dressed in their own clothes, swords and daggers in their belts, while Seris fretted over the loading of supplies.

Myrina and Iphigenia sat together a little way up the hillside, both mirror gazing, their bows and quivers beside them. Myrina looked for Kuspada and the Moon Riders' camp; she was delighted to see a fast horse race taking place. Way ahead of the others rode a girl with flying braids, who sat astride her horse like a centaur's daughter. It was Zimapo, and she won the race amid wild celebration. But where was her father? Why was he not watching his daughter in her triumph? Myrina could not see the face she searched for.

Then a small gasp beside her made her lose the vision and come quickly back to her present concerns. "What is it?" she asked.

Iphigenia had gone very pale. "Cassandra!" she whispered.

At once Myrina looked back into her own golden mirror and found the troubling vision that held her friend.

Cassandra stood over the stone trough that usually swarmed with mice, her hands tangled in her hair as though in great distress. The Mouse Boy clung to her waist and they both looked down with fear at a great space that grew in the middle of the trough. The mice surged with one accord toward the outer rim, scurrying for their lives away from the center, leaving it deserted and empty.

"What can it mean?" Myrina cried.

"Danger—sudden danger!" Iphigenia murmured.

"To whom? To them?"

Iphigenia's voice shook and she looked up. "To us, I fear! It is a warning!"

Myrina's heart thundered as she dropped her mirror and scrambled to her feet. They both looked out to sea and saw a ship slide into sight around the eastern promontory. They grabbed each other by the hand, and for just one terrible moment stood and watched. The symbol that adorned the billowing sail could not be seen clearly as yet, but still they recognized the ship, a shape they could never forget. The sail would bear the sign of the ant!

"Neoptolemus!" Myrina hissed.

They thrust their precious mirrors safely away and snatched up their bows and quivers, then ran down the hillside. "On board! Get on board!" they shouted.

Everyone looked to the high cliffs and the western horizon, fearing that Thoas pursued them. Nobody could understand why the two Moon Riders were so wildly bellowing the order to go. There was confusion. Seris swore that they hadn't enough stores aboard, but then Phoebe saw the true threat from the upper deck of the ship and began to howl. "The slave men!" she wailed. "The slave men!" She had never forgotten what the sign of the ant meant.

That quickly made everyone understand and there was panic. People ran about in all directions.

Tamsin marched determinedly over the wooden ramp that had been set up to help them load supplies. She snatched Snowboots's halter and calmly led her aboard the ship. She was not going to leave her horse behind this time.

Myrina saw quickly that her child had more good sense than she had. She led Big Chief aboard, giving the firm command for the other horses to follow; the Moon Riders' camp beyond the Sinta River would just have to wait for now.

Seris and Orestes at last understood the fear that had descended on them, and as soon as everyone was aboard they drew up the ramp and gave the order to move off. But the brightly painted ant ship moved toward them fast and before they could manage to escape the harbor, it cut across their bows and blocked the way.

The foredeck of Neoptolemus's flagship was filled with armed warriors. A shout went up. "Halt in the name of the son of great Achilles!"

Myrina's heart sank. She could not believe that they had battled their way through so much trouble only to be stopped again and dragged back into slavery by this pirate of the Inhospitable Sea. She reached up to cling to Big Chief's neck, in need of support, grateful for the feel of warm horseflesh.

A giant of a man, armed to the teeth, shouted again, "I take this ship and all on board in the name of Neoptolemus, son of the great hero Achilles!"

There was silence. Myrina anxiously looked back at the eastern promontory, wondering when the rest of Neoptolemus's fleet would follow his flagship into view. As yet there was no sign of them, but she knew that they would come. She scanned the helmets that, row on row, covered the deck of the ship that blocked their way. The men carried swords and lances, but she could see no archers among their ranks. That gave her a little hope as she quickly rallied her courage and nocked an arrow to her bow. Phoebe and Iphigenia did the same. The Ant Men would have to get past their arrows to capture any Moon Riders again.

Seris spoke urgently to his master. "We have no space to ram them," he whispered. "All we can do is back up a little and then try to make a break for it!"

There was silence again, but then suddenly Orestes strode forward and climbed up onto the balustrade on the foredeck. "Neoptolemus, show yourself!" he cried, his voice surprisingly firm and steady.

"Who has the temerity to demand such a thing!"

"I, Orestes! Son of the great King Agamemnon!"

There was a ripple of shock as his words sank in, then suddenly every warrior's face turned to stare in disbelief at the young man. This was not what they'd expected.

The huge giant stepped forward, thumping his chest with pride. "I am Neoptolemus, son of Achilles!"

Iphigenia looked uncertainly at Myrina, who nodded. "Yes, it is him—I saw his father fight, remember."

"I have no quarrel with you—Agamemnon's son! Our fathers once fought side by side!"

"Huh! There was no love lost between them," Myrina whispered.

"Hand over your ship to me and join my ranks! You and I will stand together as our fathers did!"

Orestes spoke quietly now through gritted teeth. "You took my sister as a slave!"

Neoptolemus stared at him, amazed. "Your sister?"

"My sister Iphigenia, long lost to me, was among the ranks of the Moon Riders you captured at the fight for the Thermodon."

Again there came a ripple of surprise among the warriors, but also laughter and sneers. Neoptolemus's answer was ripe with insult. "Iphigenia! She did escape the sacrificial knife then? How could I know that she'd keep company with those mad bitches at the Thermodon?" His appeal was from one thug to another.

Iphigenia opened her mouth as though she must speak, but Myrina shook her head and silenced her. "Your brother has found his courage—let him see what he can do!"

"I challenge you, Achilles' son!" Orestes thundered, drawing his sword. "Let us see how brave you are without your band of pirates. Come ashore and fight with me alone! Let us finish the quarrel that poisoned our fathers' friendship. If you win, you take my ship and all aboard; if you lose you simply let us leave unharmed!"

"Ha!" Neoptolemus convulsed with laughter while his men jeered. "I cannot lose!"

There was worried silence among Orestes' supporters. Achilles' son must be thirty years old and had his father's physique. Orestes was a mere boy beside him. Pylades looked at his friend, aghast, but said nothing. Seris whispered furiously into his master's ear, but Orestes did not move a muscle.

At last the laughter died down and the sullen silence from those aboard the *Castor and Pollux* made Neoptolemus's men look to their master for a response.

Neoptolemus's face now grew grim; all trace of laughter fled as he flushed and drew his sword. "Let the sniveling whelp of Agamemnon face his doom then! I will meet you down there on the quayside. No one else leave either ship! If the boy wishes to be slaughtered like a calf, he deserves so foolish an end!"

Orestes marched bravely to the gunwale and swung himself over, leaping lightly down onto the quay. "I accept!"

Pylades threw a shield down to him. Every person aboard both ships stumbled over to the shoreward side to see what would happen next. Iphigenia went very pale and gripped Myrina's arm. "Have I found my brother to lose him so soon?"

Myrina touched her bow. "I see no archers in their ranks," she hissed. "I could shoot the man down like a stag!"

"But you will not do that!" Iphigenia was quick to assert her sense of justice.

"No . . . you are right," Myrina agreed reluctantly. "But will they honor the agreement?"

Neoptolemus climbed over the gunwales of his flagship and clambered down, landing heavily, though the great muscles of his calves and thighs helped him to recover quickly.

Myrina watched it all, remembering with pain how Penthesilea had fought the great Achilles and died at his hand. Was this troubled young man to suffer a similar fate?

"Penthesilea, help him," she murmured.

CHAPTER THIRTY-FOUR

Orestes' Redemption

PHOEBE WAS STANDING at Myrina's side and she'd heard Myrina's whispered prayer for help. She knew the story of Penthesilea well. "Snake Lady," she said, "you often told me how Penthesilea nearly won when she fought Achilles!"

"Yes." Myrina tried to find comfort and courage in this reminder. "You are right, Young Tiger. Penthesilea could leap like a gazelle, and Orestes is much lighter than Neoptolemus; he must try to use that. And another thing"—she narrowed her eyes—"this is not the great Achilles. It seems to me that the wealth Neoptolemus has gained through trading slaves has made the man fat!"

Iphigenia almost smiled. "You are right, Snake Lady, Neoptolemus has grown fat!"

But any sense of cheer fled quickly, for Achilles' son did not wait for any signal, but swung his sword, closely missing Orestes' neck and catching him unawares. They saw that for all his height and weight the man could fight. Neoptolemus's men cheered and jeered, but those on Orestes' ship watched quietly, grim and alert, as Captain Seris moved among them, whispering orders to each of them.

Orestes had been caught unawares by this sudden attack, but he quickly rallied and Myrina saw with a touch of hope that he was not inexperienced in fighting with a sword. Pylades watched in an agony of helplessness, whispering instructions that his friend could not hear. "Beware his swing! To the east, to the east! Now duck!"

"You two learned to fight together," Myrina said.

Pylades nodded. "I have slightly the better skill. It should be me down there!"

"No!" She tried to offer comfort. "You have fought by his side for long enough. This is one battle that Orestes must fight alone, and whatever may come of it, he has earned my respect!"

There was a low moan and a gasp from Orestes' men as they saw Neoptolemus lunge and slice their master's left shoulder above the protection of his shield. But while Neoptolemus turned to his men in triumph, the younger man managed to make a quick upper thrust from below that deeply wounded the giant's neck.

Then there were angry gasps from his men as Neoptolemus staggered backward. His warriors threatened to climb down to aid their master, but Myrina grabbed her arrow. "Here's a dart for the first man to break the rules!" she bellowed.

They did not need another warning; for all their sneers, they knew that a Moon Rider's arrow was something to be feared. Orestes was bleeding profusely from his wound and his shield arm hung uselessly, but he leaped forward, sensing that he had gained an advantage. He thrust again, and this time his sword sank deep into Neoptolemus's breast. There was a hushed gasp, then Pylades leaped over the gunwales, grabbed his friend, and dragged him back to the boat. At the same moment Neoptolemus's men swarmed down like angry bees to their master, despite their fear of flying arrows.

Myrina lowered her bow; the fight was over. Neoptolemus could not recover from such a wound. The son of Agamemnon had killed the son of Achilles.

"Now," Seris shouted. "To the oars!"

As one man, Orestes' oarsmen slipped into their seats, snatching up the oars at once, for they had little trust that the followers of Neoptolemus would honor their master's agreement. Captain Seris had steadily been slipping the ropes during the fight so that the *Castor and Pollux* had slowly drifted to the east. Now he had gained a small space to maneuver and turn the prow for the open sea.

Myrina watched with admiration, remembering the

sleepy, rebellious crew she had disturbed only two days ago. The oarsmen struck the water with precision, catapulting the ship away from the shore. They moved with such strength that though the prow caught the bows of Neoptolemus's ship, it knocked it aside like flotsam and plowed out into the deep water.

Orestes had collapsed on the deck, but Myrina saw that he was in good hands, Iphigenia tending him, aided by Phoebe. The ship lurched as the oars sent it shooting forward, but they already had his wound stanched and were binding it tightly. Tamsin had set herself to soothe the horses, for they tossed their heads and stamped in protest at the unnerving sensation of a rolling deck beneath their hooves.

"Good girl!" Myrina went at once to help her. "Hush now, boy!" she crooned, fastening Big Chief to one of the stanchions, softly repeating the Mazagardi command to be still.

She looked back and saw more ships sliding into sight around the promontory; the rest of Neoptolemus's fleet had come, as she knew they must. Back in Yalushta Bay some of his men were trying to man the oars and set off in pursuit in the flagship, but most of them stayed on the shore in disarray, raging and mourning their leader.

Myrina swore under her breath. "We leave not a moment too soon!"

The *Castor and Pollux* plowed on through the waves, a strong wind blowing in their favor. They unfurled the brail sail as soon as they could.

"Thank you, Maa, for this blessed wind," Myrina whispered.

Though it was midday, with the wind came clouds, a dramatic fading of the light, and a squall of rain. Still Captain Seris kept the sail set, for though it was rough going, at least they were carried fast away from Yalushta. Myrina could not help but fear the storm that seemed to be building, remembering her last experience of the Inhospitable Sea. Nonya's story of the terrible weapon that made the waves boil and rage crept unbidden into her mind. Sometimes she thought she glimpsed the dark shapes of vessels following them, but nobody spoke of it. At last, as darkness gathered thick about them, the wind dropped a little and they lit the oil lamps. Still the oarsmen rowed, while Seris steered by the stars.

Only then did a sense of relief and safety come to Myrina, though it was swiftly followed by frustration as she acknowledged to herself that the fates had dealt a sharp blow to her plans once again. By now she'd thought to be galloping back toward the Sinta grasslands, looking for a suitable spot to camp for the night. As the ship dipped and rose, heading for the southern shore of the

Inhospitable Sea and the Bosphorus, the Moon Riders' camp beyond the river seemed as distant as the stars that shone down on them.

She put her hand down to grasp her mirror pouch, then let it go. "Too tired to mirror gaze!" she sighed. Instead she contented herself with murmuring soothing Mazagardi words to Big Chief, who still protested a little at the unsteady ground beneath him.

"Sorry, boy," she whispered, stroking his withers. "I don't know when you and I will ride the grassy steppe again, but at least we are still alive and together."

She looked around for the girls and saw that Tamsin and Phoebe were standing by the steering oar on either side of Captain Seris, who was telling them the Achaean names of the stars that he steered the ship by.

"Those two we call by the names of Castor and Pollux; twin brothers for whom we named this ship. They would have been uncles to my master and the Princess Iphigenia, but they died young. Some say they flew up to the top of Mount Olympus by magic as they were descended from gods!"

"That would mean that our Iphigenia is descended from gods, too!" Tamsin insisted, looking around at the princess with new interest.

"We Mazagardi call them the stallion and the mare!" Phoebe told him firmly. "And the three stars below are the three foals they produced."

Myrina smiled to hear this friendly conversation. The girls did not seem too troubled to be crossing a rough sea toward the Bosphorus instead of the great sea of grass. Iphigenia sat with Orestes and Pylades, helping her brother sip a soothing drink, while his friend steadied him protectively against the lurch of the deck. The princess, too, it seemed, was content to travel wherever fate would take her, more devoted than ever to the brother she'd found. Myrina sighed and tried to reconcile herself to accepting what must be.

"Achilles' whelp had much to answer for," she grumbled into Big Chief's flanks. "None of us will mourn him!" At last she pulled a warm cloak from one of her bundles and settled to snatch some sleep close to the horses, where she could drift fitfully in and out of dreams.

Myrina opened her bleary eyes to sharp sun the following morning. Her mouth was dry and foul tasting. She struggled to her feet and checked that there was no sign of pursuit, then went in search of water for herself and the horses. Seris still clutched the steering oar, and from the blue shadows beneath his eyes she guessed he'd been there all night.

"Water?" she murmured.

He indicated the water butt, then shook his head. "Not

much of it though," he warned.

Myrina scooped up a handful and drank it carefully, understanding his concern. "Is this all?" she asked.

Seris nodded. "We didn't get fresh water on board before the cursed pirates came at us! Most of our water butts still stand by the quay in Yalushta Bay! I should have ordered them aboard first."

"You were not to know we'd be set on by poison ants!"

They stood quietly together for a moment, while Myrina surveyed the deck, crowded with sleeping bodies. "What food did we manage to get aboard?" she asked.

"Two good casks of grain!"

"What else?"

He shook his head. "A butt of wine! I spent the morning patching holes, thinking that we'd load up after the midday heat. I would give anything now to change that wine for water."

Myrina took the oar from his hands. "You are to rest," she ordered. "You did right to make your ship seaworthy first. If you hadn't done that we'd all be at the bottom of the sea by now."

Seris hesitated, but he saw that she could handle the oar. "We've made good progress through the night, but I do not know this sea well," he worried. "Where we can stop and beg supplies I do not know!"

"Rest!" Myrina told him. "I have no complaints about

your seamanship now—we all owe you our lives. I will think carefully while I steer; now you must rest!"

Seris grinned at her for all his weariness. "I hear they call you the Snake Lady," he said.

She smiled back at him. "Obey or you will feel my bite!"

"I think you have already sunk your fangs into my heart," he answered gallantly and staggered away to find a space where he could rest.

The wind blew steadily in their favor and the spring sunshine warmed and cheered all those aboard, along with the reassurance that there was no sign of Neoptolemus's ships following them. Orestes troubled them all, for he ran a fever and Iphigenia worried that his wound was festering.

Myrina insisted that Iphigenia rest for a while and promised that she would sit by Orestes and see that he took water. The boy looked weak, and it was hard to believe that he had found the strength to challenge Neoptolemus so bravely.

"I hope you have no regrets about the death of the young Ant Man," Myrina told him roundly. "I say you redeemed yourself when you took him on, though I would like to have killed him myself. The whole of the Black Sea coast will rejoice and be free again."

Orestes smiled at her. "I thank you . . . Snake Lady," he said. Though his voice was faint, all trace of madness seemed to have gone from him. "Your good opinion means much to me . . . I understand now that it was you who saved my sister from the sacrificial knife!"

Myrina pressed his good arm in a gesture of friendship. "I didn't do it alone. I am glad to hear you speak such sense; I feared that distress had turned your mind. Now all you have to do is rest and recover from this wound."

"I consider myself a lucky man." He spoke with warmth. "I have much to live for now. I have my sister, and if I take her safely back to Athens, I believe there may be a chance of forgiveness from the council there, even though I haven't found the ancient image of Artemis."

Myrina shook her head and spoke with certainty. "That statue was naught but an old ship's figurehead."

"I do not care." Orestes shrugged painfully. "To have found my sister is all that matters."

Iphigenia smiled as she settled to rest, overhearing this exchange, glad that her brother and Myrina seemed to be becoming friends.

CHAPTER THIRTY-FIVE

A Warm Welcome

THE *CASTOR AND Pollux* sailed on and those aboard lived frugally. They crushed the grain and mixed it sparingly with water to make dry cakes and mash for the horses. The wine was shared and cheered them a little. But though they eked out the water as carefully as they could, after four days' sailing the grain was low and the water almost gone.

To their relief the fever left Orestes, but he was still weak and they could not provide good food to strengthen him. When dawn broke on the fourth day, there came a sudden cry from the young boy who perched as lookout in the little basket above the yardarm. It brought Myrina rushing to the prow, where Seris already stood with Pylades; Orestes struggled up to join them. There, coming up on the port side, was a coastline that seemed to run from east to west, but in the westerly direction the land fell away, leaving a great gulf of water with land on either side.

"The Bosphorus," Myrina whispered.

"We think so," Seris agreed. "Though we did not expect to reach it quite so soon."

"But we have sailed steadily, day and night," Pylades reassured him. "Your navigation has never been at fault, Seris. What else can it be but the Bosphorus?"

"But what do we do?" Seris was still cautious. "Do we land here and beg for help or sail on south down the straits, hoping that we can find a place that might welcome us in the Sea of Marmara?"

At the mention of that little inland sea Myrina smiled. "I know where we may find a welcome that will be warm as the sun; my friend King Daris of the Isle of Marble would treat us like gods. I once nursed his young wife back to health when she'd nearly died giving birth to his first son. He swore friendship to me, and his generosity has never failed."

"Bless you, Snake Lady." Orestes smiled at her, clinging to the balustrades of the foredeck. "Let us pinch in our belts for just a while longer; after Tauris, a sure welcome will be worth the wait."

Though their bellies were aching for want of food and their mouths parched, still the warm wind continued to blow, sending them steadily through the narrow straits. There was consternation and then delight when the sky above them suddenly turned black with the wings of storks, flying northeast for the summer. At last they sailed out into the warm Sea of Marmara. A few of the crew raised their eyebrows but said nothing as the last of the water and grain was fed to the horses for, as Tamsin insisted, "They cannot know that they'll soon be fed."

Before the light faded they limped into the harbor at the Isle of Marble. Myrina's hopes were not disappointed for she was recognized at once in the prow of the *Castor and Pollux*.

"The Snake Lady! The Snake Lady has returned!"

A messenger was sent at once to the palace and even before they'd stepped ashore the king and his wife were there on the quayside to welcome them, three healthy, growing children at their side.

The horses were led to the palace stables, where they were treated to clean straw and water and as much hay as they could eat. Both masters and crew were offered sumptuous accommodation, baths, and new clothes. "We will have a feast in your honor!" King Daris was eager to please.

Myrina hugged him as though she were his aunt. "Blessings of Maa on you," she murmured. "I knew I could rely on your kindness, but before we do anything else, each one of us must eat and drink just a little, for we've sailed two days with nothing to pass our lips and we all have growling bellies and little strength."

The young king stared with concern and horror—such a thing was beyond his understanding—but Ira, his young wife, had known hunger herself as a child and she took charge. She made them all sit down and quickly ordered the servants to pour them beakers of water and bring them small bowls of warm porridge, sweetened with a little milk and honey. Tamsin was so exhausted that Myrina had to feed her like a child.

The king hovered around his guests, looking worried. "Now would you like to bathe?" he asked, concerned at their grimy state.

Queen Ira smiled at him and firmly shook her head. "They go to their beds and sleep," she insisted. "Then tomorrow, when they are rested, they can bathe and in the evening we will hold a wonderful feast."

They slept through the night and most of the following morning, but by the next evening the Snake Lady and her companions appeared clean and refreshed and the king held his feast; everyone ate and drank to their heart's content. It was a feast for the eyes as well as the stomach, with roast swan and duck decorated with dates in marzipan fashioned into the shape of bees, followed by delicate rose-flavored puddings sprinkled with honeyed petals, all accompanied with well-mixed water and wine.

Musicians played while they ate, and afterward they lay back on cushions, smiles of blessed relief on their faces as dancing girls in beautiful gowns swayed and twirled in front of them. Many of Orestes' men thought that they'd died in the night and flown to Mount Olympus to live with the gods.

Three blissful days passed on the Isle of Marble. The surprise visitors were given everything they needed to feel safe and comfortable. Orestes seemed to recover well with rest and excellent food. Myrina rejoiced to see the happiness that the young king and queen shared, and Tamsin took a great liking to the oldest prince, who'd been named Myrinus, after the Moon Rider who'd saved both him and his mother.

Seris enjoyed his well-earned rest and spent each evening at Myrina's side, sometimes teasing her, but more and more he observed with admiration the harmonious family of the king and queen of the Isle of Marble. "How does he manage it?" he asked. "How does Daris keep this little haven of peace when invasion and land grabbing goes on all around him?"

Myrina smiled thoughtfully. "The island is too small to covet. Who would go to the expense of raising an army to conquer a little place like this? Daris is well content with what he has, he doesn't go seeking more; he isn't greedy."

"And his subjects are loyal," Seris said, still impressed. "Orestes has noted this well; he learns much from the man. If Mycenae is ever returned to him, Orestes will make a better king for knowing Daris!"

"I hope you are right." Myrina smiled at the thought. "Daris treats his people with kindness, even though he is so young, and in return they give him tolerance and love."

"When I was young, I would never listen to wise advice—I longed to travel and craved excitement," Seris admitted. "I never saw myself with a wife and little ones, but our latest adventure has set me thinking that peace and a family around him has much to offer a man."

Myrina listened to him, amused; she had a good idea where this line of thought was taking him. He was a fine-looking man, and having got to know him better, she found she enjoyed his company very much. On the Isle of Marble he spent time with Phoebe and Tamsin, teasing them both relentlessly, but when they asked about his travels, he took their questions seriously and seemed to enjoy the telling, exaggerating just a little for dramatic effect.

On the third evening, after another pleasant meal, Seris reached out and took Myrina's hand. She was mellow with wine and sat contentedly for a while, enjoying the feel of a strong male hand clasping hers. But as she sat there watching the dancing, a slow sense of unease began to creep over her. It would be all too easy to settle down here on the Isle of Marble with Seris and be his wife.

She'd have a charming companion and they could both live here in comfort forever, cosseted and respected by the islanders. But . . . who would she become? What would happen to the resourceful Snake Lady? The more she saw how tempting it was, the more disturbed she became. What was she doing here, sitting watching the pretty young girls dancing? She had warned Tamsin and Phoebe that they must not forget they were Moon Riders, but how long now since she had made them dance to welcome the sun?

She gently withdrew her hand, smiling at Seris to show that she hadn't been offended, but she made herself get up and walk away. As soon as she left the close atmosphere of the feasting hall, she felt better and more herself again. A warm breeze blew inland and the moon gave a good light. She sat down facing the sea, setting her back against a warm rock, and pulled the golden mirror from her belt. She slowed her breathing and let her shoulders droop, thinking not of the Moon Riders' camp, but of the man who had worked over a glowing fire for many days to fashion this mirror for her.

At first all she could see was her own face in the shadows and the grassy bank behind her, with waving stalks, silver tipped in the moonlight. Then slowly a different landscape unfolded behind the waving stalks: a wide sea of grassy steppe land that stretched bleakly over rolling hills, mile on mile. She saw Kuspada's face, dim in the darkness, his cheeks lit by the flickering flame of a small fire. There was just one tent behind him. Where were the Moon Riders? Kuspada seemed to be watching something that glinted with silver beside him; it was the river. She looked carefully for clues that would make her understand. Why did Kuspada sit there all alone? What was he waiting for? Then she realized that she knew the answer. He'd left the big camp and returned to the river; he was waiting for the Snake Lady to return.

Myrina's heart twisted with longing. She released the vision at once, letting it fall swiftly away, but as soon as it had faded, she struggled to her feet and went to find Iphigenia. Orestes was there beside his sister.

"My dear friends"—she spoke to them both and they could see her agitation—"I fear we grow too soft and comfortable; we should be moving on."

Orestes agreed at once. "I'm glad that you said it, Snake Lady. I cannot tell you how grateful I am to your friend Daris, but Iphigenia has agreed to come back to Athens with me. She will plead on my behalf to the council, and I must admit that this makes me eager to journey onward."

Myrina was relieved to hear him speak so, but then she sighed. "I must take my leave of you both very soon, for I wish to be set ashore close to where Troy once stood—

I have a strange hankering to see what is left of that sad city—and then I must travel back across the Inhospitable Sea to find the other Moon Riders."

Iphigenia looked at her with concern. "But that is a terrible journey to face—and what of the girls?"

Myrina agreed that it was a harsh journey, but she would not change her mind. "We will travel steadily on horseback toward the Thermodon, and if I cannot find a boat to carry us all across, then we'll go to the east and travel around the sea by land. We no longer need fear Neoptolemus—knowing that gives me courage; we will get there safe and sound."

Iphigenia was troubled by her resolve, but she knew better than to try to dissuade her friend. "So you and I must part after all," she whispered.

Myrina reached out to hug her tightly. "Remember what Cassandra said—we will never be apart in our hearts and we will always share our mirror visions!"

Orestes watched this, frowning a little. "Seris will take your leaving hard," he warned. "I'm sure that he has hopes . . ."

Myrina nodded. "I will speak to him," she promised. "Will you speak to our hosts and thank them so that we do not seem to leave discourteously?"

"Yes, I will do it now! Then I will try to persuade the crew!"

Iphigenia smiled and wagged her finger at him in a sisterly manner. "Remember, little brother, you are the master!"

They wandered off in different directions, searching for the right words to use, so that their decision would not give too much pain to their friends. Seris's disappointment was clear in his face when he heard her plans, and he snatched at a small crumb of hope. "I will come with you," he said. "Ask your devoted follower King Daris to give you a boat and I will navigate you back across the Inhospitable Sea, if that is where you wish to go. Orestes and Pylades can manage to find Athens without me!"

But Myrina shook her head. "I long for the nomadic life that I knew as a young girl," she told him. "To ride across the grassy steppe and stuff my pillow with fresh feather grass and sleep with the stars above my head. I need the excitement of packing up tents and moving to fresh pastures with each new moon. I must not forget that I am a warrior priestess, a Moon Rider."

Seris struggled to understand. "It is a harsh life that you describe," he said, puzzled that she should want to live with such hardship.

"Yes," Myrina agreed. "But I was born a Mazagardi and that way of life is part of me. It is not the right way for you."

344

"I have spent most of my life traveling," he objected.

Myrina smiled. "But you—you are a nomad of the sea. I have watched the way your nose twitches at the salt sea breeze and your eyes light up at the sight of a sail unfurling and you love the creaky singing of the deck beneath your feet. I am sad to say it, but we do not belong together and even if . . ." She paused, reluctant to hurt him, but wishing to be honest. "There is . . . another that I think of."

Seris sighed deeply, seeing at last that he was beaten. "You have never spoken of him," he said. "But I think I know his name; it is Kuspada!"

Myrina was amazed. "But how . . . ?"

Seris laughed. "You are not the only one who is devoted to him; he is a very lucky fellow. Both Tamsin and Phoebe chant his name at every turn. Kuspada rides like a centaur! Kuspada draws golden nuggets through the fire. Kuspada tells us tales of the sky god and his snaky wife."

Myrina could not help but smile to hear this.

"Well . . . he must be a fine fellow, this Kuspada," Seris told her generously, "to win so quick and fierce a snake lady's heart."

Myrina took his hand and pressed it with gratitude. "I will never forget that your skills saved all our lives. I want us to part as friends!"

"We are friends," Seris agreed. "And I will never forget the Snake Lady, who stabbed me in the heart, then patched me up! But . . . I know when I am beaten. I think we had better get to our beds now if my master will insist that we set sail again so soon!"

CHAPTER THIRTY-SIX

The Fates

THOUGH THERE WAS reluctance on the part of Daris and Ira to let them go, both Orestes and Myrina insisted that they must travel on. Seris swallowed his disappointment bravely and barked at his crew until they understood that their moment of bliss had passed and they must return to the old, hard life. Tamsin and Phoebe felt a great sadness at the thought of leaving Iphigenia and their new friends, but the promise of a long adventurous journey raised their spirits and sent them fettling their bows and sharpening their arrows.

"Soon I will ride at Leni's side." Phoebe looked forward to that.

"Yes." Tamsin smiled. "We will be Moon Riders again."

The whole of the next day was spent preparing to leave, and this time the ship was loaded to the gunwales with butts of fresh water, grain, oatmeal, dates, figs, salted fish, and smoked meats of every kind. The hull was newly patched, pitched, and painted. The following morning they were up before the dawn, and it seemed the whole population of the Isle of Marble had risen early to see them on their way. They all gathered on the beach carrying torches, but before crew and passengers went aboard, Myrina made an announcement.

"Now we Moon Riders must make some small return for the Marble Islanders' hospitality," she said. "We bring you the blessing of Maa!"

Iphigenia came forward with Phoebe and Tamsin on either side of her, their brows decked with silver circlets and a crescent moon. The islanders gasped with delight when they saw them and moved back to make a space for them.

The four Moon Riders joined hands, and there on the beach as the sun came up, they danced to welcome the day. Myrinus accompanied them with a steady drum beat, and his parents stood hand in hand watching proudly. They followed it with the Dance of Blessing, which would bring fertility and safety to the islanders for many years to come. As they finished, the king and queen went to kiss them. Instead of applauding, the islanders reverently whispered their thanks.

"I had thought you'd forgotten the Moon Riders' dance," Daris told Myrina.

"No, never!" Myrina shook her head fiercely.

"I am glad of that," he said.

Then it was time to lead Big Chief calmly up the gang-plank, his coat sleek with grooming and his belly full; Snowboots, Sandmane, and Moonbeam followed on.

Myrina hugged her host and hostess again. "I cannot thank you enough!" she whispered. "I fear we may not meet again!"

The young king kissed her on both cheeks and laughed. "Snake Lady! That is what you said last time! I do not believe you! The Isle of Marble is always here for you."

They sailed away, southward down through the Dardanelles toward the Hellespont, as the sun rose to its zenith. Through the morning they made steady progress, but the sea grew choppy as the two coastlines drew close together. The narrow passageway of water that linked the Sea of Marmara to the Aegean was busy with heavily loaded cargo ships, for since the defeat of Troy there were now no dues to be paid and water traffic passed freely up and down.

"What are they all carrying?" Myrina asked.

"They carry butts of olive oil and pottery to the Caucasus Mountains and bring back grain and iron," Seris told her.

"Father always told us it was the waterway the

Achaeans really wanted," said Myrina. "It seems he was right."

Iphigenia listened sadly. "Was I to be sacrificed for a waterway?" she murmured.

Myrina stroked her friend's arm. "Many were sacrificed," she said.

The ship lurched up and down as the waves grew, so that the passengers clung unsteadily to the balustrades of the afterdeck while they passed the mountains of Thrace to the west and the empty desolation that was once Priam's kingdom to the east.

As they drew close to the narrowest point, despite the swinging of the deck, Myrina prepared to leave, giving Seris and the girls a nod.

"Furl the sail!" Seris cried.

Myrina went to where Big Chief was tethered, but the wind rose so sharply that she had to grab hold of the stanchion, dropping her baggage to soothe the beasts. The *Castor and Pollux* started to toss wildly up and down as the sky turned black and a heavy rain began to pelt down on them. Many aboard cried out in alarm.

"Not again," Myrina grumbled, trying to shelter at Big Chief's side.

"Back the oars!" Seris bellowed, trying desperately to hold the ship against the violent tipping of the waves.

"There'll be no putting ashore now," Myrina told herself. It seemed the fates were blocking her every decision.

The wind blew to such a pitch that Seris had every man hauling on the oars, just to keep the vessel from ramming into the coast; no hope of making a landing. The suddenness of the storm had caught other vessels unawares, and they heard the dreadful crack that came from two small fishing boats that clashed together and lurched to the side, sinking fast.

The *Castor and Pollux* was carried helplessly down the narrow channel of the Hellespont and out into the open sea as the sky went darker still and lightning flashed across the sky. A great rumble of thunder followed another flash that caught the mast. The horses screamed and reared as the heavy wooden pole first cracked and then crashed down onto the terrified oarsmen, sending the ship spinning wildly around. Myrina could do nothing but cower beneath the stanchion, her face lashed with rain. She tried hopelessly to soothe Big Chief, but the horses snaked their heads in terror and it was hard to avoid their trampling hooves.

"*Cush! Cush!*" she whispered.

Seris shouted orders that his crew had no hope of obeying. The ship spun wildly onward, tossed by huge waves.

"The sea god is angry!"

"We should not have come!"

"Poseidon save us!"

"Why not stay safe on the Isle of Marble?"

At last the terrible whirling seemed to slow down a little, and the darkness began to lift. Myrina climbed out of the space where she'd been hiding to see that they were being carried in a great rush past a coastline that seemed somehow familiar to her. As she gazed up at the dark mound in the distance, topped with crumbling towers and broken walls, she understood that they had been blown off course and carried east in quite the opposite direction from Athens. That desolate mound, with its cracked walls that stood like broken teeth against the returning sun, must be the shattered remains of Troy.

Iphigenia struggled to her side. "Is that the ruined city?" she whispered.

"Oh yes," Myrina told her.

The fall of the mast had killed two of Seris's men outright and badly crushed five more. Myrina forced her own concerns away and staggered down the deck to help those who were hurt. Iphigenia and the two girls bravely worked with her, binding wounds and clearing up the mess of blood and vomit.

Seris endeavored simply to keep his ship afloat, while Orestes and Pylades took orders from him, trying frantically to stuff a leaking hole and hack free the broken mast to prevent it dragging the ship right over onto its side.

A watery sun broke through the clouds, and though the waves had subsided, it seemed they were now being carried along by a powerful current. They looked desperately for a sandy cove, toward which they might try to steer the tipping vessel. The coast was nothing but rocks and cliffs and they had little daylight left to them, as the sun was already beginning to set.

Seris gave the steering oar to Orestes and Pylades while he stumbled the full length of the ship to stand in the prow, feverishly scanning the horizon. Then suddenly he shouted and pointed wildly ahead of them. "Run for shelter!"

"Where, man?" Orestes bellowed.

"An island, with a sandy beach!"

They all turned to look where he pointed and saw that he was right. Ahead of them, just a little way out from the coast, was a small island with a high hill in the middle and a building perched on top of it. Myrina struggled toward the prow, staring at the sight ahead; she had the strangest sense of having seen this place before but couldn't think when. Had she dreamed it? No name would come to mind, but it did have a fine sandy beach.

Seris went back to the stern to see if they could turn the heavy steering oar and heave the lopsided vessel in the direction they wanted. The strong current that carried them eastward threatened to wash them farther out to sea, completely missing this safe haven.

"Hold tight! Hold tight!" Seris warned as the three of them threw their weight together to force the steering oar around.

Everyone obeyed, grabbing tight hold of the gunwales or the stanchions. Myrina braced herself on the balustrades as the creaking ship swung about. The strange sense of recognition fled from her mind—all she wanted now was to survive and crawl ashore.

"Tamsin!" she cried.

"I've got her!" Phoebe answered.

"Hold tight," Seris cried again. "Now!"

Seris could not prevent the impact; all he could do was steer for the softest-looking sandbank as he drove his ship aground.

The *Castor and Pollux* slid forward almost smoothly, then stuck with a sickening lurch that sent many of those aboard flying the full length of the deck. Myrina heard Big Chief and his mares protesting and then the scrape of their hooves as they skidded wildly on the deck. There were more cracking sounds as part of the thwarts shattered, then sudden quietness.

The balustrade that Myrina clung to gave way and she slipped into shallow water that broke her fall. She scrambled quickly to her feet, grateful to find that though she was soaking wet and badly bruised, all her limbs were still attached and working.

Her first thought as ever was for the girls. "Tamsin, Phoebe!" she bellowed. Two answering calls told her that they, too, were alive. Next she whistled for Big Chief, but she need not have worried about him; she was answered by a surprised snort far ahead on the darkening beach.

"Snake Lady, are you safe?" It was Orestes' voice close to her. She could see the dark shape of him as he hauled himself upright ahead of her.

"A light!" he called. "A light ahead. People are coming—is this help or hindrance?

Myrina turned and saw that there were indeed two figures moving down toward them from the hillside where she had seen the building with a tower.

Orestes moved protectively in front of her and at the same time she found Iphigenia at her side. She grasped her hand, grateful that she, too, had survived. "Are you hurt?"

"No." Iphigenia's voice was calm as ever. "Not hurt at all!"

"Nothing seems to trouble you," Myrina said, a touch of resentment in her voice.

"But we are safe." Iphigenia spoke with certainty, her voice warm and confident. "You must know that we are safe!"

Myrina's sense of the familiarity of the place returned

at once. "I thought . . ." she murmured. "I thought I knew this place, but . . ."

Iphigenia laughed; a strange sound among so much wreckage. "You and I have both been here in spirit," she said. "We have nothing to fear!"

CHAPTER THIRTY-SEVEN

A Place of Safety

M YRINA COULD SEE the pale oval of her
friend's face in the dim light and the white-
ness of her teeth as she smiled. If Iphigenia
swore that they were safe, then perhaps they were.

Orestes marched ahead of them, his sword ready in his
hand. Now they could see the two figures much more
clearly: one was tall and slender and carried two gleaming
oil lamps in either hand; the other, marching ahead, was
a young boy. He carried a strong staff to help him walk,
but as Myrina saw the strange shadow that followed his
every movement, she gave a small joyful cry of recognition. Now she knew where they were.

She reached out for Iphigenia's hand. "I can't believe it!
Young Chryse and Cassandra!"

Iphigenia could hardly speak for the tears of joy that
welled up in her throat. "But it is true . . ." she stammered.
"We are really here on the island of Sminthe and . . . I am

to meet my other little brother at last!"

The magical gray shadow swirled about the boy's feet, and every step he took brought forward a swarm of dark mouse bodies that rippled together as though they were one. But when the boy saw Orestes coming toward him, sword at the ready, he raised his strong staff in both hands and rushed forward aggressively.

Orestes pulled back, seeing this was little more than a child; but as the boy ran at him, he was forced to put up his sword to defend himself.

"Stop! Stop at once!" The tall slim woman who carried the lamps hurried forward and Myrina and Iphigenia saw with delight that it was their dear Cassandra, a little older looking and not quite as thin as she used to be.

"Put away your weapons!" Cassandra ordered. "You would not attack your brother, would you?"

Orestes and the Mouse Boy both stopped at once, utterly amazed.

Myrina and Iphigenia could not speak; their eyes had filled with tears, but huge smiles spread across their faces.

"Wh-who are you speaking to?" Chryse turned to Cassandra in confusion.

"I am speaking to you both! For you two are brothers!"

Orestes looked from the strange boy to the older woman. "Then you . . . must be Cassandra, Princess of Troy!"

She smiled at him. "That was long ago! Now I am

priestess of the temple here. I serve both Sminthean Apollo and Maa."

Orestes stood still, amazed and helpless, his sword still dangling in his hand.

"Send your men up to the temple." Cassandra took charge, holding out a lantern. "There is food and shelter for them all."

Orestes seemed too stunned to direct his men, so Pylades strode forward, understanding the strange nature of this meeting. He took the lanterns from Cassandra and led the men up the hill. They followed him, coughing seawater from their lungs and carrying their wounded.

Orestes hung back, still shaken by what Cassandra had said. Though they now stood there in darkness, a heavy cloud rolled back, revealing a fine bright moon.

"Maa smiles down on her Moon Riders tonight," Iphigenia whispered at last. Then she stepped forward and bent to kiss Chryse on the cheek. "I am your sister," she told him gently, "and I have longed to meet you."

Chryse's mouth dropped open in wonder. "Are you Iphigenia? I should have known," he said. "The mice were wild this afternoon, running round in a circle, faster and faster. Cassandra swore that we were to have visitors and a great blessing coming to us, but . . . when I saw the man with the sword I feared you were pirates come to steal us away."

Everyone smiled at his words, and Tamsin came forward, holding out her hand to him. "I have heard of you," she said.

"And I," said Phoebe shyly.

Iphigenia got up and held her arms wide to Cassandra, a huge happy smile on her face. "I thought never to see you again!" she murmured, her voice full of emotion.

They threw their arms around each other and wept with joy. Myrina watched with tears pouring down her face. Then Cassandra looked for her and stretched out her arm. "Snake Lady!"

She went to them, and all three hugged each other and cried again with happiness.

"We three have never really been apart!" Cassandra whispered.

"No, we have not!" Myrina agreed. "But no vision can be as good as this!"

At last they raised their heads and wiped their tears away, for there were others who might need their help and a good explanation.

But Orestes was already recovering from his shock. He went down on one knee, holding his hand out to the Mouse Boy. "You must be Chryse and I know your story," he told him. "You and I share the same father, but we have different mothers. My father did your gentle mother great harm, and for that I am truly sorry!"

Chryse eyed him uncomfortably for a moment, but then he took the offered hand and at last the two hugged each other. "You never harmed us," Chryse whispered.

"I almost did!" Orestes held him at arm's length again and smiled at him.

The Mouse Boy giggled. "I will fight you properly tomorrow!"

"It's a promise," Orestes said.

Myrina remembered the horses and whistled for Big Chief. He came at once, the mares following him, blowing happily, heads erect, glad to be on firm land again.

Chryse smiled shyly at Tamsin and Phoebe. "We've made a feast for you," he told them. "Come and see."

Tamsin marched eagerly up the beach beside him. Phoebe followed, looking older and a little awkward.

Myrina and Iphigenia walked arm in arm with Cassandra, one on either side of her. They went slowly up the hill together toward the temple hidden in the trees. Myrina hesitated halfway up the hill.

"What is it?" Cassandra asked, concerned.

"Am I really here with you or am I dreaming?"

Cassandra laughed; it was a lovely sound.

"I just can't believe we are here," Myrina insisted, rubbing her eyes. "I swore the fates were treating me ill, but it seems those capricious ones were kinder than I knew. If I wasn't so wet and bruised, I'd think I was dreaming!"

"I feel as though I'm dreaming, too," Iphigenia agreed.

As they emerged from the trees they saw ahead of them a wonderful scene. Three fires burned in braziers, and a long table was laid with food and drink. Orestes' weary crew were already eating and drinking and warming themselves.

Myrina stopped. "You knew that we were coming!"

"Of course we knew—the mice told us." Cassandra smiled. "But I have watched you in my dark pool every step of the way. If you had looked into your glass you would have seen me preparing your supper."

"There was no time for mirror gazing!" Myrina told her sharply. Then they all laughed again.

Myrina ate and drank a little, but weariness blurred her mind and she could remember little more. She woke warm and dry in a simple bedchamber, on a comfortable straw-stuffed mattress, and couldn't think where she was. How had she got to bed? Tamsin was still fast asleep beside her. She saw that Iphigenia and Phoebe slept on another mattress in the same room. It was only when she sat up and groaned as she moved her bruised legs that she remembered.

"Cassandra!" she murmured.

Gritting her teeth against the aches and pains, she got up quietly, leaving the others in peace. She wandered out into the main temple building, eager to explore. Two powerful decorated columns stood at the entrance to the temple: one bore an image of the god Apollo with his bow and arrows, sitting astride a huge mouse.

"Sminthean Apollo, the Mouse God." She bowed to it.

The other column depicted a fat female shape, with large breasts and a swollen stomach that the woman cradled protectively with her hands.

"Maa!" Myrina smiled and bowed again. "Thank you for bringing us here."

She turned at the sound of a footstep behind her. It was Cassandra. "Do you like my new addition?" she asked.

"You have set the image of Maa up here?"

"This place was sacred to Maa long before they built Apollo's temple. I decided to bring her back as companion to the Mouse God. I was promised to Apollo as a child, but then I became a Moon Rider, so now that I am free to choose I give my respect to both of them."

Myrina understood that very well. "But what did the people who live in these parts say when you changed their temple?"

Cassandra spoke with confidence. "Respect for Maa was always there, hidden away in their dances and songs. They are glad to have her restored to her proper place— you will see for yourself; they'll be coming soon."

CHAPTER THIRTY-EIGHT

The Mouse Boy

YRINA STARED OVER toward the mainland as, shading her eyes, she saw many people gathering on the shore.

"Where are the boats?" she asked.

Cassandra smiled, amused. "They do not need boats; this is a magical island—they walk on water. Look . . . here they come."

Myrina watched with growing amazement as a trail of people, young and old, some leading little children, seemed to march into the water and set off toward them. Cassandra laughed at her expression of astonishment.

"We are not really an island," she explained. "At least not for much longer!"

Myrina frowned. "It's a causeway!"

"A causeway built by Maa, you might say. It's a sand spit that seems to grow each year, and every storm washes a little more sand around the island to build the pathway. In years to come we will be part of the mainland."

Myrina smiled as she watched the procession. She could see now that they must proceed almost in single file, the sand spit just wide enough for a mother and child. They marched confidently toward the temple, looking just as if they were walking over the sea, the water swishing at their ankles.

"Even though it's only a sand spit, there is something magical about it. It's as though Maa leads them over here to find you."

"I'd like to think that was true," Cassandra said.

"What do they come for, and what are the little bundles they carry?"

"They come for advice! They come for healing! They come to share their troubles, and the bundles are our payment; bakers bring us bread, goatherds bring us milk, weavers bring us rugs and linen."

Myrina laughed. "You seem to have found a perfect way of living and a true purpose here," she said, "just as Centaurea did on Lunardia, her Nest of Maa."

Cassandra took her hand. "Dear friend," she said, "I have found real peace on this half island. I am happier than I have ever been, and the people here treat me with more respect and honor than ever I was given as princess of Troy."

"But it must be hard work," Myrina insisted, "serving so many folk."

"They don't all come for my advice; I have a helper. Come and see!"

Cassandra led her by the hand down to the gardens, where the dark pool lay surrounded by weeping willows. The people were already arriving, and a few of them gathered beside the pool, waiting and whispering hopefully as Cassandra came into view. Beyond the pool in a sunny, open space Chryse crouched beside the shallow stone trough that teemed with mice, just as Myrina had seen in her mirror visions. He dipped into the middle and lifted one small mouse out from the many. Then he rose to his feet and handed the creature to a little girl. The child took it carefully in her hands, then solemnly followed her mother into the temple.

Cassandra went to greet the people who waited patiently by her pool, but Myrina stood quietly in the sunshine to watch what Chryse would do next.

As soon as the young girl had left carrying her mouse, a father immediately pushed forward in her place a boy who'd seen four or five springs. He stood by the trough, white-faced and yawning, dark shadows beneath his eyes. The father looked exhausted, too, and he spoke with quiet desperation. Myrina crept closer to hear what he said.

"Our son Machus will not sleep," he told Chryse. "He

is restless all night and wanders away. We cannot sleep ourselves for we fear he will go outside and fall down the well. We are all worn out, and my wife and I begin to blame each other!"

Chryse listened intently, then he reached out to touch the man's shoulder in a kindly, soothing gesture that seemed mature beyond his years. He studied the mice carefully, then he picked one out and turned to Machus.

Involuntarily, the child's hands went out, palms up. "I give you my friend Poppy," Chryse said solemnly. "You must weave a little house for him to live in, made from willow wands, with many holes to give him air. He needs clean water to drink each day, sunflower seeds to eat, and soft dry grass to sleep in, and when he curls up to sleep, you must watch over him to see that he is safe. But you must remember this—when he wakes at night to drink and feed and run about his little home, then it is time for you to close your eyes and sleep. You and Poppy will be two sides of one coin. When he sleeps you will stay awake to look after him and while you sleep, Poppy will stand guard and keep you safe. Do you understand?"

The boy solemnly nodded, still holding out his hands.

Chryse gently gave him the mouse, and both father and child watched with wonder as the small brown creature curled up in the child's soft palms and went straight to sleep.

"Guard him well until he wakes!" Chryse said. "When he wakes, what will you do?"

"I will sleep," the boy promised. Then he turned and followed his father toward the temple.

Myrina watched the Mouse Boy with pride, remembering the poor weak baby he'd been, born within the war-torn walls of Troy.

As soon as Machus had moved away, a woman pushed a small girl forward, who looked healthy enough to Myrina. "Can you help us, Mouse Boy?" she begged. "We cannot get a word out of this little one. We've six all bigger than her and we can't keep them quiet, but little Dor won't say a word. All our family have great loud voices, but not little Dor—she won't make a sound!"

Chryse didn't answer; he just nodded and put his finger to his lips as though to hush the mother. The woman fell silent at once. Chryse studied his mice again, then he picked one out while Dor watched, wide-eyed. "This is Squeak," he said to her softly. "Squeak has no words of her own, so you must speak for her—you are to be her voice. You must tell others what she needs—do you understand? Your brothers and sisters must do the work."

Dor held out her hands and took the small brown, trembling creature. The mouse looked up at her and squeaked. The mother opened her mouth as though to speak, but Chryse hushed her. "Dor is her voice!" he reminded.

The mouse squeaked again, and Chryse waited patiently. Dor looked anxious. "You are her voice," Chryse told her gently. "What does she say?"

Dor still looked worried, but her lips suddenly moved, as though with a great effort. "N-needs a . . . a little house," she managed at last.

Her mother's mouth dropped open in surprise to hear her voice; there was clearly nothing wrong with little Dor's hearing.

Chryse turned his sweet smile on the child and she glowed. The mouse squeaked again.

"And what else?" he asked, his voice still low.

"W-water and s-sunflower seeds."

"And who must get them for her?"

"My brothers and s-sisters."

"And who will tell them?"

"I will." Dor spoke with conviction.

"Thank you," the mother whispered as she led her child away.

Myrina looked on with tears in her eyes, as she thought of Chryse's babyhood. In war-stricken Troy, while fighting raged all about the walls, both she and Cassandra had struggled to help the gentle priestess of Apollo accept the child that Agamemnon had forced on her. They had won that battle, and Chryseis had grown to love her son dearly. "He was well worth the effort," Myrina murmured. "A gifted child."

She left the busy garden and went into the temple to find a growing collection of small offerings laid out on a table in the main entrance hall. She poured a little goat's milk into a beaker, took up a small bowl of figs and carried them out to Chryse.

"You work hard," she told him. "You deserve a little rest and food."

The Mouse Boy looked at her, surprised, but then he smiled and thanked her.

"Your mother would be very proud of you," she told him warmly. "This is important work that you do. Nobody could do it better."

Later that day, Orestes emerged from a long sleep and wandered out to see how Chryse spent his time. He watched, impressed. "I thought to spar with him as young boys do," he confided to Myrina. "But my little brother has the wisdom of an ancient one."

"I think he would still like a bit of brotherly fun," Myrina told him.

That evening, when the long trail of visitors had left, Orestes and Chryse clashed fighting sticks together on the temple lawn, and the quiet place grew noisy with laughter and shouts. Tamsin and Phoebe watched them impatiently for a while, voicing their criticisms, hands on hips.

"Let's show them what Moon Rider girls can do," Phoebe said at last, all shyness gone.

"Come on, Tiger Girl," Tamsin agreed.

They found themselves sticks and joined in with gusto. Pylades came to help his master, fearful that he needed it against so fierce a crew.

That same evening, after they had eaten, Cassandra, Iphigenia, and Myrina danced together on the lawn. Tamsin and Phoebe swore they were too exhausted to perform, but the truth was that they wanted to watch this dance, for they saw that the Snake Lady's eyes shone as never before and her smile was wild with joy as she spun and swayed. Those three friends, who'd seen so many years of struggle, had the appearance of agile young girls, their hair swinging out as they moved in harmony, their limbs lithe and strong.

Orestes and his supporters looked on with awe and a deep sense of privilege. There would never be another night like this, and nothing but the dance could express the love and happiness that the three friends felt.

CHAPTER THIRTY-NINE

Parting

THE NEXT MORNING brought practical talk of what they should all do next. Captain Seris set about repairing the damage that had been done to his ship, and the word soon spread around the Sminthean countryside that the priestess and the Mouse Boy had shipwrecked visitors who needed help. Instead of pots of honey, people carried across the sand spit planks of wood and pots of pitch. Carpenters came to offer their help, and by the time the Month of Flowers had arrived the boat was fully repaired and strong again.

Many of the provisions they'd been given on the Isle of Marble were salvaged and stashed safely aboard the ship, and then a touch of restlessness seemed to come to Orestes. After they'd worked hard all day to see the *Castor and Pollux* shipshape he spoke to his sister at supper, putting his thoughts into words. "Seris says there is time to reach Athens before the hottest weather comes," he murmured, looking at his sister anxiously. "If we are to return to Athens, I think we must set sail soon."

Iphigenia nodded sadly.

"I hate to take you from your friends," he told her. "You are free to change your mind and stay here with them. There could be no better place for you to be."

But Iphigenia shook her head, determined to go with him. "We have work to do," she said. "I think the council of Athens may listen to me. You and I are the only ones who can wipe out the bitter curse of our inheritance and bring peace to the troubled land where we were born."

Orestes nodded in agreement. "I don't return to the council with the image of the goddess they told me to seek, but I think the living person of my sister safe and well will impress them more."

Cassandra sat on the other side of Iphigenia and heard his words. She smiled. "You have found more than you know," she told him mysteriously.

They looked at her, surprised, but Cassandra refused to say more.

On the day of their departure they all gathered at the beach to make their sad farewells. Seris made his offer of marriage to Myrina one last time.

She hugged him tightly, but shook her head. "I will never forget you," she whispered.

He sighed heavily and kissed her forehead. "He is a lucky man, that one who waits. You had better not make him wait too long."

Orestes and Iphigenia both hugged Chryse. "We are so glad to know our little brother," Iphigenia cried, tears in her eyes.

"You can always find a home with us on Sminthe," Chryse offered in an almost fatherly way.

Orestes kissed the young boy's hand. "Your love and forgiveness does much to heal all wounds," he said. 'We children of Agamemnon can give one another peace."

Myrina led Moonbeam down to the ship. "Take her with you," she told Iphigenia. "With Moonbeam at your side, you will always be a Moon Rider."

Iphigenia clasped her as though she could not let go, but at last she managed to pull away and began with shaking fingers to untie the pouch that contained her ancient magical mirror.

"This precious gift should now be returned to its true owner," she offered, holding it out to Cassandra.

"No." Cassandra was firm. "I'm glad that you value my old mirror, but I have no need of it these days, and believe me, its true owner is you. If you keep it, just as before we will never be apart, but there is more to this mirror. Take it out and examine it carefully."

Iphigenia looked puzzled, but she obediently pulled

the dark glossy round of rough-cut obsidian from its pouch. Both Orestes and Myrina crept close, intrigued by her words, frowning and trying to understand what Cassandra might mean.

Myrina remembered only too well that Atisha, the old leader of the Moon Riders, had spoken with reverence when she'd first seen the shining hard black shape. Now Iphigenia held it up, so that the sun gleamed on its simple glassy surface. They could see nothing but the images of themselves reflected there, staring back with curiosity.

Cassandra smiled. "Tip it just a little to the side," she said.

Iphigenia obeyed and they all gasped: as the smooth shining surface tipped, they could suddenly see that it was marred in four places, but those four breaks had been carefully placed. They were so slight that they were hardly there, but once you had started to look at them, it didn't take too much imagination to see that the marks represented two eyes, a nose and a wide, generous mouth.

Once she had seen it, Iphigenia gasped. "A face that smiles at us! Why have I never seen it before?"

"You never needed to look for it before."

"No . . . the face is full of sadness," Orestes insisted. "But who . . . ?"

Myrina suddenly felt that she understood. "The goddess!" she whispered, her voice low with excitement. "It shows us the image of the goddess!"

Orestes saw what she meant. "Could this be the image that I have been seeking? I was looking for the ancient image of Artemis!"

"This goddess can be Artemis to you Achaeans, or Rhea to the Hittites," Cassandra replied; "to the Moon Riders she is Maa. We see whichever goddess we want to see. The magic is in the simplicity; it shows the face that all true seekers wish to find."

Orestes smiled in wonder, shaking his head. "My sister had the precious image there beside her all the time. She and the magical image are one and the same. I am blessed."

Iphigenia smiled with joy as she turned to him. "The curse is already lifting. The fates are beginning to smile on us."

So with this treasure, Orestes and Iphigenia at last managed to tear themselves away from Sminthe and their friends. Myrina stood beside Cassandra on the beach, watching the lift and dip of the new oars as the *Castor and Pollux* moved out into the deep blue Aegean Sea. Seris swung the steering oar about and ordered the sail to be unfurled.

"You knew about that mirror all along," Myrina accused, her mouth twitching with humor.

"There's a right moment and a wrong moment for

telling," Cassandra told her firmly. "That was the right moment."

They watched the sail bell out to catch the wind as the ship headed away from them, shrinking smaller and smaller as every moment passed. At last they turned away and walked back up the beach. Myrina was quiet and thoughtful; Seris's generous warning not to wait too long to return to Kuspada had touched her.

"And has the right moment come for you?" Cassandra asked, as though she picked up her thoughts. "I cannot see my fierce Snake Lady staying here forever in the peace of Sminthe."

Myrina looked at her with sadness. "It is hard to think of leaving," she acknowledged. "But I do long to live as a Mazagardi once again, and when I gazed in my mirror last night, I saw the devoted man who still waits for me beside the Sinta River. I must travel north to release him from his dreary watch, but I fear to drag the girls away from this lovely place on such a long harsh journey."

"It is a long journey," Cassandra agreed, "but you need not make it all alone."

"You would come?"

Cassandra shook her head sadly. "I am needed here too much, but here, close to the foothills of Mount Ida, we are well placed to watch all the comings and goings, the traders and the camel trains. I had word this morning from a trader I know who was once a captain of the guard in the city of Troy."

"Aah." Myrina looked at her with interest. "A camel train, you say!"

"Cornelius is on his way from Ephesus, having heard of the death of Neoptolemus. He will be here in three days' time, with his camel train of goods, and will go as far north as the Caucasus Mountains. The young Ant Man's death has freed up the old traveling routes."

Myrina caught her breath with pleasure at the thought. The journey would follow many of the old ways along which her own lost tribe, the Mazagardi, traveled when she was a child. "We would go past the Place of Flowing Waters," she said. "And travel close to the Nest of Maa, where Centaurea raises her fledgling warrior priestesses. Such a journey would bring much joy," she admitted.

Cassandra smiled encouragement. "The girls are young and brave, always ready for a new adventure. They will have so much to tell their friends when they reach their journey's end."

Myrina saw that this was true. "I cursed the fates when they smashed our mast and sent us skittering off course, but I would never have seen you again, if it were not for that storm."

"The fates can never hold you prisoner." Cassandra

spoke solemnly. "Our brave Snake Lady must go where she will."

"Will your trader friend be willing to take us, do you think?"

Cassandra had no hesitation. "Cornelius carries oil and olives up through the Caucasus Mountains and comes back with heavy iron goods. He would appreciate the support of a good archer on horseback—there are bears in those mountains as well as thieves."

"Quite an adventure!" Myrina grasped her friend's hand. "You understand me so well."

Cassandra clung to her for a moment and her mouth trembled with love as she spoke, but she was determined to say what she must. "There was once a friendless princess, rejected by her own family, for they thought her mad, but . . . she met a crafty sharp-tongued snake lady, who became her friend and the only one she could really trust. She will never forget that crafty one."

Myrina kissed her and they sat together holding hands until the sun had gone.

Both Phoebe and Tamsin stamped a foot when they heard of the journey that Myrina planned. "Why go? We love it here," they said.

Myrina knew that it was the sweetness of the Mouse

Boy's smile that made them both wish to stay. She could not blame either of them, for Chryse had won her heart, too. She felt guilty at the thought of dragging them away, but the image of the watcher by the Sinta River was strong in her mind.

"I could leave you here with Cassandra. I'd trust my oldest friend to care for you better than I do. I will not force either of you to come with me to the cold northern steppe. But if you do, I promise that I will beg Kuspada to make you both fine golden mirrors like mine. Then I will teach you the real magic of a Moon maiden and you will be able to watch those you love, wherever they are, and Sminthe will not seem so very far away."

Chryse saw the terrible uncertainty that his young friends struggled with. "If you learn the Moon maiden's magic, I will send you messages. If I hold up my hand like this, it is in greeting. If I touch my heart, it means that I am missing you."

They smiled at him. "And this," said Tamsin, closing her fist, "means I wish I could spar with you!"

They all laughed and made up more signs, but then Phoebe turned serious again. "But you have no magic mirror," she told Chryse.

"I can look for you every day in Cassandra's dark pool," he promised solemnly.

"Well then, we had better get ready for our journey," Phoebe agreed.

"I will need a mirror with two lizards." Tamsin was already making her plans. "Their tails twisted together at the top."

Myrina smiled at Cassandra. She would have been true to her word, but it would have wrenched her heart to leave either of them behind.

Cornelius arrived at Sminthe on the evening of the full moon. He left his camels and drovers camping on the mainland and came to spend the evening at the temple of Sminthean Apollo. Cassandra had prepared a feast for them all, and Myrina watched with approval, remembering the stick-thin princess who would not touch her food. This time it was Myrina who could not eat; her heart pounded with excitement at the adventure that lay ahead, at the same time feeling heavy with sadness at leaving her friends and this place of safety.

The camel drover ate and drank well, appreciating what Myrina could not. He went to his bed replete, while Cassandra, Myrina, and the two girls went down onto the sandy beach, followed by Chryse, who had brought out the oud that his mother had taught him to play. Beneath the full moon they performed the familiar steps of the sacred moon dance, twisting and turning their hands in graceful harmony. At the end they linked hands and arms, circling one way and then the other, full of loving smiles and tears.

"Do our sisters in the north dance, too?" Myrina wondered.

"Oh yes," Cassandra assured her. "They dance beneath the moon just as we do, and they long for the Snake Lady to return."

Epilogue

ATE IN THE Month of Falling Leaves Cassandra
sat by her pool, wrapped in a warm shawl, looking into the still water, her pale face serene.
Then, deep in the mysterious depths of the pool, she saw
something that made her smile.

"Chryse," she called. "Come and see!"

The Mouse Boy left his stone trough and went to her.
He had to still himself for a moment and let his eyes gaze
vaguely beneath the glinting surface, but it wasn't long
before he, too, saw the same wondrous vision as the
priestess.

He smiled. "The man does not see them coming."

There in the dark waters they saw three riders. The
older woman rode slightly ahead through falling snow
toward a small snow-flecked tent, set upon the edge of a
winding riverbank. In the far distance a great camp could
be seen, sheltering beneath overhanging rocks that

seemed to have the shape of an eagle. But this man had set up his tent away from them; he sat alone by the river, feeding a struggling fire with twigs. He looked up constantly toward the west, as though he thought he might see something, or someone, crossing the river. His horse stood beside him, very still and patient, midnight black.

At last the black stallion pricked up his ears and turned, aware of the riders approaching from the east. The front rider urged her horse on faster and faster and the man got up as he heard the thud of hooves in the snow.

Cassandra and Chryse watched as Myrina swung down from her horse and ran straight into Kuspada's arms. He swung her off her feet and kissed her as tears rained down his cheeks.

"Now what is he doing?" Chryse asked as they saw the man take an arrow from his quiver and hold it to the embers of his fire until it caught light. He shot the fiery arrow high into the sky, toward the rocks.

The other two riders slipped from their horses and flung themselves at the man. Soon lights appeared in the distance. A great crowd of people dressed in warm skins came toward them through the snow—men and women, many with young babies in their arms, wrapped well against the weather. Some of them rode on horseback; others ran on foot. All waved and danced, their necks gleaming with gold. They surrounded the weary travelers, hugging them passionately. Then they made a circle around the man and the three newcomers, singing and dancing with wild abandon.

Cassandra and the Mouse Boy watched with huge smiles on their faces. "I think the Snake Lady's journey is over," Cassandra said. "And the welcome she has found is warm."